I0645093

# HEAVY
## in the
# GAME

J. Love

*Keep It Pushin' productions*
*P.O Box 56457*
*Los Angeles, CA 90056*
*www.jlovebooks.com*

*This book is a work of fiction. People, places, events, and situations are the product of the author's imagination. Any resemblance to actual persons, living or dead, or historical events, is purely coincidental.*





*First published by AuthorHouse    11/09/2006*

*ISBN: 1-4259-2892-7 (sc)*

*Photographs taken by Lisa Love*

*Printed in the United States of America*

*This book is printed on acid-free paper.*

This book is dedicated to
my mother's unconditional love.
I can never thank you enough.
I love you Ma!

# ACKNOWLEDGEMENTS

First and foremost, I would like to give thanks and praise to the Source that fuels me with Life, Love, and Laughter on a daily basis. Throughout all the struggle and pain, those three L's have kept me moving forward and that is truly a blessing.

Next I would like to give a very special thanks to my sister and twin in spirit, Temple Love. Many people are unable to see your heart when you are messing up and making mistakes in this life, but you have always seen and believed in my heart. You have truly been there for me and I love you so much.

To my parents, Henry and Dorothy Love, I know it took a whole lot of strength to have dealt with my many short comings and I am so happy and proud to have parents that never turned their backs.

To my son, Jermane Love, your belief in me has always been there throughout the tough and difficult times. You have been an inspiration and I am so thankful for that.

To my special supporter and friend, Gayle Whitaker, there were many times when I felt down and doubted this project and it took your motivation and kind words to lift me up again. I thank you so much.

To the special flower, Barbara Knoll, your support from day one is greatly appreciated. That kind of belief in someone is rare and I'm very thankful you believed in me. You are so kind and sweet. And may your beauty and heart continue to blossom like a rose.

To my dear friend, Jennifer Patterson, your support has been greatly appreciated and I thank you for your patience and effort you put into helping me create the prototype to my book cover design. Your encouraging words and beautiful smile have both been inspirational.

To my sister in-law, Lisa Love, I am very thankful for your time in taking my photos for this book and much love for always laughing at my jokes.

To my friend, Laverne Gentry, I thank you for your prayers and keeping me in your thoughts.

To my first four paying customers and friends: Carrie Walker, Sherry Federici, Sue Wilkie, and Patty Meredith. It takes a lot to purchase a book from a first time author and I really am grateful for your trust in me.

To Michelle Martinez, I thank you for everything you have done. Honesty is hard to come by and yours came just in time. Your support and motivation was there to strengthen me when I needed it. You are very special and possess a gift that's waiting to be unwrapped.

To Ken & Vida, I do realize that true friends are very rare in these times that we live in and so I'm more than thankful for the friendship and support that you both have given to me.

To Kristie Odom, I still can't believe all the energy you have given in the name of help, support, and friendship. You are my proof that angels do exist on earth, and I am very thankful for all that you've done.

To Robert Edwards, I thank you for constantly staying in touch with me and bringing me to Authorhouse.

To Jenifer Brandt, your patience and time has been so appreciated during the whole process of putting this book together for the readers.

And finally I would like to thank my brother Darrell Love, my play mother in-law Rhonda Love, and my grandmother Ma'dear a.k.a Jo Betty Love. Your spirits and loving memories will always have a place in my heart. All of you have played an important part in my life and your roles will never be forgotten. I thank you.

# PRELUDE

*Darkened by destruction and I can no longer see the light*
*I'm headed down a one-way street where futures don't look so bright*
*Death or to jail is where many say that this road will lead*
*Trails of blood lay off to the side as mothers continue to grieve*
*Having knowledge of this I still can't resist*
*The pursuit of ghetto fortune and fame*
*Supplying the demand of my own people who crave to fry their brains*
*The selling of souls at a very low price goes on day after day*
*As a house full of broken dreams pass the pipe*
*While outside their children play*
*Going nowhere fast but here I come with a pocket full of dope*
*Hurting the kids' future and destroying their parent's hopes*
*Living the good life is what people think but I'm full of misery and pain*
*Feeling that there is no way out, I'm trapped in this hustling game*
*I can't turn back now, this is all I know*
*I've been doing this since I was a teen*
*I've been running my own business by way of a triple-beam*
*Watching over my shoulders every step that I take*
*For there is one thing that I know*

*Somethin' is out there trying to get me, is it the police or a jealous foe?*
*Either one I'm blinded to the facts, ignoring every warning sign*
*As if my fate is already sealed like a patient that knows he's dying*
*If I had the chance to do over again, I wonder if I would change*
*Live the legal life and be able to sleep at night*
*Unlike when you're Heavy in the Game...*


Written by: Youngster

# 1

October 28th, 1991 ~ It's been three long years and Youngster, a tall slim black male, is still having nightmares of a night that is surrounded in mystery, warning, and his fate. Waking up in a cold sweat has become the norm for this young man who constantly has the same dream of being cornered by nine gang members in a dark creepy alley. The decision of allowing himself to become a product of his environment is continuing to haunt him due to the uncontrollable situations of the streets and the circumstances that come along with being involved in it.

***

A jolted charge of fear runs through his frozen body as nine gangsters approach him with very bad intentions toting guns from .38 revolvers to all types of semi-automatics. Nervous and shaken by the sight of nine large figures, some wearing red beanies while others red baseball caps, slowly approaching and closing the gap between him and them. He stands in silence from the uncertainty and suspense of the moment. He stares ahead extremely scared as he is only able to see the white of his predators eyes. They all have red bandanas tied tightly around the bridge of their nose. He sees the bandanas hanging down each one of their necks so they wouldn't be identified by him or any possible witnesses while they carried out the slaying of their jittered prey.

Having nowhere to turn and run, the young man has no choice but to conjure up the courage to defend himself. His only option is to go out in a blaze of glory or else he would certainly die like a coward on this night. His heart beats furiously as he pulls out a black 9 millimeter Smith & Wesson from his waist belt to let off rounds on the nine gang members. He aims his weapon in their direction. He starts to press down on the trigger hoping to end the pursuit of the threats headed towards him. Nothing happens. He grips the weapon tighter. He attempts to squeeze the trigger again only to receive the same results, nothing.

All of his courage quickly vanishes as he realizes that his gun has jammed on him. He feels a fear that overshadows his entire body. He becomes stiff and numb. He watches the gang members advance towards him. They are getting closer and closer threatening his young life which seemed to be coming to a tragic end. He braces himself and prepares for a short-lived life to no longer exist. He closes his eyes tight while listening to the yelling of gang slurs and taunting. The sound magnifies and his fear grows. He pleads to God but he feels helpless. All hope is gone and it is confirmed when he slowly opens his eyes to watch his demise at the hands of a gang.

On this somber night, death will soon follow the sight of a group of arms rising up against him aiming their deadly arsenals towards the very terrified male known as Youngster.

***

Youngsters' worst fear haunts him as he awakes from another nightmare perspiring at the forehead. His heart was pumping and limbs shaking like he had just narrowly escaped death. He turns his head slightly to the left towards his nightstand to check for the time. The black digital clock read 8:05 a.m. He rose up and sat at the edge of his black lacquered queen size bed. While wiping the sweat from his forehead and thick black eyebrows, he began to gather his thoughts. He attempted to regain the strength mentally to prepare for another day of the uncertain journey in the street life.

After a refreshing shower, Youngster put on a pair of blue Guess jeans, a matching Guess shirt, and a pair of all white Reeboks. He then walked towards his nightstand to grab his all black pager. He headed downstairs to the kitchen to cook his famous cookies, (cocaine in the form of a cookie instead of the normal rock shape) in the microwave. He wraps each cookie in aluminum foil with them all weighing fourteen grams each. He sells each cookie for three hundred dollars and he gets rid of about ten to twelve a day.

Youngster is doing very well for a young black male. He is twenty-two years old surviving in the rough brutal city of South-Central Los Angeles. He rents a two bedroom, two and a half bath townhouse just outside of the city in a place called Hawthorne. He has some of the best furniture and clothes that money can buy. He drives a brand new fully loaded green Volvo wagon that he is very proud to own. Youngster is six feet tall and carries around an innocent face with dark brown eyes. He has a thick black mustache, nice trimmed goatee, and keeps a shiny bald head.

He has come a long way from selling dimes and twenties of rock cocaine on the corners and in the dim alleys behind apartment buildings four years back. He now picks up at least three hundred dollars a drop. He conducts his business for the most part from inside of his car instead of on the blocks. If there is such a thing as an illegal entrepreneur, he personifies the characteristics of one. He has the mind set equipped with the ambition to reach the very top. His mind constantly stays on getting there.

A little after ten, Youngster's pager began to alert him by vibrating. He took the pager from off of his hip to check the number. After seeing the number, he went to grab the kitchen telephone hanging on the wall. He dialed the number displayed across the pager and listened to two rings before someone picked up on the other end of the line.

"Hello." A mellow deep woman's voice answered.

"Hey, what's up Betty?" he asked in a smooth heavy tone.

"Not too much, what time can you come see me?" she asked.

He looked around the kitchen to estimate his clean up time. He then answered, "I'll be there in about twenty minutes."

"Well, call me when you get here," she said.

"Alright, I'll call when I'm close."

Betty is a long time customer of Youngster's. She is one of his main money makers. She has a dark complexion, tight eyes, wide nose, and is very thin. She is a little over five feet and six inches tall and always has her hair in a ponytail that hangs just above her shoulders. Betty is in her forties but the wear and tear of the streets has aged her at least twenty more years in looks. She has two sons; Kevin and Calvin, both in their teens. She does a steady job of mixing her business with pleasure and has been doing it that way for years. She sells just enough drugs to support her habit which is the use of the same product that she sells. Betty has been loyal to Youngster ever since he started out hustling when they were introduced to one another at an old spot where he once sold rocks.

Thirty minutes after he hung up with Betty, Youngster approached the building in which she lived. He dialed her up on his mobile phone so that they would meet in the back of her building at the same time.

"Hello." Betty answered.

"Betty, I'm out back."

"Okay, I'll be right out."

In less than three minutes, Betty appeared in her powder blue robe. She stepped out from behind a brown iron security gate that led directly into the alley.

"What's up Youngster?" she asked as she approached the car.

"Not much," he replied as he handed her a cookie while she tossed him the money wrapped in a rubber band. "I'll be out here till about eleven tonight." He informed her as he gripped the tightly rolled money.

"Okay," she responded as she was backing away from the car. "I'll be givin' you a call again later on because I know this won't last me till tomorrow."

"Alright then, holla at me." He put his first three hundred dollars of the day in his pocket, rolled up his window, and pulled off at a moderate speed.

When Youngster drove down the street and approached a stop sign, a suspicious car pulled up beside him. He slowly looked over to see who was in the car beside him while preparing for the possibility of a threatening situation. He was relieved when he saw the heavy set dark figure known as Gee leaning back in his old red Buick Regal. He was wearing a thick gold herringbone and a red long sleeve T-shirt along with a useless hardcore expression on his face.

Youngster retreated from his motion for his gun before he rolled down the passenger side window. While the window was rolling down, he heard, "What's up Youngster?"

"Not much," he replied in a calm manner.

"Blood, what's the deal with you still comin' up in here and shit? You know that you're in violation and that shit ain't *bool*." Gee tried to play the real hard gangster role by replacing some words that begin with the letter *C* with the letter *B*. This was done by rival gangs to show a sign of disrespect towards each other.

"Nigga please!" Youngster quickly responded. "I grew up over here just like you, so you can miss me with that bullshit!" Youngster switched from a calm tone to a very serious one in his voice. He also had the look to complement it. There was no hiding the fact that he was irritated at Gee's same old routine. He let it be known in his voice and by the look on his face without hesitation.

"Alright Blood, you better watch your back." Gee spoke wearing a grim look on his face as he slowly pulled off from the stop sign. He tried to look fearless but also wanted to avoid further confrontation before he dug a hole too deep to get out.

"Oh yeah, Fuck you!" Youngster yelled out but his vile words fell upon deaf ears as Gee was too far away to hear them.

Gee would always pull up on Youngster acting hard. He would talk the same old mess to Youngster but Youngster never paid it too much attention. Gee is from the Jungles. He has been banging for quite a few years. He is twenty years old and a few inches under six feet tall. He wears a funny short hair cut along with a funny looking scar under his bottom lip. A scar that he received during his initiation a few years back. His eyes were bigger than the size of silver quarters and his lips were fat matching the rest of his facial features.

Youngster feels that Gee is just a wannabe. He thinks of Gee as an actor trying hard to fit in a place that he didn't belong. Youngster would usually just brush him off. His feelings were that Gee was just someone that wouldn't let go of what happened back in '88. He felt Gee wasn't a danger nor a major factor to him. Although Youngster was well aware that one never knows what an individual is capable of doing at any given time, he could just sense that Gee feared him too much. Gee didn't really want to go there with Youngster but would always just put on an act whenever he would run into him. It was like he was rehearsing for a role in a movie where he played the villain and Youngster was his nemesis.

Youngster was never caught off guard in the streets. He was always prepared for drama and stayed strapped during his business hours. So if Gee or anyone else wanted to actually bring some noise his way, he would be more than ready to accommodate them with the help from his fully loaded black 9 millimeter. He kept his black 9 in a stash spot under the steering column of his car. Everyone in the Jungles had the feeling that Youngster kept some type of protection near him at all times. They figured that if he was crazy enough to still come in the Jungles after the situation jumped off in '88, he was definitely packing artillery. They knew with some certainty that he wouldn't mind using it if or when duty called.

The Jungles is the territory that the Bloods claim as theirs. It's located in an area of South-Central L.A that is filled with apartment buildings side by side on every block. There were no homes in the Jungles so the clustered apartment buildings gave the look of a modern version of the projects. It had become just one of the many supermarkets for drug users to shop for what they wanted. What made the Jungles unique and different is unlike most of the drug infested areas located in the hostile ghetto environments on the east side of L.A, the Jungles was located on the west side. This was near the so-called middle class and upper class black community. This meant a better and more of a steady money flow on a daily basis instead of the headaches of waiting for the 1$^{st}$ and 15$^{th}$ just to make some real money.

The Jungles was the place where Youngster first embraced the grind and hustle of the street life. It was the place where most of his customers were stationed. This also was where his nickname came from. Due to the fact that Youngster was the youngest among a group of hustlers at the spot he first sold dope, a woman that witnessed him grinding each night started calling him Youngster. The name stuck with him while he became well known for his focus and the quality of dope he sold. This is why for Gee to pull up on him talking about a violation was like talking to him in Chinese or any other foreign language. He felt that he was not going to stop making money in the Jungles just because of what happened three years earlier no matter what anyone said, especially those that were not even around when the ordeal took place.

Youngster felt that he had just as much right to sell dope in that neighborhood as anyone else did. This is because the *O.G.'s,* who he had known ever since elementary and Jr. high school, gave him a pass to hustle and make his money in the hood. The older gangsters' knew that Youngster was not a gang member. It became evident to them that the only color that he would fight for or maybe even kill over was the color of money. They had respected him for that long before the incident occurred.

Youngster had big dreams when he first started out hustling in the Jungles. It wasn't all about the jewelry, fancy cars, and lots of women to him once he had seen the steady cash flow. He saw that there was so much money to be made in the Jungles if the Bloods would only get more organized. Millions of dollars could be made easily in the area. He felt that if he could possibly get the Bloods together, he would see his dream come true. He soon learned that it was an impossible dream to achieve when dealing with the one track minds of gangsters. Youngster was one of those kids growing up that had always been fascinated with the Mafia and their ways. He had studied all the documentaries on the Mafia while admiring the Godfather movies along with his favorite movie, *Scarface.* He believed that if the Bloods could be more organized and concentrated on making money inside their territory more than trying to terrorize it, they could be the richest gang in Los Angeles. He felt that he had the brains to put it together and make it happen if he could have only gotten the Bloods to overlook the fact he wasn't a member of their gang and would never be interested in becoming one. His only interest was in something much greater and more prosperous than gang banging. His only interest was in getting paid.

The Bloods, just like most gangs in Los Angeles, would always be on some other type of madness. Their strive to be hardcore blinded their vision which should have been to get out the ghetto instead of remaining there only to worsen its condition. Their perception of an organized gang was to just terrorize and earn stripes for a neighborhood reputation that didn't earn dollars which didn't make any sense to Youngster. This would be the road block in Youngster's dream of leading the Bloods into the direction of an organized hustling family full of riches. However, he wouldn't let this stop him from his own personal dream of prospering and turning his illegal earnings into a legitimate business. Youngster knew that the Jungles would play a major part in achieving this dream of his. It was his birthplace as a hustler and he viewed the Jungles as the very foundation for building an empire that would eventually grow all across the city of Los Angeles. An empire that he would achieve by doing things his own way.

# 2

Youngster turned a few corners to see if anyone was out and about. He was hoping to catch some of what he called *unexpected money*. These were sales that he would get just by being in the right place, at the right time. Whether it be on his way to a delivery or just after making one, there would usually be at least that one person that would flag him down claiming that they were just about to give him a call. On this particular day, there would be no such luck of someone he wasn't expecting on spending money with him. He rolled around a few minutes thinking he should just head back home until his pager began to vibrate. He glanced down at it to read off the number to himself. He then picked up his mobile phone from the passengers' seat to dial the number that was displayed across the pager. The sounds of N.W.A was booming from his speakers so he had to turn the volume down in order to hear when the person answered on the other end of the line.

"Hello." A sweet and pleasant voice came through the receiver.

"Hey, what's up Angel?"

"What's up Youngster, are you around?" she asked.

"Yeah, you know I'm always around for you."

"Can you come through?" she managed to ask while she smiled from his comment.

"No problem. I'll be there in a few minutes," he told her knowing what she wanted already. He tried to keep the conversation short over the phone.

"Okay, bring me two of them," she said.

"Alright," he quickly stated and hung up the phone.

Angel is another one of Youngster's long time customers. She is thirty-six years old. She used to be a *strawberry* back when Youngster first met her. He was introduced to her at the same spot he worked from when he met Betty. Angel was one of the finest *strawberrys* in the neighborhood. She has hazel eyes, a butterscotch complexion, and a shape that was nowhere near that of a crack head. Her father is Jamaican and her mother is Puerto Rican which gave her a very exotic look. She used to be on every trick's most wanted list which allowed her to get as high as she wanted to every single day and night. However, being the best looking hoe in the neighborhood also has its disadvantages. She would often tell Youngster some of the horrible stories when she would hang with him at the spot during the times she would rest. Many nights she would just chill out from all the street walking and talk to Youngster about her desires to put an end to her addiction. She would tell him how much she wanted to stop selling her body for the use of cocaine and reveal to him the different things she would have to go through for that high that her body yearned for daily.

The one story that would always stand out in Youngster's mind was the story about those same police officers that would harass him, picking her up and taking her to secluded areas to receive oral sex in exchange for not taking her in on prostitution charges. To think that those so-called officers of the law can go from roughing up a person, claiming to uphold the law, and the next minute break the law, ate at the core of Youngsters' soul. It would really disgust him to hear about how those no good dirty cops would take advantage of someone using their badges to protect their wrongs while serving their lustful desires. It would often remind him of what an old man once wrote, "Wolves in sheep's clothing are found in higher places many more times than in the lower ones."

Angel no longer sells herself for the use of dope. She doesn't have to deal with situations like those any longer. She has gotten herself together and now raises her ten year old daughter, Trina. Angel rents an apartment in the Jungles and makes her money from slangin' rocks in her building. She still will use cocaine occasionally and Youngster would get on her every time he would find out about it. He would remind her of how far she has come. He would tell her how good she still looks after living such a hard life. He would also tell her how proud that he was of her for overcoming it all. When Youngster and Angel had time for a serious discussion, he would mention all the nights she would be out while leaving Trina with her mother to watch. He then would say to her that she had a lot of making up to do with her little daughter. Youngster is very fond of Angel in a caring way. He always stayed on her in hopes that it would lead to her giving up the use of drugs completely.

Youngster called Angel before turning into a long alley so that she would meet him in the back of her apartment building. Her building was located at the very top of the alley. This would give her enough time to meet him out back before he arrived. Like clockwork, he reached her building just as she stepped out into the alley. She was wearing black tights and a short red pajama top with matching furry slippers.

"Hey Youngster, how are you doing today?" she asked as she stepped towards the car.

"I'm doin' alright Angel. What's up with you?" he replied as he handed her two cookies covered in foil. He then watched as she reached down in her bra to retrieve the money.

"Everything been movin' pretty smooth this week," she said as she gave him the money. "I'm just going to go back up here and post up all day."

"You haven't been messin' around with that, have you?" he asked gesturing towards the wrapped cookies that she held hidden in her hand.

"No, I've been too busy to even think about it."

"Good," he replied. "And you keep on being too busy not thinkin' about it." With that said, she just smiled at him. Youngster continued, "I'm not playin' Angel, save your money and get your ass and Trina up out this damn Jungle. Ya'll deserve better than this and you know it." She looked at him directly in his eyes as if she had just met the man of her dreams. Youngster has been the most kind and concerned person in her life besides her mother. He held a special place in her heart.

"Sounds like you ready for me and Trina to come move in with you or somethin'," Angel said after glaring into his eyes. "And if that's the case, you can have these damn cookies back and I'll get to start packin' right now."

Her comment brought a laughter from the both of them as she retreated back to her building swaying her nicely shaped hips back and forth. It was her way of giving him something to think about and to take notice of while he went about the rest of his day. Angel arrived at her gate to enter her apartment building. Before walking inside the gate, she turned back towards Youngster. She caught him staring which was nothing new. She then said in an alluring way, "Don't play with me Papi, you know I'll put this thing on your ass and have you saying I do in front of a preacher." They both wore a smile on their faces as Youngster shook his head before saying to her, "You so crazy." He slowly pulled off as she watched him pass by her still wearing a smile on her face.

When Youngster finished flirting with Angel as he would do most of the time when they handled their business, he made a few more drops before noticing that it was a little after twelve. This time of the day meant only one thing to him, it was time to eat. He would always head towards his favorite spot to eat breakfast around noon each day when he would be out making his moves. Roscoe's Chicken & Waffles was the name of the restaurant. There are two locations in Los Angeles where Roscoe's could be found. One of these locations is on the Eastside while the other could be found on the Westside of L.A. Youngster would drive over to the Eastside instead of going to the one that was much closer. The reason for this was that he didn't like to sit and eat close to where he conducted his business. The one that was located on the Westside was too close to where he made his runs. He felt that it wasn't a good thing for security reasons. A man tends to let his guard down during feeding time, so Youngster preferred to eat far from his business activities. He also liked the way the waitresses looked and the way they treated him at the particular Roscoe's on the eastside. There was more of a comfortable atmosphere there.

He arrived at the restaurant at about twelve forty-five. He pulled into the plaza located on the corner of Manchester & Main to park. As soon as he walked in the restaurant, he was greeted by a beautiful waitress.

"How are you doing today, and where's the little one?" she asked referring to Youngster's two year old son, Jay.

"He's with his mama for a change, probably cryin' for me to come back and pick him up," he replied in a joking manner while he stood at the entrance smelling the aroma of fried chicken and fresh waffles.

The waitress smiled and then asked, "The usual for you?"

"Yeah," he answered. He then walked towards the corner of the somewhat empty restaurant.

"Okay, coming right up." She wrote down his order on her tablet while walking towards the back where the food was being cooked.

"Thanks!" Youngster took his favorite table tucked away in the corner where he could view everything and everyone that entered. It was a table where the pictures of Sojourner Truth and Malcolm X hung above the area. They were adjacent to one another.

Youngster's usual was an order of well done chicken wings with a side order of eggs scrambled with cheese, a large waffle, and a glass of lemonade. All of the waitresses knew that was his regular order from the menu. They were all fond of him due to how he carried himself. They all felt that he was very polite. They would all gossip among one another trying to figure out the burning question, what was a twenty-two year old black male doing to where he was able to bring his son in to eat almost everyday during normal work hours? Youngster knew that it could be difficult to figure out his illegal occupation because he was never one to fit the stereotype by wearing jewelry or flashy clothes. He dressed conservative and never wore any jewelry besides his watch. He would always be well mannered in the public eye. He kept to himself, within himself, and would always act as if he was a law abiding citizen in the watchful vision of those that didn't know him. This came from a lesson an old man taught him once, "Never fit the stereotype of your profession when your main objective is to keep the heat off of you and the others off balance."

After about fifteen minutes had past, the food was ready and on its way towards the table.

"Here you are," the waitress said as she placed the food down on the table in front of him.

"Thank you," he said graciously.

"You're welcome and your drink is coming right up. Will there be anything else I can get you?" she asked as she made eye contact with him.

"No thanks!"

"Well, if you need anything, just let me know." Lisa smiled as she slowly turned away while he watched the back of her blue jeans take on a life of its own.

Lisa is one of the nicest waitresses at Roscoe's. She is also one of the finest. She is light-skinned with a lovely shape. Lisa has long brown wavy hair that she keeps in a ponytail and always seems to maintain a beautiful smile on her face. A smile that would just brighten her light-brown eyes up and put her thick lips on display. Youngster just loved to see that smile. He liked the way Lisa carried herself and thought that she had a very nice personality. But Youngster didn't allow his attraction towards her to show. He couldn't get up the nerves to let her know that he wanted to get more acquainted with her. At times, he could be quite a shy person. Especially when it came down to trying to get to know someone that he had been seeing in the same restaurant for over a year. It had gotten to the point where it was just too odd. It had become strange to attempt to get at Lisa in that way.

Halfway through his meal, Youngster's pager went off and he glanced down at it on his hip. He pushed the display bottom recognizing Shell's number across the screen. He grabbed his mobile phone laying on the table and began to dial her number.

"Hello." Shell answered.

"Hey, what's up?" he asked.

"Nothin', what's up with you?" she replied.

"I'm at Roscoe's right now eating a little somethin'. Where's Jay at?"

"He's layin' right here. Why? Are you comin' to get him today?" Before Youngster could answer, she continued, "He's been whinin' for you since you dropped him off yesterday."

"I thought you said you wanted him for a few days?"

"I know but I can't take this whinin'."

"Well, if you want me to, I'll come get him as soon as I get through eating."

"About how long do you think that's going to be?" she asked with a big sigh of relief in her voice.

Youngster looked at the phone in disbelief and answered, "I'm almost finished over here, so not that long."

"Well, just call me when you done."

"Alright, I will."

"See you when you get here."

"Alright," Youngster hung up the phone and proceeded to finish his meal while he thought about the phone conversation he just had with his baby's mama. He just could not believe that a mother could be so quick to get rid of her own child.

Shell is the nickname of the mother of Youngster's son. Her real name is Michelle. She is nineteen years old and stands just a little over five feet and five inches. Shell was only sixteen when she first met Youngster but she was already a *vet* when it came down to using her sex appeal. Youngster used to always tell the story of the day when he first saw her getting off the bus on Crenshaw & Slauson Avenue. He would joke and say, "It is a day that I will always regret and never forget." Youngster was known for being a little shy, especially back when he first met Shell. But when he saw Shell step off that bright orange R.T.D and began to walk down the street, he felt that he just had to turn around. He just had to attempt to get at her, no matter what. Youngster was driving a two toned black and silver El Camino. He was on his way to his grandmother's house to watch a big boxing match between Sugar Ray Leonard and Marvin Hagler with the rest of his family. However, after seeing Shell get off that bus, he had forgot all about the fight. All his attention was drawn to Shell as he made a U-turn to catch her before she caught the next bus on Slauson.

Shell was dressed in a pair of white pants that had fit her perfectly to display her assets. She was wearing a black silk top, three gold chains, and had long jet black hair with pretty dark eyes. At first sight, Youngster couldn't tell whether she was Black or Hispanic because of her very light complexion and long wavy hair. He later found out that she was Creole but on the day he first met her, he just wanted to know her name and number.

After receiving her number that day, he called her later on that week. From there, things happened quite fast. They became inseparable. Shell wouldn't let Youngster out of her sight. He took to her just the same. However, since she was his first real relationship, Youngster kept himself from falling in love with her. He wanted to prevent getting attached emotionally. He felt that by being so young and Shell being his first true intimate involvement, that there were many more fish in the sea. He felt that he had just begun to throw out his fishing rod.

***

"Will there be anything else?" Lisa asked while Youngster was daydreaming.

"Oh, I'm sorry. No thank you!" He responded just before she was about to repeat herself.

"Missing your son, or thinking about your girlfriend?" she asked with a smile.

He smiled back as he stood up, "Just some business I have to take care of." He lied.

"Well, you have a blessed and wonderful day," she said while placing the tab on the table. She then walked away to attend to another table.

"Same to you," he replied while he reached in his pocket. He dropped a ten dollar bill on the table and walked to the counter to pay for his food.

Youngster stepped outside and was greeted by a very bright sun, a warm gentle breeze, and an elderly black man with a beard. The man asked Youngster for some spare change. Without a word being said, Youngster reached in his pocket and handed the man five dollars. Youngster then took in his surroundings for a brief moment. After the man thanked him, Youngster proceeded to walk to his car. Once inside his car, he dialed Shell's number right after starting up the engine.

"Hello." She answered.

"Hey, I'm on my way."

"Okay, I'm gonna get his stuff ready," she replied.

"Alright, I'll be there in about twenty minutes."

"Alright, we will see you then." They both hung up and Youngster merged into traffic.

Shell lives with her grandmother in Compton. Compton is another gang infested area of California about twelve miles away from South-Central L.A. She moved in with her grandmother once she was released from the hospital after giving birth to Jay. She had no other choice after the split with Youngster. Shell's grandmother's name is Anne. Anne is an elderly woman in her sixties. She stands at five feet and three inches. She has long grayish hair and keeps her reading glasses hanging around her neck. She resembles a Native American in her entire appearance but when she speaks, the fact that she's from down south is unmistakable. Anne didn't like the fact that Youngster broke up with Shell and left her in such a bad condition. She always had something negative to say about Youngster during Shell's eleven months of rehabilitation. However, she was well aware that there is always two sides to a story. Knowing that fact, would eventually allow her to give him the benefit of the doubt. Anne never treated Youngster ill behind the break-up with her granddaughter. She would always be very polite to him every time he would come in her house.

Youngster pulled up in front of the light brown home about twenty minutes after leaving Roscoe's. He stepped out of his car and entered the yard that was surrounded by a small steel gate. Once he arrived at the porch, he noticed Anne standing behind the iron security screen door. The type of door that is a must when living in the settings of poverty, crime, gangs, and drugs.

"Hello Anne. How have you been?" he greeted her as she opened the door for him.

"I'm just fine Jayshawn, come on in," she said in her southern accent with a bright smile on her face. She then called out to her granddaughter, "Michelle!" After no response, Anne just turned to him and said, "She's right there in her room with Badness, go on in there."

Shell's room was the first room off to the right of the living room. It was the only bedroom of the three that was located in the front part of the house. Entering Shell's room was always an adventure for Youngster. He never knew what to expect when it came down to going into her bedroom. If Anne had only knew how her granddaughter would carry on sometimes, she would have never allowed Youngster to enter without her being present.

Most of the time if Jay was asleep when Youngster came to pick him up, Shell would lock the door to her bedroom and attempt to win him over. She would undo his pants to please Youngster the best way that she knew how. She knew he couldn't resist her oral skills. She always hoped that he would take her back each time she would finish pleasing him. Then there were the other times when she would just sob, shed tears, and tell him how sorry she was for letting him down. She would just plead and beg him for another chance. Needless to say, Youngster would look forward to Shell's oral skills but couldn't stand the crying and pleading. This particular day, there would be neither of the two because Jay was wide awake and ready to leave.

"What's up Jay, are you ready to go?" Youngster asked once he entered the bedroom.

Jay quickly jumped off the bed as the answer to Youngster's question. He ran straight towards his daddy with open arms.

Youngster grabbed Jay under his arms and hurled him to his chest. He squeezed his little toddler tight, kissed him on the cheek, and said, "Boy you are gettin' heavier each day."

"Yeah, that's from you takin' him out to eat all the time and that fast food that you keep feedin' him," Shell snapped.

"Girl, we eat at home more than you think we do."

"Yeah right, but anyway," she paused and then asked, "What do you be doin' to my son?"

"What do you mean?" he asked with a look of confusion.

"That boy has been up since this mornin' whinin' and askin' for you. All he does is whine for you when he's over here." Shell got up off her bed to hand Jay's diaper bag to Youngster.

"It's not what I'm doin' to him. It's what you not doin'." He joked, "A child be knowin' things, they can sense and feel the real love from people." Youngster wore a sarcastic look on his face as he threw Jay's bag over his shoulder while still holding Jay in his arms.

"You are always tryin' to be funny Jayshawn. Where are ya'll about to go anyway?" Shell asked.

Youngster looked at her to try to see just where she was going with the question before he answered, "I don't know, probably over my mother's house for a minute, make some runs, and then head back home." He turned to exit the bedroom. He looked at his son and said, "Come on Jay, let's go."

He held Jay as he walked out into the living room with Shell following close behind. Anne was sitting on the couch when they all came walking through.

"You takin' Badness away from me already?" Anne asked. "He just got here yesterday." Badness is what Anne affectionately called Jay.

"Grandma, you know I can't do anything with him when he is cryin' for his daddy," Shell stated.

"Well, let me get my kiss before ya'll leave," Anne said while shaking her head. She struggled off her couch while Youngster walked over to her with Jay in his arms. "Bye Badness," she said right after kissing Jay on the cheek.

"Bye," Jay responded in his cute voice while waving his hand. He then quickly turned his head towards the door as if he was anxious to leave.

"Jay is leavin' already?" Shell's little cousin Rudy shouted as he ran towards everyone from his room in the back. "But he just got here."

"Don't blame me," Youngster said in his own defense. He then nodded his head towards Shell to give Rudy a hint where to place the blame. Youngster started out the door while Rudy waved and said, "Goodbye." Jay waved back at Rudy. Shell followed them to the door saying, "Wait a minute, let me get my kiss before ya'll leave."

Youngster stopped on the porch for Shell to kiss Jay. After she kissed him on the forehead, she whispered in Youngster's ear, "I want to spend the night so come back later and get me, alright?" She waited for an answer as he left her standing on the porch. Youngster walked towards his car as if he didn't hear her. He would play games with her often like that so this was no surprise to her. Shell just continued, "I know you heard me Jayshawn, so stop playing with me and let me know something."

"Yeah I heard you," he replied.

"So what's up?" she asked.

Youngster had her waiting for a response while he strapped Jay in the car. He then slowly put Jay's belongings in the back seat. He continued to ignore Shell's question just to aggravate her.

"You know you make me sick when you play like that, right?" she asked as she stood on the porch with her hands on her hips.

Finally, he turned towards her saying with a grin on his face, "I don't know yet, I'll think about it and I'll call you later on."

"Don't have me waiting all night without hearin' from you!" She demanded as she watched him walk around to the driver side of his car.

"Yeah, yeah whatever," he brushed her off before getting in his car. He started the car up and pulled off.

The music booming from out the speakers of the Volvo was pretty loud when Youngster first started the car. He began to pull off with the booming sounds but soon turned the music down to speak to Jay. "What's up boy, did you miss me?" Jay looked up at his daddy before nodding his head up and down with a big smile on his face.

"Daddy missed you too. Do you want to go see your grandma?"

"Yeah," Jay answered.

"Okay, we're on our way. You want somethin' to eat first? Are you hungry?" he asked looking over to Jay who shook his head from left to right a few times.

"Well, here's somethin' to play with until we get to grandma's house," Youngster reached in the back seat and handed Jay one of his toys that was hanging from the side of Jay's bag. Jay took the toy from his daddy and began to play with it.

Youngster turned his music back up and started rolling back towards South-Central. About ten minutes later right after passing a McDonalds, Jay tapped Youngster on the arm. He gave Youngster a slick grin before saying, "Daddy, I want some fren fries."

"You want some French fries?" he asked. "Boy you're just saying that because you saw that McDonalds back there. I thought you weren't hungry."

"Dat was a long time ago," he said innocently as his daddy looked over towards him.

"Boy that was just a minute ago. You call that a long time ago?" Youngsters' question only received a big bright giggle from his little one. "Boy you crazy," Youngster managed to say. He then shook his head as he continued to drive until he reached the next McDonalds. He then pulled into the drive-thru to order Jay a bag of French Fries.

Jayson King is simply known as Jay. He is Youngster's terrible two who was soon to be three years old. Jay is his road *dawg*. They are seen together rolling around Los Angeles most of the time throughout the day. Youngster enjoys his son's company. He loves the many experiences that comes along with being a parent and raising a child. The one thing that disturbs him is that Jay looks just like his mother. Jay does not look anything like him. Under the circumstances that caused the break up between Youngster and Shell, he has had his doubts about Jay actually being his son. He has learned to deal with his doubts though. At times he has found it to be pretty amusing watching Jay's expressions. He would look just like Shell when Youngster would fuss at him. Youngster has truly embraced the responsibility of raising his son. He has realized that his doubts are not as strong as the overwhelming enjoyment of parenthood in which he wouldn't trade for anything in the world.

Youngster has been keeping Jay ever since Jay was four months old. Unlike the many horrible stories of raising a newborn like the crying and not getting no sleep tales, Youngster has not experienced any problems with Jay. He eats when Youngster eats, sleeps when he sleeps, and he loves to roll around in the car listening to Rap, R&B, and Youngster's Bob Marley collection. Jay has even started to learn some of the lyrics to most of the repeated songs that would be played in the car.

Jay is a very smart little boy that picks up on things quickly. He is observant, curious, and attentive. Youngster would often brag about how it took him only a week to potty train Jay but he knew that the fast training was more of Jay being able to learn quick than it was him being this great teacher of potty training. His simple tactic of sitting Jay on his little pot every morning in front of the television to watch cartoons until he used the pot, worked like a charm in just one week. There was no more buying diapers and changing Jay after that. This was a very good thing for Youngster with all of the running he had to do. Changing diapers would often slow him down which would make him late for appointments.

Youngster took pride in his achievements in parenting and had big plans for his son. His hopes of sending Jay to a private school so that Jay could receive the best education was one of his main goals. His desire for Jay to make something of his life without having to taste the life of the streets was dear to him. The sad thing is that he knew his mother had wished the same for him when he was a young boy. He knew he had let her down. Although she did her best, Youngster chose the direction of hustling in the streets rather than to make an honest living which would have made his mother proud of him.

Despite realizing that he had let his mother down, Youngster has no regrets about deciding to choose the life of the streets. In fact, he would often say that he would recommend that every black man in America receive some form of street knowledge growing up. He felt it would give a black male a fighting chance in White America. He would say that there was nothing better than to have some street knowledge when it came down to dealing with the white man in the white man's world. He would say that the black man can best believe that the white man wants to pimp the black man like he was a prostitute in this world, so the only way to learn to fight fire with fire is with the knowledge that one can get only in the streets.

Youngster would feel so bad when he would think about how he had disappointed his mother. To think that she has to go to sleep every night not knowing if her son would live to see another day or if the streets would finally claim him bothered Youngster. The worried look on her face would always appear soon after the relieving expression she would have when she greeted him and Jay at her door. This would happen each and every time they would stop by her house.

Youngster didn't have the sad story of growing up on welfare. He couldn't tell tales of living in a house full of drugs and alcohol abuse. He couldn't even say that he grew up in the Jungles where the living was hard. Youngster grew up across from the Jungles where the nice homes were and the neighbors were mostly Asian families. There were only a few black family home owners where he grew up. They were sprinkled among the Asian families.

Even with the fact that his father was never there due to a life sentence in prison, this once straight "A" student never used that as an excuse. He was well aware that his mother went out of her way to provide and fill the void that a single parent has to fill. His mother did her best for both him and his little sister. She played the roles of the mother and father in the household. She would do all that she could, the best she knew how, to provide for her children. However, the one thing she couldn't provide for her son, the neighborhood was there to give it to him with open arms.

Youngster's mother was as square and as wholesome as they came in the big city. She tried hard to raise him and his younger sister the right way. While it seemed to have worked for his sister who lives on the legal side of society, it has been a complete failure as far as the outcome for Youngster. This would bother him and sometimes confuse him. Not knowing why he had to be the outcast of the household and the bad seed in the family would get to him often. He would always hear his mother compare him to that of having his father's ways over and over again. This was from childhood to the present which often confused him even more. But in those moments of confusion, Youngster would just think about what the old man wrote to him in a letter that read, "You'll never be able to change what is meant to be, so accept the circumstances and strive to change the final outcome."

# 4

A daily routine for Youngster was to stop by his mother's house and hang out for a little while. This would be his way of letting her know that he and Jay were all right. He would also do this so that she could see there was a normal side to him. He knew that his mother's perception of his lifestyle was far from the truth. It wasn't as dangerous and horrible as she thought it to be. She always pictured her son standing on the corner with Jay by his side surrounded by dope fiends selling crack all throughout the night. By stopping at his mother's house daily, Youngster felt that he was showing her that his life was a bit normal and calm. He wanted her to see that it wasn't as reckless as she imagined it. He would try to ease her mind by showing up each day. He would raid the kitchen and tell a few jokes while he hung around her house before making more runs. Even if it was for a few minutes, it made him feel good inside to see the relief in her face when he would stop by for a brief moment.

His mother, Louise King, is a forty-two year old tall brown skin woman with shoulder length dark hair. Most of Youngsters' facial features and his slim build has come from her. Louise works for the Post Office from seven in the morning to four in the afternoon. She has been working there Monday through Friday ever since Youngster could remember. She has maintained the house notes and bills all alone from the day of her husbands sentencing. They had just purchased the house from the money James, Youngster's father, had saved from all his illegal trips he had made. He was making his final trip before getting caught, locked up, and taken away from his family.

Youngster's sister Lavette is a nineteen year old tall brown skin young lady who looks just like her mother with one exception, her weight. Lavette took after her father in the weight department and carried a few extra pounds around more than her mother. A little over a year removed from graduating high school, she now works a few miles away from home at a big supermarket. Youngster and his sister are very close and are sometimes called twins for their similar ways and their resemblance to one another.

***

Youngster rolled around throughout South-Central Los Angeles with Jay making his usual drops until the late afternoon. When there was no one else to meet, he decided to head in the direction of his mother's house until he received some more calls. Jay's face gleamed the closer they came to his grandmother's house as he looked at the familiar houses on the block. When they finally came within a few houses to his grandmother's, he prepared to leap out his seatbelt. He wanted to be the first one at the porch.

"Well, if it isn't my prodigal son and my miracle baby." Louise said with a light-hearted voice. She stood on her porch wearing a smile as she greeted her grandchild and son.

"Jay, come give your grandma a big hug." Jay rushed towards the porch to embrace his grandmother.

"Mmm," was the sound that Louise let out as she squeezed her little grandson tight. She then pulled away. She took a quick look at him and said, "Now give me some suga baby."

"Ma, you gettin' a little old there ain't you?" Youngster joked.

"Boy, what are you talkin' about?" she asked.

"Come on now, give me some suga," he paused. He gave his mother a silly look before saying, "Now that's old."

"Boy be quiet, and tell me when are you gonna let Jay stay over to spend some time with me on the weekend?"

"I don't know yet, maybe next weekend Ma," he replied as he passed her walking through the living room. He headed straight to the kitchen to see what was there to snack on.

"You know that you've been sayin' that for the past few weeks and you haven't dropped him off to spend some time with me yet."

"I know Ma, I just been doin' things with him on the weekends," he lied to hide the real reason.

"Well, his grandma would like to do things with him also. So you just can't have him all to yourself."

Louise is crazy about her grandchild, Miracle Baby. Miracle Baby is what she sometimes would call Jay. She named him Miracle Baby because she says that it had to be a miracle that Jay was even born. With Shell being in the condition that she was in due to the incident that occurred, Louise believes it could have only been the work of God that allowed Shell to be able to pull through and deliver a healthy baby boy.

Youngster and his mom have developed a strange relationship. This would be the reason why Jay wouldn't spend the night at his grandmother's house too often. Over the past two and a half years since Jay's birth, Youngster has been studying the teachings of the Nation of Islam. He has been listening to many Malcolm X and Farrakhan speeches during this time. He had grown up under Christianity and his mother was now in that stage in her life in which Youngster had labeled a Church Addict. This was someone who when every time the church doors would open, they just had to walk in no matter what time, day, or occasion. They were there and in the front row.

Youngster didn't want his son walking through those doors with his grandmother. He had no desire whatsoever for his son to learn what the Christians' taught and he sure didn't want him to taste the flesh of that filthy animal; pork. Despite his wishes, Louise would totally ignore her son's ideas because she viewed them as foolishness. She would take Jay to church whenever she had the chance and fed him pork each time he would spend the night over to her house. This would irk and upset Youngster so much that he would just avoid letting Jay stay over as much as he could. He didn't understand why his mother couldn't respect his wishes and respect him as a parent. This was his child and his attempt to raise his child the way that he saw fit. But Louise just looked at her son as a child also, rather than an adult with a child. This made no sense to Youngster. This would be the reason why there was such a strange relationship between the two because Louise never learned to respect her son as a man. She would only treat him as her little boy no matter how old he would get. He would just remain her child that needed to be overruled by her.

"Ma, where is Vette at?" Youngster asked as he grabbed a can of root beer from out of the refrigerator.

"I think she had switched hours with someone at her job so she'll be comin' in a little later than usual."

"Oh, okay."

"You know she said that they are hiring up there again." Louise tried another one of her vain attempts to get her son to consider earning his money legally.

"That's good Ma, I hope they hire someone that really needs that job." Louise could only shake her head in disgust and pray that her son would eventually come around.

Youngster sat over his mom's house for a few hours. He also managed to make a few runs while she watched Jay for him. It began to get late in the evening and he decided to give Shell a call before he went home to see if she still wanted him to pick her up. Although he made it his business not to let it show, he thought about her a lot. Deep down inside he wished that things could have worked out between the two of them.

Shell meant a lot to him but she also really hurt him like he had never experienced before in his young life. This would make his feelings for her so mixed up and confusing. The positive thoughts and feelings that he did have for her would not be seen through her eyes. Youngster dealt with the situation with Shell by going on a personal rule that he developed within himself which was pride over emotions. He would never allow his emotions to overcome him. He would stand firm on his pride.

After getting Jay buckled up in the car and situated, he started the car. He then dialed Shell's number as he slowly pulled off from his mom's house.

"Hello." She answered.

"Hello," he echoed to mimic her.

"Hey, what's up? Are ya'll on ya'll way?"

"On our way? Girl we're out in the front of your house right now."

There was a pause over the phone. Being that Shell's window had a view of the front yard, there was a short moment of silence as she peeked outside before returning to the phone and saying, "You play way too much Jayshawn."

"What?" he asked as if he had no idea what she was talking about.

"You are not in front of the house," she said.

"Oh! Well, we'll be there in about twenty minutes then."

"Well, I'm going to get my stuff ready so call me when you get out front."

"Alright, I will."

It was a little after eleven that night by the time Youngster had arrived in Compton. He was a bit upset at himself for staying out that late with Jay. He was trying to hurry home to put him to bed. Jay was wide awake during the time it took to get home. He was so happy to see both his mother and father together. He was doing his best to stay awake and enjoy the moment. Seeing his mother and father actually together was a rare sight for Jay. He was for the most part either with one or the other. It wasn't often that he was with the both of them at the same time. This issue bothered Youngster a lot because he was all too familiar with what his son was missing. He hated that his son had to be brought up not seeing his parents sharing the same household. He didn't like the fact that Jay couldn't be raised among them both. It saddened him that Jay didn't get to go places with both his parents like to the park or to the movies. He knew that it could have an effect on Jay later on. Because growing up with just one parent whether it be only the mother or the father, a child would always seem to miss out on what the one parent can't give.

Youngster never planned on having his child grow up in a single parent household like he had to do when he was a child. He used to always tell his little sister that when he grew up, that his children would get to enjoy living in a complete household. He vowed to never leave his family hanging like his father left them. He was only three and his sister was just born when their father was taken away. The situation with Jay's mother, he felt was out of his control. He had hoped that his son would understand why his mother and father weren't together when he became older. Although he never understood his own father's abandonment as a child, he hoped that Jay would actually understand the situation better than he did. Youngster never stopped to think about the thin line he walked that could get him into the same position that took his father away from his family. Youngster always thought he would be much smarter.

When they arrived at the apartment, Youngster headed straight upstairs with Jay to put him to bed. Shell followed right behind them making a right turn towards Youngsters' bedroom while saying, "Goodnight baby," to her son.

"Goodnight mama," Jay replied rubbing his eyes. As tired as he was, he still attempted to fight his sleep.

Shell entered the bedroom and turned on the light that sat on the nightstand on Youngster's main side of the bed. That nightstand was the closest upon entering the bedroom. She then grabbed the remote off the nightstand and turned on the television. She pressed the mute button and sat on the edge of the bed waiting for Youngster to come in the room. Shell never knew what to expect when it came to dealing with Youngster. She would often compare it to dealing with Dr. Jekyll and Mr. Hyde. She would take her chances on which side would show up nevertheless. She understood the pain she caused Youngster. She only hoped that she could make things right between them. She had learned to deal with his ways, the mood swings, and the attitudes he dished out. She wanted him back so much that she was willing to do all that it took to accomplish that.

Youngster stood in the doorway of Jay's Batman decorated bedroom waiting for him to finish using the bathroom. When Jay finished handling his business, he washed his hands and came out walking towards his daddy. He was looking to get picked up so his daddy would tuck him in bed. Jay had two twin size beds in his room. He would sleep in the one closest to the bedroom door. With his daddy's bedroom right next to his, he felt more secure in sleeping in the bed right next to the wall separating the two rooms.

After Youngster sat Jay on the bed, he gave him a big hug before tucking him in under the blankets and sheets. He looked at his son and said, "Night, night Jay."

"Goodnight daddy. I love you!" Jay told his daddy as he gave him a tight squeeze around the neck.

"I love you too," Youngster turned on Jay's little night light by his bed. He then walked to the bedroom door to turn off the main light to his room. "See you in the morning," he told him and closed his door behind him as he walked out.

When Youngster entered his bedroom where Shell was waiting for him, he saw her on his bed with the look of seduction and desire written all over her face. He knew that she had only one thing on her mind. It was the very reason why he called her.

"Come over here and lay down so I can relax you," she said with a low sexual tone in her voice, "I know you've been busy all day and you want this."

"Relax me?" he responded, playing naïve. "How are you gonna do that?" he pretended not to know what she was trying to insinuate.

"Jayshawn, why do you always wanna joke around with me? Even when you know I'm being serious with you. You know why you picked me up tonight so stop playin' and get over here." She stood up and began to undress, slowly revealing her shapely form.

Youngster closed the door shut. He stared for a very brief moment before approaching her nude invitation. When he stepped towards her, she dropped down on the bed to loosen his belt. She discovered that he was more than ready to come out of his jeans. She accommodated the obvious excited part of his body by gently freeing it from the suffocating jeans and the black boxers he was wearing. She then immediately began giving his released stiff chocolate bar her full attention. There were only the sounds of his appreciation and the moans of Shell's delight in knowing that she was pleasing him as she continued to work on his desire.

Shell guided him to the middle of the bed. She completely undressed him as he lay there craving for more pleasure. She then went to grab a condom out the top drawer of his nightstand and returned to him. She caressed his neck and chest with her tongue making her way back down to the center of his body while listening to his moaning approval. He was enjoying her work so much that he was almost ready to explode. But he wanted to spend some time inside of her wet walls before reaching his climax. At that moment, he let her know that he was ready to feel her warm interior by pulling his body away from her occupied mouth and tongue. Without a word being said, she ripped open the condom and placed it on his hard chocolate bar. She then mounted him. She immediately started riding him nice and slow until she began to feel her own climax building up. It was then that she started moving at a much more rapid pace. She began to ride him as if she was on an untamed bull. Things had gotten very intense as her body pulled on his sexual forces. Youngster was giving it his best shot not to give in until she reached her orgasm. He wanted her to *cum* before he did. He fought long and hard not to climax until she had reached hers but time was not on his side. He could feel the build up getting stronger and stronger. He was ready to release from the pressure.

Finally, after motions and sounds of passionate lust, Shell let out a scream of satisfaction. His entire source of energy completely left his body at the same time. They both trembled from the aftershocks and let out whispering sounds of sensual relief. Shell dropped down on Youngster's damp chest and remained for a moment to soak in the wonderful feeling she just received. Youngster could only lay still because his body had stiffened. He was momentarily paralyzed due to the hard release that was weeks overdue. One couldn't tell from their subdued reaction and drained physiques, but they were both very thankful. The cause and effect from the act of lust gave them both a gratifying feeling.

After a few minutes went by, Shell rolled off Youngster and looked over at him. She looked to see if it was alright to cuddle with him but her answer was given as soon as he turned away from her. He curled up with his back facing her and fell into a very deep state of unconsciousness that sent him straight to his past.

1988

**5**

It was a few days before Halloween and Youngster had just finished breakfast around nine that morning. He noticed the time and went into his bedroom to prepare to go to Los Angeles. He had to get ready to do his usual routine of selling double-up packs in the Jungle. He had planned on leaving from West Covina at ten to avoid the usual traffic jams on the 10 freeway going west. Shell had a job in West Covina but this particular day she was off. She began to bug Youngster as she always would when she didn't have to go to work.

"Jayshawn, can I go with you to L.A?"

"No!" He quickly replied. Before Shell could plead her case, he continued, "We didn't move all the way out here for you to be following me back and forth. We moved out here for you to be away from what I do and for me to be able to get away from that shit when I finish each night."

"What makes you think that I like stayin' out here by myself while you're out there doin' who knows what with who knows who?"

"What the fuck do you mean who knows who? Are you tryin' to say that you don't trust me or somethin'?" he responded very angrily. He was on the verge of getting upset.

She paused a few seconds as she looked up at him. She gave him the cutest sad face that he had ever seen before she spoke softly, "I'm not saying that I don't trust you but you tell me all the time that those damn *jungle bunnies* be always trying to get with you and I know that they'll try extra hard when they continue not to see me with you. I'm off work today and I'll only be bored if you leave me out here."

"And what's wrong with that Shell?" he asked. "I'd rather be bored and safe, than out there in the streets not knowin' what the fuck might happen to me."

Shell was still wearing that cute sad face, "We were together all day and night before we had moved out here so that is somethin' that I would have to get used to and right now I'm not used to that yet Jayshawn. I want to be with you today." At that moment, her eyes were watery and she asked for the fourth time, "Let me go to L.A with you today, alright?"

He took a long look at her and that expression she wore before giving in, "Alright, hurry up so we can beat the traffic."

She instantly started glowing and her face filled with joy. She leaped off the bed and rushed towards him. She embraced him and began pecking at his face with kisses of gratitude.

"Okay, okay," he said slightly pushing her away. Shell took a step back. She gave him a bright smile before rushing off to the shower. She was feeling wonderful as she hurried to get dressed. She felt very happy knowing she would be traveling with her man.

They arrived in L.A a little before noon. Youngster was rushing to get to his mother's house to call back a few pages that he had received while driving. He didn't own a mobile phone so he operated from his mother's house. It was like his dispatching center or headquarters for a cocaine take-out. He would make his calls from there and would hang out there until he received a page for a delivery. Not having a mobile phone didn't bother Youngster that much. He felt that it was in his best interest not having one because there were many rumors of the police and other government authorities tapping the mobile phones to bust the young black drug dealers. He heard too many stories about others in his profession getting raided and the District Attorney using their mobile phone conversations as evidence against them. Possessing a mobile phone at that time was the stereotype of a drug dealer. This only applied if one was a young black male driving with a phone. It had become one of the many probable cause tools used by the police force to pull over and harass the young black men. As if being black was not enough, seeing a black male with a mobile phone gave the authorities more of a reason to pull blacks over to search their car.

Youngster had just made a drop in the Jungles and turned up Hillcrest Street when he spotted Stone in his rearview mirror. He saw Stone trying to flag him down. He pulled to the curb to allow Stone to catch up to him.

Stone was a Blood from the Jungles that stood about six feet and was twenty years old. Stone had a very light-brown complexion, bird like nose, and he had the most up to no good pair of eyes ever placed on a human being. He wore his hair in a flat top and wore a gold earring of the letter *S* in his nose.

"Hey Youngster, how much you'll let three ounces go for?" Stone asked as soon as he got to the window.

"Each one is six hundred a piece Stone. I thought we had this discussion last week." Youngster said without trying to hide the sarcasm in his voice.

"Nah Youngster, I asked about one ounce last week," he replied, "But three of them should be about eighteen hundred, right?"

"That's right Stone, so what's up?"

"Well look, I'm gonna see what's up and page you if I need it." Stone backed away from the car after completing his sentence.

"Alright then, I'll holla at you." Youngster pulled off and headed up the street.

When he arrived at a stop sign on the corner of Hillcrest & Santa Rosalia Drive, he looked at Shell and said, "I don't trust that nigga at all."

"Why you say that?" she asked.

"Because all that nigga do is ask about prices and shit, he haven't bought no dope from me and I rarely see him out sellin' dope. It's like he is just tryin' to see how much shit I got. He got me really thinkin' that he is up to somethin'."

Youngster went on about his business up until six in the evening. It was at that time he had ran out of dope. He needed to re-up. He drove back to his mother's house to page his connection named Ace. Ace is four years older than Youngster. He is six-two, brown skinned, and wears his hair short with brushed in waves. He had an athletic built with wide shoulders and big hands. Ace is part of an organized drug family whose members are his older brother Ali, his two cousins Kareem and Brad, and his younger brother Eli. Ace returned his call about ten minutes after Youngster had paged him. He instructed Youngster not to say much on the phone. He told Youngster just to meet him at the bowling alley at 7:30 p.m. Youngster stayed posted until 7:20 before leaving his mother's house with Shell to meet with Ace.

The bowling alley was not too far from where they were so being there on time was no problem. Just as Youngster was pulling off to meet Ace, his pager went off. He came to a complete stop at a corner to see who was paging him. The number that showed up on the pager was Teddy's. This was one of Youngster's homeboys he has known since his early school days. He didn't want to go back to his mother's to call Teddy so he just continued to drive until he reached a phone booth. He drove to a small shopping area around the corner from his mom's house. He jumped out the car when he arrived at the phone booth and dialed Teddy's number.

"What's up?" Teddy answered after a few rings.

"Hey Teddy, this is Youngster."

"Oh, what's goin' on Youngster? What's up with you?" he asked in a slow dragging voice.

"Not much, I'm about to go handle somethin' and then get ready to close up shop for the night."

"Well, check this out Youngster, I got this old man that might need five of them big cookies in a minute. Can you handle that?" Teddy asked.

"Yeah I can handle it Teddy, but how much did you tell him that it's gonna cost him?" Youngster asked. He was trying to hurry the conversation along because he had to get to the bowling alley. He soon would be running late and it was freezing.

"I didn't tell him anything yet," Teddy replied. "That's what I need to know from you. He just liked what I showed him earlier after we had hooked up and wanted to know if you could give him a deal on five of those big ones."

"Well, look Teddy, tell him that they are six hundred a piece but since he is gettin' five, I'll take one twenty-five off. So page me back to let me know what's up because right now I got to go handle somethin'."

"Okay, I'll page you right back," Teddy said before they both hung up the phone.

It was rare for Youngster to handle orders as large as five ounces in that stage of his illegal career. He ran a small operation but was working his way up. The people that he dealt with had no idea that he wasn't the man on the top. He was only buying five ounces during that time. He was breaking the ounces down into two grams each and selling them for fifty dollars a piece. Youngster was only making a hundred and twenty-five dollars off each ounce he sold after breaking them down. He would re-up about twice a week which added up to a profit of twelve hundred and fifty dollars. It was because of the way that he carried himself and his connections that made the people he was dealing with think that he was on a level that he was really only striving to reach. This level on the top was known as *Big Time* in the streets. To reach this level meant that you were moving kilos of cocaine. Moving that much weight meant making thousands each day. For most of the people around Youngster that he had known and grown up with, this was their American Dream. Youngster was determined to make it his reality.

# 6

The bowling alley was pretty crowded when Youngster and Shell walked in. It was a little after seven thirty. It had taken them a few minutes before they were able to spot Ace and his cousin Kareem who were with two females bowling. They walked over to them and everyone spoke to one another. After exchanging greetings, Ace looked at Youngster and said in his always calm cool voice, "So what's up my brotha, talk to me."

"I need the same as always and might need you again before ten tonight."

"What's this, you trying to move it like that now?" he asked. Ace chuckled as he began to walk towards Youngster. He handed Youngster the keys to his car, "It's under the passenger seat. Get it and leave the money up under the seat."

"Alright," Youngster replied as he took the keys and headed off towards the parking lot with Shell by his side.

Shell had the money in her purse folded in two separate stacks wrapped tightly in rubber bands. She handed the money to Youngster once he opened the car door and sat down in the passengers' seat. He put the money under the seat before handing

Shell the dope to place in her purse. He stepped out of the car. He checked his surroundings before heading back inside. Youngster and Shell noticed a suspicious black car in the parking lot but didn't think anything of it. They just continued on about their business without giving it a second thought. They didn't think that they were being watched. When they approached Ace back inside, Youngster returned Ace's keys to him.

"Is everything cool?" Ace asked.

"Yeah, everything is straight like always," Youngster answered.

"Ya'll going to stick around and get some of this ass kicking I'm dishing out?" Ace asked.

"Nah, I heard you've been on a roll lately, so we'll wait until you start to cool off. Besides, I have to go put up this package and get ready to hit the freeway. But if this other thing comes through, I'll be hittin' you back soon."

"Well, page me later to let me know that everything is safe and sound," Ace said like always after he has met with someone.

"I sure will," Youngster told him. He then exited the bowling alley with Shell right beside him.

Youngster drove back to his mother's house to stash the dope in her garage. He then chilled there for a few minutes just in case Teddy had paged him or someone else had called before he headed back to West Covina. Once ten o' clock finally rolled around, Youngster hadn't received a page from anyone. He decided to leave his mom's house to head home. His mother and sister were sound asleep but he had to disturb his sister. He had to wake her to lock the door. He had forgot the keys to his mom's house in West Covina which his sister didn't find amusing.

"Man, you better not forget your keys again. I have to get up and go to school in the morning." Lavette told him as she was getting out of the bed sounding very tired, drained, and upset.

"Just come lock the door," he interrupted before she could continue to fuss.

After Lavette locked the door, Youngster and Shell went to the car. Youngster started up his car but sat there before pulling off. He was making sure that he wasn't leaving anything. He wondered if he had closed the lid properly to his stash spot in the garage. He thought about it for a minute and proceeded to drive off. As soon as they got around the corner, his pager went off.

"Damn, who the hell is this," he said aloud as he reached for his pager on his hip. He looked at the number and said, "It's that nigga Teddy pagin' me 911."

"Well, what you gonna do?" Shell asked.

"It's too late now, it's past ten and he knows that I go in at ten. He know he supposed to call me before ten." Youngster continued to drive. After a few seconds, his pager went off two more times back to back. It was Teddy's number each time followed by 911. At that time, Youngster was about three or four blocks from his mother's house. He decided to drive back over there to call Teddy and tell him that he would have to get with him the following day. When he reached his mother's house, he remembered that he didn't have the keys to her house with him. "Damn!" Youngster yelled. He asked Shell to go ring the door bell to see if his sister would answer. He waited a few minutes. He then yelled to her from the car, "Shell, wait here just in case someone answers the door, I'll be right back."

"Okay," she said with a strange look on her face as if something was wrong.

"I won't be gone long," he told her before pulling off.

Youngster drove around the corner to the phone booth. When he arrived at the phone booth, he rushed out his car and dialed Teddy's number. He let the phone ring four times. There was no answer so he hung up to try again. The second attempt received the same results. He began to get irritated at the fact that Teddy would blow his pager up and not answer his telephone. "One last try before I go get Shell and get the fuck out of here," he thought to himself. On the third and final attempt, a car pulled up behind his car. He turned to see who it was. Three guys dressed in red jumped out of a black four door Ford Escort. They were all carrying guns. Youngster dropped the phone from his ear. His heart started to pump at an unbelievable rate as he attempted to get a better look at the danger approaching him. He wanted to get a feel if the danger was aimed towards him before they were too close. But it was too late.

One of the guys holding a .357 magnum walked right up on him pointing the gun at his chest saying, "What's up Blood?" The other two followed his lead. Youngster's first thought was that the guys were trying to see what neighborhood he claimed. He recognized one of the guys who was the furthest from where he stood. It was Stone. Youngster started to feel a little at ease as he thought that Stone would see him. He thought that Stone would let the other two know that he didn't gang bang and that he wasn't from the Crip gang. He was wrong. As soon as he tried to get a word out, the guy holding the magnum said, "You know what time it is Blood, get your ass in the back of the car." He snatched Youngster's keys from his hand. The two guys that he had never seen before led him to his car while Stone, acting as if he didn't even know Youngster, walked back to the Ford Escort. Before Youngster sat in the back seat of his own car, he attempted to say something again. He couldn't get a word out as the barrel of the .357 hit his back. "Didn't I say get your ass in the back Blood. I'll let you know when I want you to talk muthafucka."

Youngster sat in the back of his car with the tough talkative guy. They both were sitting in the back seat while the other guy jumped in the driver's seat. The guy put Youngster's keys in the ignition and quickly drove off with Stone following close behind. At that point Youngster had no idea what was going on or what was about to happen to him. He was becoming more and more nervous by the minute. Six minutes later was when everything began to get a lot clearer. It was then that they drove him to a dark alley, pulled in the middle of it, and stopped.

"Okay Blood, where's the shit?" Nudging the gun in Youngster's side, the tough guy asked.

"What shit?" Youngster stuttered with fear.

"Don't play with me Blood, you know what the fuck I'm talkin' about. Tell me where the *birds* at or you'll die right in this fuckin' alley tonight," he convincingly stated to Youngster which added to Youngster's fear.

By the time the tough guy finished his statement, Stone came to the door on the side of Youngster and opened it. Stone pointed an Uzi at the tip of Youngster's nose. At that moment, there were two things that Youngster knew for sure. One was that the guys were dead serious, and the other thing was that it wouldn't be long before he would be a dead man if he didn't come up with something in a hurry. They wanted a large amount of dope but he definitely didn't have any kilos in his possession.

"Blood, do you wanna die or what? Cause we don't have all night." The tough black guy stated with more intensity and urgency in his voice.

The tough and talkative guy was very dark, short, and kind of muscular with a rough look on his face. His eyes were red like that of a drunk. He seemed to be a lot older than the rest of the crew and it was obvious that they had all agreed to let him lead the way in their robbery attempt.

"Man, I don't buy *birds*. I ain't got it like that." Youngster spoke truthfully with the sign of fear showing in his face along with every stuttering word.

"This nigga is lyin' Blood. I've seen this nigga with Ace's crew before." Stone said as he moved the Uzi from the tip of Youngster's nose and placed it on his forehead.

"Blood, take us to the fuckin' *birds* or else you're dead," the driver said as he turned towards Youngster pointing a 9 millimeter semi-automatic towards his chest. He was very dark with spooky eyes. He wore a jerry-curl that seemed to be very dry. His face was chubby matching the frame of his body. The driver seemed to be the youngest of the group.

"Do you wanna die or what, nigga?" The tough guy yelled into Youngster's ear.

Youngster didn't know what to say but he knew that he didn't want to die in that alley. The only thing that he could think of was getting back to his mother's house. He thought that he might have a fighting chance to see another day if he could only get to his gun. He kept a gun hidden in his sister's bedroom. He had hoped that the day would never come to where he would have to use it.

"We have to go to my mother's house," Youngster said sounding as if he was giving in and ready to turn over everything he had.

"Your mother's house! Where the fuck is that at?" the tough guy asked.

"It's not too far from here."

"Blood, you better not be fuckin' with us because if you are, I promise you that you'll never see the light of day again."

"I'm not bullshittin', we just got to go over here across from the Jungles."

"Alright Blood, let's go," the tough guy said. He then nodded to Stone for him to retreat back to the Escort.

Stone walked back to the car he was driving. He followed closely as Youngster instructed the driver of his car to his mother's house. When they pulled in front of his mother's home, Youngster looked to see if Shell was still outside. He was relieved to see that she was nowhere in sight. Everyone stepped outside of the cars. Youngster led the way towards the house after receiving his keys back in his hands. He had no way of getting inside of the house without awaking someone. All three guns were pointed in his direction as he walked ahead. When they reached the porch, Shell stepped from the side of the house and came into view. The youngest one swiftly aimed his weapon in Shell's direction. Shell's entire body leaped off the ground at the sight of the gun.

"Who the fuck is this?" the young one asked as he aimed at Shell.

"Blood, that's his girl." Stone answered before Youngster could speak.

"Where the fuck did she come from?" the tough one asked.

"I left her out here when I went to use the phone," Youngster replied as his worst scenario was beginning to unfold right before his eyes. He had hoped that if Shell didn't make it in his mother's house before they came there, that she had at least remained out of sight. He didn't want her to be involved in whatever was about to go down.

They all stood on the porch facing the front door in a tactical formation. The three gunmen positioned themselves to keep watch on both Youngster and Shell. The tough guy holding the .357 was standing directly behind Youngster with the barrel of his gun aimed at Youngster's back. Stone stood to the side of Shell with his gun on her while the youngest guy stood a little further off to the side behind everyone else. He was watching the whole scene carefully.

Youngster turned slowly towards the tough guy before ringing the door bell and said, "It's gonna look strange with all of us goin' in here this late at night."

"Blood, who the fuck is up in there?" he asked.

"My mother and sister," Youngster answered. "I just don't want us lookin' all suspicious. It will be better if only one of ya'll come in with me so they won't trip on a bunch of niggas in the house this late."

The tough guy paused for a moment and then said, "Alright Blood, ya'll head back to the car with her. I'll go in."

After about three silent minutes went by, Louise came to the door and opened it. She immediately wore a disturbing look on her face. She glanced at her son and the suspicious person standing directly behind him. She didn't say anything to them. She just turned away. She went to her room as Youngster and the tough guy stepped into the house. Youngster waited for a minute before he said a word as they just stood in the living room. It was not until he heard his mother close the door to her bedroom that he went into action. He felt more at ease in the house because he noticed that the hardcore tough guy had become a little passive. He didn't seem as aggressive as earlier. In fact, he was not saying a word as if he was just waiting for Youngster to lead the way to a pot of gold.

"Wait here, I'm gonna go in this room right here," Youngster said before pointing to the first room near the living room.

The tough guy stood there. He nodded his head giving Youngster the okay. Youngster walked to the door he had pointed to. He stood in front of the door a second before opening it. After opening the door, he entered into his sister's room and closed the door behind him. He turned on the light to his sister's room. He looked over to her but she didn't budge. She was sleeping like a baby. He quietly walked over to her closet and opened it slowly. He stepped inside hoping not to wake Lavette. He reached for his duffle bag laying in the back. He opened it and retrieved his .38 revolver that was inside a small box within the bag. He checked the gun to make sure that it was fully loaded. He grabbed the duffle bag before closing the closet door softly. He turned to his sister not knowing what the outcome of his situation was going to be. He looked at her as if to say, "I love you." He then walked to her door. He paused at the door to say a prayer inside his head ~ "Please God, have mercy on my soul for what's about to take place and protect me and my family."

With his left hand holding the straps of the bag, he opened the door and walked out. He took three small steps outside of his sister's door. There was the target sitting on the couch glancing up at him. The target stood up to receive what he perceived as an easy payday. He saw the yellow duffle bag in Youngster's hand but as Youngster made a left turn to face his target, the tough guy saw something else in Youngster's right hand. When he saw that his life was in danger, it was too late for him to protect it. He didn't have time to react as Youngster pulled the trigger twice back to back. Two bullets hit the unexpected target in his chest both times before he fell to the floor. Youngster took a step towards his victim.

He noticed that the gun dropped right beside the body. He took no chances. Youngster fired a third shot that entered straight into the head of the fallen gangster.

Youngster quickly grabbed the corpse's gun. He placed it on the kitchen table and proceeded out the front door to help Shell. When he stepped outside on the porch, he saw Stone walking towards the house. Stone was startled at the sight of Youngster's breathing body.

"He shot Juan! He shot Juan!" Stone shouted as he quickly turned on his heels. He started running back to the car where Shell and the young male were sitting in.

Youngster took off towards the side walk. He wanted a better shot at Stone before letting off three times in his direction. Youngster emptied his gun in an attempt to hit Stone. Stone was able to maneuver and avoid being shot. The sound of gunfire immediately began to ring out in what Youngster thought was return fire. He ran back inside the house to reload his six shooter. When he stepped back inside the house, there were both his mother and sister. They were standing in the hallway stunned with disbelief in their eyes. Staring at a dead body lying in the living room, it took a second before they even recognized Youngster. Louise started screaming and shouting as soon as she noticed him, "Jayshawn, what have you done? What have you done, boy?"

He didn't have time to explain. He just ran to the kitchen to grab the duffle bag for some more bullets. He heard his sister ask, "Jayshawn, what are you doin'?"

"They got Shell, Shell is outside, they got her!" He yelled while he rushed to put bullets into his gun.

Louise was holding her phone in her hand. She had spoke to someone before Youngster had arrived back in her house. She relayed the message hysterically, "Jayshawn, the police just got through calling here and they are on their way! They said to make sure you did not have a weapon on you so you won't get hurt! You can't go back out there, can't you hear? They are already out there!

They're going to put you in---." Her voice drowned out due to the sound of sirens and helicopters outside. But even with all the noise, Youngster knew what she was saying. He will be going to jail for a very long time.

The police stated over the loud speaker, "Step slowly outside one by one." Youngster left his gun in the kitchen and went out first. It looked as though the entire police force from every division in the county of Los Angeles was on the block. The helicopter light lit the street up as it flew above, circling the house. Before three officers rushed him, Youngster was able to get a quick look down the street. He saw Shell lying by the curb a couple of houses down the street from his mother's home. She was being cared for by the paramedics. Youngster couldn't make out whether or not she was seriously injured due to the speed of the events taking place. The next thing he knew, he was being handcuffed. His head was being lowered by an officer to place him in the back of a police car and he was taken away down to the police station.

# 7

Youngster was taken to a secluded room at the police station where he was left all alone. The room reminded him of an interrogation room straight out of a movie. There were two chairs, a desk, and a long dark glass on one side of the wall. Youngster sat there for hours not knowing what was going on. He wondered how Shell and his family were doing. He had no clue on their conditions. Visions of what seemed to be his last moments of freedom were flashing before his eyes. The thought of eating breakfast in his apartment, wanting Shell to stay home, Stone flagging him down, and Teddy paging him like crazy, these thoughts flowed through his head. All the strange signs throughout the day that led up to the death of a man, Shell in the streets bleeding, and now the possibility of him spending the rest of his life in jail, pecked at Youngster's brain. The longer he sat in solitude, things were getting worse.

After hours of sitting in the secluded room, he started pacing back and forth. He started to hit the walls and shouted, "Hey, hey is anyone out there? I'm starvin' in here, get me somethin' to eat. I'm hungry in this bitch! Can anybody hear me? Get me the fuck out of here!" Youngster started to experience a slight nervous breakdown. He was sitting in an empty room with an empty stomach and there was no clock to tell the time. Youngster was clueless. He didn't know what was going on with his girl, what was happening to his family, or what was going to happen to him. This really was beginning to disturb him. Finally, two tall black men entered into the room. The first one to enter said, "Mr. King, I'm Detective Johnson and this is my partner Detective Jones. Come with us."

They led Youngster through a long hallway to an office with a table and a few chairs. They all entered the office and Det. Johnson said to Youngster, "Have a seat and lets get down to business." Det. Johnson seemed like he was the cool cop because he had an easy going look on his face. He was being very polite while Det. Jones looked on with a blank expression on his face. Up to that point, Det. Jones hadn't said a word. It looked like he was just ready to kick some ass and Youngster was his opponent.

When Youngster sat down, he looked around the room. He saw lots of pictures pinned on a bulletin board of homicide victims laying in pools of blood. They were all young black males. After observing that gruesome site, he noticed a clock hanging on the wall. He asked, "Excuse me Detective, but is that the right time?"

Det. Johnson glanced at his watch on his wrist. After checking his watch, he looked up at the clock on the wall and said, "That is correct, it's six twenty-five." Youngster couldn't believe it. He was actually in the other room alone for at least five hours or maybe longer.

"Okay Mr. King," Det. Johnson said as he sat down across from him, "First I will inform you that your family is safe and back at home. As for Michelle, she has been taken to the hospital after receiving multiple gun shot wounds. She is in stable condition and they have discovered that she's about a month pregnant."

Youngster went numb listening to Det. Johnson. He just sat there while the Detective reached into his coat. Det. Johnson pulled out a pen and pad. He looked Youngster directly in the eyes before saying, "Mr. King, tell us what happened last night."

After pausing for a minute, Youngster began to make up a story as he went along. He was hoping that the Detectives wouldn't notice his spontaneous lie. "Well, I was at a phone booth around the corner from my mother's house when all of a sudden these guys pulled up in a car and jumped out on me yelling a bunch of gang stuff and asking me what *set* was I from and was I a Crip. They pointed guns at me and made me get in the back seat of my car."

Youngster went on telling his amazing and untrue story about three gang members that just happen to roll up on him in an attempt to try to rob him but before he could finish his story Det. Jones interrupted him, "Look Mr. King, cut the bullshit. We have been all through your mother's house, searched through the front and back, and found a scale, razors, and some dope in the garage. Now the good news is that we do not work narcotics so we do not give a shit about all that. We are homicide detectives and that means that our only concern is how that body ended up dead in that house and what did he do to deserve it. Now the bad news is that you'll be going to jail for a long ass time if you do not cooperate with us and tell us the whole damn truth so we can help you."

Youngster thought about his dilemma for a moment before he figured that he had better cooperate. He began to tell them exactly what happened in full detail. When he finished telling the complete story, Det. Johnson told him that he would not be going to jail. He told him that the other two suspects had fled the scene of the crime. He informed Youngster that they were still on the loose. He instructed Youngster not to go too far and to be careful. He told him they will be getting back in touch with him real soon. He made it clear to Youngster that he is to make sure he could be reached and to be sure that he stayed out of trouble. The two detectives then drove him back to his mother's house. As soon as they hit the corner to the house, the media could be seen camped out in front of his mother's home. Det. Jones noticed the puzzled look on Youngster's face. He turned completely around to face Youngster before saying, "You don't have to talk to them if you don't want to. All you have to say is no comment and keep on steppin'."

Det. Johnson pulled in front of the house. He put the car in park but kept the engine running. He handed Youngster a business card to get in touch with him or Det. Jones if he had any questions. He then said, "Don't bother looking for the dope and guns. And make sure you stay out of trouble." Youngster gave him a nod of the head and said, "Alright." Youngster stepped out of the car to face the anxious news reporters that wanted to hear his story of what happened. They wanted to know what had taken place in the middle of the night that caused one man's death and a young lady being shot several times. Three different news reporters from different television stations hurried towards Youngster. They were closely followed by their team of camera men. As soon as Youngster crossed the street, he stepped on the sidewalk and heard, "Excuse me Mr. King, but would you be so kind to give a minute of your time for a brief interview to explain what took place last night?" The tall brown-skinned woman holding a microphone to her side asked Youngster very politely while the other two with their camera crew waited for a response from him.

Youngster was confused. He was undecided about whether or not he should give an interview in front of a camera that would be broadcasted on national television. He asked the reporters to give him a minute to go freshen up. He was anxious to check on his family in the house. He went inside his mother's house to learn that Louise and Lavette were still trying to recover from the shocking events that took place hours ago in their home. The blood stained rug hadn't been removed and the signs of the police investigation still showed around the tranquilized subdued house. He went to the restroom to wash his face and returned outside to face the many questions of the reporters.

Youngster gave a beautiful performance of an innocent citizen that gang members attempted to victimize. He told his story that he attempted to get over on the Detectives. This time it worked like a charm. When the news aired, Youngster came across as a neighborhood hero. All three stations reported, "An attempted robbery by three gang members late last night went bad, leaving one suspect dead, and a young girl shot and in critical condition. Two fugitives are on the run. The victim; Jayshawn King, was taken by gunpoint from a phone booth and kidnapped late last night. From there, he was driven to an alley where the suspects threaten to kill him if he didn't give them what they wanted. They then drove Jayshawn King to his mother's house where Jayshawn was able to get the drop on his would be robbers. In self-defense, the heroic Jayshawn King took the life of one of the suspects; Juan Givens, in order to save him and his entire family. In his attempt to save his girlfriend; Michelle Wilson, who was being held by the other two robbers, Michelle was shot six times before the two gunmen fled the scene. Word on the streets is that last night events were drug related, but Jayshawn King says that the unfortunate events was just a failed robbery attempt."

Youngster second guessed himself about whether he should have given the interview. He was uncertain soon after he finished telling his tale. His concerns quickly shifted as he jumped into his car to go see about Shell's condition. He wanted to confirm what the detectives told him about her being pregnant and was hoping she was doing better.

During the drive to the hospital, Youngster could only vision the look on his mother's face. How silent she was when he had entered her house. He felt that her disappointment of him had skyrocketed since the ordeal happened. The guilt moved throughout his mind and body. He thought to himself that there was nothing he could ever do to repair what he had just subjected his mother to. She had warned him time and time again that something like that could take place but he continued like it would never happen to him. However, in a blink of an eye, a life was gone and one came close to ending. Now it seemed that a brand new life would be soon entering the cold and cruel world in which Youngster dwelled.

When he arrived at the hospital, he was greeted by cold and condemning stares from Shell's family. The mother who put her own daughter out four months prior to that day, and the father who never was there for his daughter looked at Youngster like he was the one that just shot their daughter. He spoke to the frozen faces as he passed to enter the intensive care unit room where Shell was located. Shell was somewhat sedated and still trying to regain her senses after coming out of surgery not too long before Youngster had arrived. She had an I.V in her arm with large bandages covering her left cheek, the left side of her neck, and her left shoulder from flesh wounds. All caused by gun shots. She had been hit six times. The most serious damage was done by the shots that entered the left side of her body. A bullet entered under her ribs and in her hip on her left side.

Shell's eyes slowly opened recognizing Youngster as he stood over her expressing sorrow and grief silently. She reached out for his hand, squeezed it tight, and struggled to say, "Don't look so sad Jayshawn, I was hopin' that you would be here when they finished operating on me. Did they tell you that I'm pregnant?"

Youngster nodded his head but remained silent while he continued examining what he believed to be his fault.

"The doctor is tryin' to talk me out of havin' the baby. He said that it would be dangerous due to my recovery and my diabetes." Shell lifted the left side of her hospital gown to reveal the colostomy bag on her stomach. "It's this and somethin' about my hip bone. These things are the reason for my projected long recovery." Her eyes quickly swelled full of tears, "The doctor said that I'll be hospitalized up to a year." She turned her head away from Youngster and let her tears flow as she cried.

"Don't do that, you gonna make me feel even worse than I already feel." Youngster finally broke his silence and spoke.

"Why do you feel bad? If I would have just listened to you and stayed home, I wouldn't be layin' in this fuckin' place." Shell made a point and he wasted no time to disagree with her.

Youngster stood there thinking to himself, "What if Shell had not come along with me to L.A?" Without her as a distraction for the other two gang members, he wondered if he would have been able to get the drop on Juan. He wondered if all three of his kidnappers had come in the house if she weren't there. He thought to himself that he could be the one lying there instead of her. He even went as far as to think that he might have been dead if it hadn't been for her.

"Shell, you have to be strong and stop that cryin'. You have a life to bring into this world. We are about to be parents." He brought a smile to her face as she gave thought to what he just said. She began to wipe the tears from her face and glow from the thought of becoming a mother. She started to imagine being married to Youngster. She reached out for his hand and held it tight. She just stared into his eyes for a moment before saying, "Jayshawn, I love you so much."

Shell's mother, Helen, walked into the room saving Youngster from a sentimental moment that he felt way too young for. He wasn't used to saying I love you to anyone. He thought that nineteen wasn't the age for love so Shell had never heard it from his mouth.

"How are you feeling?" Helen asked looking down at her only child.

"I'm feelin' okay," she answered.

"Your father has been out there waiting to see you."

"Momma, you know that's the last person in the world I want to see," she stated with a mean spirit in her voice.

"Well, I told him that you might feel that way but he insisted on waiting until after your surgery and seeing you." Helen was hoping that her daughter's heart would soften towards her deadbeat dad at such a crucial time.

"Let me talk with Jayshawn a little longer first and then you can send him in here."

"Okay," Helen replied and walked out the room.

After Shell's mother left the room, Youngster and Shell began to discuss what had happened. They went over Youngster's strange feelings about Stone. They discussed how Stone must have been plotting earlier that day when he flagged them down. They talked about seeing the black car that Stone was driving in the parking lot of the bowling alley hours prior to Youngster's abduction. Just like two detectives, they put the pieces of the puzzle together. They realized that Teddy must have been in on the whole thing also. When Shell told him about the moment when she got shot, it had become clear to Youngster that when he thought it was him that was being shot at, it was actually Shell being shot instead. When Stone saw him coming out of the house, he ran back to the car yelling that Juan had been shot. This frightened the young male who was sitting in the car with Shell. He jumped out of the car and faced Shell who was in the back seat. He aimed his gun in her direction and started shooting Shell while she was in the back seat exposing her left side to him while curling up in a ball. He shot her six times before both him and Stone fled on foot towards the Jungles. Her recollection started to bring back the tears in her eyes. Youngster saw her beginning to break down and put an end to their discussion.

"Hey, I'm gonna have to get up out of here if you start that up again." He firmly stated. "You know that I can't stand to see you cry."

"I can't help it Jayshawn, it was just so stupid of me to want to follow you down here and now look what happens." Her hands went up in the air to gesture her hospitalized condition.

"Stop thinkin' like that Shell," he said to calm her down but inside he was convinced that she was telling the truth. "Look, don't blame yourself. Start concentrating on gettin' well for our baby. If you gonna have the baby, then you are goin' to need all of your strength and energy focused on doing just that to have a smooth delivery and recovery."

He struck Shell's happy nerve once again. He brought her back to thoughts of her, the baby, and him as one big happy family. She felt that having a baby by him, would secure her hold on him. She thought that marriage would definitely be in the near future. She knew how responsible he has proven to be just on the fact that he was able to get them an apartment soon after her mother put her out. She knew how Youngster felt about not wanting to treat a child of his like each of their fathers' did them. This made her feel that he would definitely do the right thing when she gave birth to his child. Shell's father never being there for her and Youngster's father receiving a life sentence when he was just a little boy, was something that she knew he didn't want for a child of his own. Although Youngster ran that same risk as his father, she just felt he was much more careful and smarter than his father. Her wonderful picture of happiness would quickly tear into pieces unknowing to her at the time.

Just as Shell was beginning to smile from her thoughts, a nurse entered the room with a clipboard in hand. She placed the clipboard on the side of the bed. She started tending to Shell while Youngster observed. When the nurse was checking Shell's vital signs, Youngster was checking out the informative clipboard. He stood off to the side until the nurse had finished. After she walked out, he started to do some examining of his own.

"Well! Well! Well!" Youngster began to chant as he walked back towards Shell.

"What is that supposed to mean?" she asked.

"June twenty-seventh, nineteen seventy-two," he slowly stated.

Shell realized that her lie about her being a year older than she actually was, had just been revealed to Youngster.

"Oh that," she said.

"No! Not just that. What were all those other things about with those disease names and shit?" Youngster inquired.

"They had to run those tests to make sure that I didn't have any diseases Jayshawn."

"Oh, is that right?" His suspicion was on the rise and the odds of him being wrong when he suspected something were very low.

"Yeah, that's right. You can go ask any of those nurses out there." She hoped that he wouldn't continue to go in the direction that he was going in. She knew that her secret would come out if he pursued it.

"Shell, I want the truth!" He demanded in a very stern voice.

"I just told you the truth," she said.

"Tell me the truth or---"

"Jayshawn," she attempted to stop his sentence but to no avail.

"I'm gonna walk out that door and you'll never see me again." He made it clear to her from the look on his face and from the words that were spoken, that he was very serious. He was ready to follow through with his threat.

She thought for a minute. She was well aware of what he wanted to hear. She knew that it had nothing to do with the chart that read all the tests were negative. He wanted the truth about what went on with the situation six weeks prior to that day. She decided to take a chance. She didn't want to hold back the truth any longer. She felt that maybe it was the best time to make her confession, and so she did. Shell told him that when he dropped her off at her mother's after their argument six weeks ago, that she called an old friend because she needed someone to talk to. She went on to say that he came and picked her up from her mother's house. She continued to explain that somehow they ended up at a motel room. She told Youngster that they had sex and that must have been when she contracted the disease that she eventually passed on to him.

When Shell completed her story, she found herself in the I.C.U room all alone. Youngster had stormed out the hospital with a pain in his heart and a lump in his throat. He drove all the way home thinking about how that doctor from five weeks ago must still be laughing in his office at him. Youngster had stood there arguing with the Doctor about how he couldn't have contracted a venereal disease because he only had sex with one partner. The Doctor gave him a questionable look before Youngster left out the office. He can only imagine how long that doctor laughed at him from being so naïve. "What a muthafuckin' fool I am," he silently thought to himself as he drove on the freeway with one hell of a twenty-four hour experience.

# 8

The scent of turkey bacon making its way up the stairway towards Youngster's bedroom combined with the signs of a brand new day, awakened the drained young man from his deep sleep. The dream of the worst 24 hours that seemed he would never forget had finally ended. His mind tried to convince his body to regain some strength. He wanted to see what was being prepared downstairs in the kitchen. The bright light from the sun rays was shining through his bedroom window located right above his headboard. The room had began to heat up from the sun as he looked over to check the time. His door was wide open as he lay there completely naked. He tried to figure out why Shell would leave the door open with him being so exposed. He didn't like the idea of his little son seeing him completely naked. He felt that his son had too much sense not to know what was going on between him and his mother if he seen him exposed. He had fussed at Shell many times in the past about leaving the door open when she would spend the night. This would be just the reason to trigger his anger early in the morning. After a dream such as the one that he just had, this wouldn't be a good thing for her.

Shell was well aware of Youngster's temper, especially after they would have sex. The smallest thing he could find, he would erupt to engage her in an argument. This would be done just to have an excuse to get rid of her. He couldn't stand to be around her after one night with her combined with his dream. His switch from Dr. Jekyll to Mr. Hyde all stems from Shell's mistake three years ago and she knew it. So many times he would go off over simple things that meant nothing at all. She would call herself guarding against his anger by trying to do everything in her power to prevent his rage. Nevertheless, he would always find something to get it started.

"Shell!" Youngster yelled as he came down the stairs wearing a black silk pajama bottom, a white tank top, and a pair of black corduroyed house slippers. "Shell!" He repeated without giving her a chance to respond the first time. "I know damn well you hear me!"

"Give me a chance to answer you," Shell responded. After responding, she was ready to apologize. She knew that Youngster might have taken it the wrong way. "What's wrong?" she asked as she turned to face him just as he entered the kitchen.

Jay was dressed and at the kitchen table waiting for his mom to finish cooking. He was a little troubled at the presence of his father due to the tone of his voice and the look on his face when he appeared in the kitchen.

"What do you mean, what's wrong? Why the damn bedroom door was left wide open after I've told you over a thousand times to not leave that door open like that?"

"I didn't think about it since we was down here," she said hoping that her answer would pass as a sufficient excuse.

"You didn't think about it, as many times we've been through this same subject and you didn't think about it?" He paused before going on, "What do you think that tells me?"

"Look Jayshawn, I'm sorry for leavin' the door open but I really didn't think it was a big deal because I had gotten

Jay dressed already and he was down here watchin' T.V. The only reason it was left opened was because I had ran up to grab somethin' and ran back down here. Before that, your door was closed just like you wanted it." She didn't leave to much room after her explanation for him to build on. He couldn't get the argument he wanted out of her. He just stood there in silence observing the breakfast. He decided to wait for his next opportunity he would have to stir something up. He was sure to get the results he was looking for.

Not too much was said during the whole time they sat at the kitchen table eating breakfast. Shell sat there with the feeling that Youngster wanted something to argue about. He sat there in deep thought knowing that he would soon have to go to his bread and butter. The subject that they both knew would get his temper to flare. All he needed was the right opportunity to present itself.

***

It was as if they had never slept together the next time Youngster and Shell were in the same room. While Jay was downstairs watching television, the drama filled show was just beginning upstairs. Youngster gave Shell the coldest stare when she had walked through his bedroom door. He had already took a shower and was dressed by the time she had finished cleaning up the kitchen.

The thought of Shell and her so-called mistake had saturated in his mind so much that when she finally appeared in the room, he was more than prepared to let her have a verbal lashing.

"Why are you lookin' at me like that?" she asked sensing trouble.

"Lookin' at you like what? You mean like a slut?" He continued before she could say anything in the middle of her changing facial expressions. "Now why are you lookin' at me like that? Is it because I'm right?"

It wouldn't have mattered if this same routine went on every single day of her life. Shell's surprised expression on her face would be her first reaction, each and every single time. She never could figure out why at the oddest moments, Youngster would start on her.

"What did I do?" she asked.

"You know damn well what you did. The question is why?"

"Jayshawn, do we have to keep goin' over this?" she asked as she walked to the opposite side of him to sit down on his bed.

"You damn right!" he said looking directly at her with hate in his eyes. "We gonna keep goin' over this until I can finally understand how you can keep on tellin' me that you love me after going out and fuckin' somebody else. To make the shit even worse, you give me a muthafuckin' disease as the proof and undisputed evidence that you fucked somebody else. Yes, we gonna keep goin' over this shit until I understand how a slut can claim to love someone."

"Jayshawn, I told you that I don't know what made me do that dumb thing but it was three years ago. It was a big mistake and I'm sorry." The tears started to flow from her eyes after she had fought hard to hold them back just to complete her sentence.

There was no letting up on her. Youngster's anger didn't allow any sympathy to creep within him. "I'm sorry!" He yelled. The hate embedded in his eyes traveled where it could be heard through his voice also. "Here's a news flash Shell, just in case you forgot. Sorry don't erase the fact that you let that nigga's dick inside you. Sorry don't erase that fuckin' disease you gave me. And sorry definitely don't erase that I got to always look at Jay and wonder if he is really my son or not. And guess what Shell? It's all because of your sorry ass." His voice along with the anger that was delivered in every word he said had overwhelmed Shell to the point where she was crying real hard and uncontrollably.

He got up off the bed. He walked to the bedroom door full of rage. He gave Shell a look of displeasure and said, "Just hurry up and get dressed so I can drop your, I'm sorry ass off." He slammed the door as he left. Youngster headed down the stairs to get things ready for his day of hustling.

A good thirty minutes later, Shell was ready to go. She slowly walked down the stairs while Youngster and Jay watched the television in the living room.

"Are you ready?" she asked as she stood behind the white Italian leather couch. She was holding her sleep over bag in her hand. Sorrow and pain wouldn't only describe the look on her face, but her very presence at that moment was full of despair. Her heart was heavy. Her mind was occupied with regrets. Youngster, on the other hand, showed no signs of remorse or concern for what Shell was going through. He had no feelings for what had just taken place between them. Instead, he just stood up without even looking in her direction and responded with a simple, "Yep!" He headed towards the door with her and Jay following close behind.

Youngster sure knew how to work his self up over Shell cheating on him and he couldn't calm down until she was completely out of his sight. Even though it has been three years, he still continued to treat the situation as if it had just happened the day before. But it would only be brought up when she would ask to be back with him or soon after an intimate session between the two of them had taken place followed by the dream. He has been putting her through this mental and emotional abuse ever since finding out about her betrayal. There was no end in sight. Shell doesn't even know whether or not she is coming or going. As for Youngster, he didn't know any other way to deal with the fact that Shell actually cheated on him. His verbal abuse was the only way he knew how to express his disappointment.

"Well, I'm going to call you later on. Okay?" she stated as she got out the car in front of her grandmother's house.

She only received the cold shoulder from Youngster as he kept a mean stare on his face and focused straight ahead above his steering wheel. He just sat there anxiously waiting to pull off as soon as she closed his car door. Her sad feeling only worsened. It became deeper as she stepped away from the car. She looked at Jay and said with a cracking voice, "Bye baby." She closed the door while Jay responded with a wave. Youngster quickly drove off as Shell sadly looked on hearing the sounds of Ice Cube penetrating through the loud speakers.

Things returned to business as usual for him once he left Compton. He arrived back in South-Central making deliveries. He made his regular drops to Betty, Angel, and a few more everyday customers before stopping at his mom's house to chill. Jay arrived at the porch before he did as always to ring the door bell. Youngster was still in the driveway trying to grab a few things out of his car. By the time he reached the porch, his sister Lavette had opened the door.

"Hey little Jay, where have you been?" she inquired before picking the smiling boy up. She embraced him and kissed him on the cheek.

"Where have you been? That is the question." Youngster stated while entering the house. He continued to give his sister a hard time. "You the one been missin' in action. We been over here a few times and you were nowhere to be found. You better not be runnin' around with one of these niggas in the streets. You know these niggas out here ain't no damn good."

"And you should know, right?" Lavette sarcastically questioned.

"Ha ha ha, very funny."

Youngster would often take on the role of the concerned older brother playfully. He never truly worried about his sister because she reminded him so much of himself. She always has proven to have a mind of her own and is never easily influenced by her peers.

"Boy, unlike some people that I know, I have to work," Lavette said to her brother who was passing by her heading towards the kitchen.

"Well good, maybe you can start treatin' me with some of that workin' money instead of me treatin' you with this non-workin' money," he fired back while he grabbed a root beer out of the refrigerator.

"Negro please, you the one with all the money. Real job or not, your butt can continue doin' the treating."

Before he could hit his sister with something smart and clever, his pager started vibrating. He took the beeper off of his hip to read off the number. He then said with a smile, "Speakin' of money." He walked over to his mother's cordless telephone sitting in the kitchen. He began to dial the number which was followed by a brief conversation. When he finished his phone call, he went to his sister's bedroom where she and Jay were, "Yo Sis, watch Jay for a minute while I go make a run."

"Okay, just don't forget about us and end up gone for hours."

"Girl, I'll be right back," he stated as he turned and headed out the door to make his drops.

By the time he returned, Lavette had been relieved from her duties by Louise. Louise had returned home from work and welcomed her grandsons' company. She had agreed to watch Jay a little longer when Youngster arrived back. He was able to make a few more runs without Jay having to ride with him. On his return to his mother's, he decided to go in earlier than his normal time. He felt like cooking dinner at home. He only had a few cookies left on him, so it wasn't that big of a deal for him to try to call it a night sooner than his regular time.

Youngster and Jay had just finished dinner and were getting ready to watch a movie that they had rented. Youngster was walking towards the living room with popcorn and soda in his hands when his pager started going off. He looked at it to see who was trying to reach him. He saw Ed's number. Ed was one of his homeboys that cops dope from him from time to time. Youngster looked over towards Jay who was still in the kitchen. Jay was closer to the telephone so he asked Jay to hand the phone to him. Jay brought the telephone to him and Youngster dialed Ed up.

"Hello." Someone other than Ed's voice answered the telephone.

"What's up? Is Ed there?" Youngster asked.

"What's up Youngster? This is Raymond."

"Who?" he asked. He didn't recognize the voice.

"Raymond and Ken from Dorsey. We been trying to hook up with you. Didn't Ed tell you?" the voice asked.

Youngster paused for a moment to think about some of the guys he had went to high school with. He tried to put some faces with the names that were just given to him.

"Oh yeah, what's goin' on with ya'll?" Youngster had suddenly remembered them from a class they all had together in the eleventh grade. He also remembered that Ed had just mentioned to him that Raymond and Ken were looking for him a few weeks ago. Ed told him that they had needed a few ounces but they didn't show back up on that particular day.

"Nothin' much," Raymond said. "We are just tryin' to get a few of those things from you."

"Right, right," Youngster said. "So where's Ed at?" he asked with a suspicious feeling inside of him. It wasn't like Ed to have other people answer his phone.

"Oh, he is outside with Ken right now." Raymond replied.

"Well, what are ya'll lookin' for?" he asked feeling a little at ease but still not too comfortable with Ed not answering his own phone.

"How much is nine of them large ones?" Raymond asked referring to nine ounces.

"Soft, or hard?" he inquired.

"Hard," Raymond answered.

Three thousand, seven hundred and fifty dollars would have been the answer if Raymond would have said soft, but since he wanted it cooked for him, Youngster had to charge a little extra for his time and labor. "That's gonna be four thousand."

"Okay cool, what time can you get here?" Raymond sounded pleased with the price given as if he had been shopping around and the four thousand was the best price he had heard.

Youngster glanced at his watch. He saw that it was almost nine and thought it would take him about thirty minutes to get the order ready. "Give me about an hour."

"Cool," Raymond said. "We'll be waiting."

Youngster then hung up the phone. He looked over at Jay who was sitting on the couch. He thought for a moment about how strange the conversation was that he just had. He paused for a minute. He never did get the chance to talk to Ed. He received a funny feeling that made him decide not to go make the run he had just agreed to make. He just decided to leave them hanging without even calling back to discuss his decision. He didn't want to show up over there with his son. He thought about the danger he would be putting Jay in. It would have been a possible dangerous situation that late at night. The four thousand dollar pick up would have only been a five hundred dollar profit for him. Having to take Jay with him to deal with two guys that he didn't normally deal with, just wasn't worth it. He decided to spend the rest of the night eating popcorn, drinking root beer, and watching an animated cartoon movie he had let Jay pick out at the video store.

9

The morning of a brand new day. Things seemed to start just like any other normal typical day for Youngster. He received a page while downstairs. He took a look at the number and saw Ed's number displayed followed by 911. He figured that it was Raymond and Ken paging him again. He thought maybe they wanted to see what had happened with him not showing up and he had hoped that maybe they still needed the nine ounces. Being that it was now daytime, he would be more comfortable meeting with them. He was in the kitchen wrapping up some cookies while Jay was upstairs watching television. Jay was anxiously waiting to roll out with his daddy. Youngster grabbed his cordless telephone he had brought downstairs with him. He began to dial Ed's number. He was hoping to make the five hundred dollars that he decided to turn down the night before. The telephone was picked up immediately after the first ring.

"Hello." Ed answered sounding very disturbed.

"Yo, Ed what's up? This is Youngster."

"Man, what's up?" Ed dragged his words. He sounded unusual. "These niggas had me tied up all last night waitin' for you. I didn't get fuckin' loose until about four this mornin'. I can't believe this shit Youngster. I can't believe this fuckin' shit!"

"Hold up Ed, and slow the fuck down. Now what the hell you mean by tied up?" Youngster asked very confused.

"They were tryin' to use me to get to your ass!" Ed explained with excitement in his tone. "Those niggas got your number from me after they drew down on me and then they tied me up to my chair and put duck tape over my mouth. They were out to get your ass man. They wanted to *jack* you for your shit."

Youngster just held the phone while thinking to himself how he had felt something strange about last night. He was right.

"Youngster, are you there?" Ed asked.

"Yeah," he replied. He was getting worked up over the thought of some guys trying to actually rob him. "Hey, where those niggas hang out at Ed?"

"I usually see them on Fridays at the barbershop on Crenshaw around one o' clock, other than that I don't know where else they can be found." Ed answered. "But I ain't gonna let that shit go down like that Youngster, believe that. Those niggas must think that I'm a punk to let that shit go down and not do anything about it. Man fuck that!"

Ed, a short plump fellow with fat cheeks and tight eyes, attempted to sound like the hardest man on the planet. He was always one of those people that came off with a loud and thunderous voice but without actions to back it up. Like a big bold talker without a backbone or spine.

"Well, holla at me if you happen to see them again," Youngster said calmly. He didn't want to disclose the plans that he had of his own. "Are you going to be alright?" he asked Ed.

"Yeah man, I just don't believe this shit." He responded in disgust.

"Don't trip my nigg, I'll holla at you later." Youngster hung up the phone deeply upset.

He stood in the kitchen for a minute thinking. He knew in order for Raymond and Ken to let Ed live, they must have felt that Ed was a punk. The code of the streets was that you never draw a gun on someone and let them live unless you thought that they were a bitch-made person. This was someone that would not retaliate. There was no doubt in his mind if that was the case, they would boldly be right at the barbershop on Friday to get their hair cuts with no fear of Ed trying anything vengeful. He figured that they wouldn't have a clue that Ed told him about their Tuesday night plans of attempting to rob him for his dope. It was now Youngster's time to plan. It was his opportunity to seek them out before they ever have the thought or chance to attempt another robbery on him.

Youngster made a phone call to a gun connection to purchase a throw-away. He made the arrangement to pick up a .38 snub-nose later on in the day. He went about his business from that day till Friday without anyone being able to detect or even guess what he had in store for them on Friday. He just carried on as if everything was normal while he burned inside.

***

The clouds were blocking the sun from shining on this gloomy Friday afternoon in South-Central Los Angeles. Youngster circled the block a few times scoping out the Right-on barbershop near the corner of Crenshaw & 43rd street. "The weather couldn't have been any better," he thought to himself. He slowly crept through the back alley where most of the customers would park their cars. Most of them would use the exit as the entrance instead of going through the front. The main entrance was located on Crenshaw Boulevard where traffic was always busy. There was very limited parking in the front with meters in every space. This made parking unbearable and using the back more convenient. It also would make Youngster's plan easier to carry out.

Observing that Raymond and Ken hadn't arrived, Youngster drove on by the shop. He decided to park his car about two blocks from the barbershop. He parked on a residential street to wait a while before going back to the barbershop. After about an hour of listening to N.W.A blast from his speakers, he started the car up. He decided to drive by the front of the shop again. When he approached the front of the shop, everything started to move in slow motion. Youngster turned to look inside the front of the Right-on barbershop and recognized Raymond sitting in one of the barber's chairs getting a hair-cut. Ken was sitting off to the side looking through a magazine. Youngster swiftly drove back to that same residential street. He parked his car and jumped out. He rushed back to the alley where he was sure that Raymond and Ken had parked. He patiently waited in the alley sitting on a small brick wall steadily checking his surroundings. He mapped out a route that would allow him a smooth get away. He made sure that he positioned himself between the exit of the barbershop and the customer parking lot. The brick wall that he sat on was about fifty feet away from the back door of the barbershop where the customer parking was located. He sat there so he would be able to see everyone that entered or left.

Thirty minutes had past before Youngster was able to see what he was waiting for. The moment had arrived. The back door of the barbershop had opened. A tall, medium build, light-complected male stepped out followed by another tall, slender dark figure. The light-skinned male with green eyes was Ken. Raymond followed right behind him. They headed in Youngster's direction with fresh hair-cuts just right for their funerals. They both were looking ripe for a decent burial. They were conversing back and forth to where they weren't paying attention to their surroundings. This was a perfect opportunity for Youngster to make his move. Youngster was wearing a Raider jacket, white T-shirt, a pair of loose fitted blue jeans, and had on a pair of black gloves. He quickly leaped off the wall, and rushed towards Ken and Raymond. His hands were in the pockets of his jacket. His right hand was firmly gripping the .38 snub-nose loaded with hollow point bullets. He walked at the same pace and rate of his adrenaline rush. He approached his prey quickly with deadly intentions.

Simultaneously as they lifted their heads up, they both wore the same expression as though they were facing death. Youngster pumped two lethal injections of hollow point bullets into Ken's body and two in Raymond's back as he attempted to turn and run. They both fell to the ground as if their legs were chopped from under them after being hit by the lethal hot lead. While hunched over on their sides on the concrete, Youngster walked up on them closer. While avoiding the blood draining out both their bodies, he fired another shot in each of their heads. From a temporary rage to a calm, he dropped the gun right where he stood. He quickly dashed through an office building directly adjacent from the barbershop. He made a clean get away to his car. He sat in his car, took a deep breath, and exhaled while taking in the brief moment of complete silence. Youngster then started his car and smoothly pulled away from the curb with *Appetite for Destruction* pumping through his speakers.

# '10

Youngster nervously retraced in his mind his every move from earlier hoping like hell that he didn't leave any evidence. That nothing could link him to the murders that had taken place near the Right-On barbershop. "So far so good," he thought to himself as he finished watching one of the local news reports. The report only concluded that the murders may have been gang related. He sat in his living room contemplating his next move. He flicked through the channels on his thirty-two inch television screen feeling a little disturbed. Killing someone has never been on his agenda when he started hustling in the streets but he has come to find out the hard way that for the most part, killing comes with the territory. It was almost a certainty when rising in the illegal business of dealing drugs.

Youngster was leaning towards making a few more moves before returning home to take time out for himself. There was no better time to chill out and lay low for a minute than at this time. Jay was finally spending the weekend over his grandmother's house so it would be perfect for him to smoke and relax. He hadn't smoked any weed in over a week and considering all the circumstances that had taken place the past week, it was well overdue. As he prepared to make some runs and cop some chronic, his pager alerted him. Ed's number followed by 911 came across the screen. Youngster dialed him up right away.

"Hello." Ed answered.

"Ed, what's up?" Youngster asked.

"Youngster, you haven't seen the news?"

"What news?" He played the dumb role.

"Ken and Raymond was killed at the barbershop."

"Get the fuck out of here, are you serious?" Youngster sounded as if it was his first time hearing about it.

"No bullshit Youngster. I just seen it on the news."

"Well, ain't that some shit. I guess I wasn't the only one that they tried to set up. Somebody caught they ass slippin'."

"Yeah, somebody got they ass before I did," Ed lied knowing he had no real intentions of doing anything like committing a murder.

"Well, somebody just saved you the time Ed."

"Alright Youngster, I just had to let you know about that shit so you don't have to worry bout those niggas anymore. I'll be hittin' you up when I'm ready to see you."

"Okay Ed, thanks for the information."

"No problem Youngster. Be safe."

"Same to you my nigg," Youngster hung up and went about his business.

It was late in the evening when Youngster returned home with a couple of Philly blunts in his hand. He walked through his door with a fifty sack of the best chronic in Los Angeles in his pocket. He had a homeboy that kept top quality weed all the time. He would cop from him once a week. Youngster wasn't what one would call your normal weed head. He considered himself a closet smoker. He would only smoke home alone. He didn't smoke on a daily basis and would only smoke the best weed in town. He would never smoke what he called *border weed* or others would call *stress*. He also didn't believe in sharing a blunt with anyone.

Therefore, he had defined himself as a closet smoker. Smoking chronic was his only recreation. He preferred doing it alone and in peace. A few years back he tried alcohol once, but he didn't like the taste nor the feeling that rushed down his throat and through his chest when he swallowed it. Alcohol was horrible to him.

Youngster checked the evening news for any new developments on the murders. He found that there weren't any. In fact, if he would have blinked his eyes, he would have missed the whole little bit that was mentioned about the double homicide off Crenshaw & 43rd street. Youngster started to break down his weed and concentrate on rolling his blunt. He sat on his living room floor in front of the television. A few minutes later, he was all set. He was ready to leave reality for the time being and enter a chilled out world with a relaxed atmosphere.

The smoke floated throughout the living room as well as his lungs while his head rid itself from the weight of the world. His mind traveled to a place where there were no worries and stress allowed. He began to feel real relaxed in his town home as the once loud coughing and choking dwindled down to a smooth calmness. He felt at ease. There definitely wouldn't be any nightmares in his sleep on this night for sure.

The next day while he was carefully making moves through the city, he still was hoping that he hadn't made any mistakes that could connect him to the murders. He didn't want anything that he might have done wrong to lead to his name being brought up. However, while he was worried about the police and his name being connected to the murders, his name was being mentioned somewhere else for other reasons besides the double homicide that he had committed.

***

The entire grass area was covered in a sea of red clothing as the Bloods gathered for their weekly meeting at the park. The park was located right above their neighborhood so most of them would just walk to the meeting while a few of the older gangsters that were making money would drive. These older gang members invested their drug dealing money into fixing up their low riders and classic cars.

The meeting that the Bloods would have each week was mandatory. It was held for both male and female members from the Jungles. This meeting was for new members to get initiated, old members to get things off their chest, and it was held to discuss problems between them and other gangs.

"Well, is that it or what Blood?" one of the *O.G.'s* known as Chicago yelled out with an impatient tone in his voice. He wore a black patch over his left eye. He lost his eye in a shoot out years ago. He was dark, large, and muscular. "Ain't nobody got no mo' shit that needs to be said at this muthafucka or what? I gots shit to do if not."

Most of the crowd looked to one another with a blank face. They all seemed to be ready to end the meeting. After a brief moment of silence, someone yelled out, "Yeah!" The loud voice came from out of the crowd. The voice stepped forward. Chicago was obviously ready to get the meeting over with so he wore a look of disgust on his face along with the body language to express his impatience.

"I wanna know how much longer we gonna let this muthafuckin' Youngster keep comin' up in our hood makin' money. What's up with that shit Blood?" The person asking the question and trying to stir up the meeting was none other than Gee.

"Blood, do you know the nigga?" an older black male in a wheel chair known as K-9 had spoken in Youngster's defense. K-9 has known Youngster ever since junior high before getting paralyzed during a drive-by a few years later in front of the high school they attended. K-9 never returned to Dorsey High after getting shot and recovering. He just became a full time gang member and dope dealer.

"I don't need to know him. I know what he did and that's enough for me Blood," Gee responded with anger in his voice. He had a look to match hoping to find some supporters that felt like he did about Youngster.

"Well, what you would have did?" Chicago interrupted K-9 before he could speak, "If someone was trying to *jack* your ass, tell me what you would have did, Blood? Now I'll tell you straight up like this, I would have done the same muthafuckin' thing that Youngster did if some niggas had tried to *jack* me."

"You damn right!" K-9 shouted in agreement with Chicago.

Gee felt out numbered as everyone else listened. His attempt to get some of the others from the hood to feel the same way he felt was failing. "Blood, he killed our homeboy and got two of the homies serving life. Ain't that enough to fuck a nigga up over?"

"Look," Chicago started, "The homies was stupid for that shit they tried to pull."

"Stupid or not, that muthafuckin' nigga killed the homey and nobody haven't said shit or did shit like everybody scared of this nigga. Like they ain't got the heart to fuck his ass up." Gee was really trying his best to get the crowd angry. He wanted them to feel enough hate to hurt Youngster on sight. Chicago wasn't having it, so he decided to pull Gee's card.

"Well, it ain't like a muthafucka here ever put no bulletin out sayin' don't touch the nigga the whole three years since that shit happened. So what's wrong with your muthafuckin' heart, Gee? You got the green light, Blood." Chicago knew that Gee didn't have the heart to do anything but talk. He put him on the spot and of course he received no response from Gee. He became silent.

"Man, let's end this damn meetin' and get the fuck on Blood." A very husky, short and dark figure wearing a red Dickie suit with a large round stomach stepped in the circle noticeably irritated. "If a muthafucka wanna touch that nigga then let him touch the nigga. All I know is that he got the best work around this bitch and he's been *bool* with me ever since I met his ass, so let's squash this shit and get the fuck out of here, I'm hungry."

The intensity broke as laughter rampantly spread throughout the crowd and everyone started to disburse. Some headed towards their cars while others walked down the hill to enter back into the hood. Gee remained standing at the park with two of his little homeboys, Kevin and Calvin. They were better known as Lil' Red and Boo. Gee was very upset and there would be no disguising it.

"Blood, you must really hate that nigga Youngster, huh?" Lil' Red asked Gee while pulling on the peach fuzz on his chin. He was searching for some kind of reasoning from his homeboy.

Gee looked directly at Lil' Red and slowly said, "Juan was my true homey and that nigga killed him."

"But damn Gee, that was three years ago," Boo broke his silence to join in the conversation.

Gee stared at both of them very hard for a moment before saying, "Ya'll little niggas just don't understand."

Lil' Red and Boo were put on the hood just less than a year ago. Lil' Red was sixteen and Boo was fourteen. The both of them have been knowing Youngster ever since their mother has been dealing with him. Their mother is Betty. Youngster would always warn Betty not to let them hang with the Bloods in the neighborhood but with Betty's drug use, it was inevitable. She was not able to pay close attention to her children and steer them from the street life.

"It's like this," Gee began to explain, "Regardless of the facts, this nigga killed one of ours and he is still allowed up in this bitch makin' plenty of paper like it ain't shit. Meanwhile, one of the homies dead and two is in the *pen* with all day to serve. That should mean somethin' to these niggas. "

Lil' Red continued to pull on the hair on his chin while he listened carefully. Boo also listened with a serious look on his dark face. Boo looked nothing like his older brother. He was black as night and Lil' Red was very light-skinned. Boo took more after Betty in features than Lil' Red. Lil Red was six feet tall and still growing while Boo stood at the same height as his mother. Lil' Red was the spitting image of his father and Boo was the opposite. He was the male version of his mother.

Gee saw the concern in his two protégés' eyes. He began to think that he might have something to build on in a matter of time. He decided to cut everything short while he would prepare for his strategy to manipulate. He looked at the two concerned faces that stood before him and said, "Let's go Blood, we missin' money out here."

## 11

A little after 5:00 p.m., Youngster entered the A+ Carpet Cleaning service office. It was located in a small business district alongside seven store fronts. This area was on the outskirts of Los Angeles hidden away from the heavy black population.

"Hey yo Ace," Youngster called out after greeting Carla; a tall brown-skinned model type woman who was Ace's older sister. She was sitting at the front desk of the office when Youngster walked inside. Carla was holding the phone to her ear very closely. She was being very attentive to the person on the other end of the line. She was only able to flash Youngster a smile and added a slight wave of her hand due to her phone call.

"Back here!" Ace managed to yell out before letting out a loud cough.

Youngster walked past Carla's desk. He made a left turn to enter one of two rooms that was inside the office. The aroma of chronic floated throughout the room as he stepped inside the door before it closed shut behind him.

"What's up my brotha?" Ace asked as he sat up from behind his desk and shook Youngster's hand.

"Not too much," Youngster stated. He acknowledged the two other men that were in the room with a nod of his head before he continued, "I'm just comin' to check on that thing that we talked about earlier."

Ace took a long hit from the blunt that he was smoking on and while holding in the smoke, he attempted to hand the blunt off to Youngster.

"You know that I don't get down like that Ace," Youngster quickly refused to take the blunt.

"What, you mean to tell me that you don't smoke any more?" Ace inquired while trying not to let out all the smoke at the same time.

"Yeah, I still smoke but you know damn well that I don't smoke with nobody. Especially ya'll niggas."

"There he goes with that shit again," Kareem said as he got up from his seat in the corner of the room to grab the blunt out of Ace's hand.

"Look, ya'll know how I feel about that shit. I don't know where ya'll niggas mouths been but I can only imagine with some of ya'll nasty asses." He finished his sentence while looking directly at Ace.

"Man, fuck you!" Ace said. The room began to fill with laughter.

They were all well aware of Youngster's story of smoking a blunt with Ace a few years prior.

While smoking with Ace, Youngster was listening to his wild sexual adventure with two females. The vision didn't set well with him as Ace talked about what he did to them and what they both did to him. Ace's nasty sexual exploration was only hours prior to the both of them smoking a blunt together. From that day on, Youngster has refused to smoke with another person knowing that their lips and tongue has been in places that he don't want to even imagine.

"Hey Brad," Ace stopped laughing to get one of his cousin's attention. "Go and get that thing out of the van so we can get rid of this closet smokin' brotha right here."

The dark man named Brad was tall and very muscular. He always wore shades even when he was inside places. Along with his shades, he was wearing a tan khaki uniform with an A+ Cleaning Service logo patch above his left pocket. Brad immediately stepped outside of the room after Ace spoke to him. Within a few minutes, Brad returned with a medium size brown paper bag in his hand. He approached the desk where Ace was sitting and placed the brown bag on the desk.

"There you go my brotha," Ace stated to Youngster.

Youngster looked inside the bag with an expression of approval. He then took the bag in his hand and said to Ace, "I got you in the car so walk with me to the car so I can be on my way."

Ace stood up from behind the desk and followed Youngster to his car. Before Youngster reached his car, he pushed the remote to the alarm on his Volvo. There was a chirping sound while the doors unlocked. He hopped in and gestured to Ace to get in on the passenger's side. He reached behind the passenger's seat and pulled out from under the seat a dark black plastic bag with a stuffed T-shirt inside of the bag.

"It's all there," he said after handing Ace the bag.

Ace just felt the stuffed T-shirt without inspecting the contents. He then looked over to Youngster and said, "I'll count it when I get inside."

"Okay," Youngster responded.

"So, what's goin' on over there with them boys in the Jungles? Are they fuckin' with you over there?" Ace asked.

"Nah, shit been straight over there besides one asshole but it's all good."

"Well, you just make sure you watch your back and let me know if some shit start smellin' too funny over there."

"You know I will."

Ace opened the door and stepped outside of the car, "Be safe and sound my brotha," he said just before closing the car door. Ace then walked back inside the office. Youngster started up his car, pulled off, and carefully drove home with the medium size brown paper bag containing a kilo of cocaine at his feet.

Every week Youngster would stop by the carpet cleaning office to meet up with Ace. He would pick up a kilo of Peruvian flake and drop off fourteen thousand and five hundred in cash before heading straight home. Ace has been Youngster's drug connection from day one. From the very first day that he had copped his first fifty dollar double-up sack, Ace been his supplier. That was a little over four years ago. Ace and his crew don't serve much coke in the streets of Los Angeles any longer. Their main thing is transporting big weight out of town to a variety of states with the backing of a Columbian cartel connection. They would use the carpet cleaning business as a front. This would be their meeting spot every morning discussing major drug trades and transactions.

Youngster has known Ace since childhood but with Ace being four years older than him, they didn't hang together much back in the day. He has learned a lot from Ace. He has always admired the way Ace and his family were so organized. Ace has been trying to lure Youngster into joining their organization but Youngster preferred running his own thing the way he liked it. He felt more comfortable doing things in his own way and on his own time.

Youngster made it home safe. He placed his package of dope in a hidden compartment upstairs in his bedroom closet. He had quite a few ounces left so there was no need to bust down the kilo that he had just bought. He was still feeling uneasy about the murders that he committed while he lay across his bed in deep thought. He wondered how he should play his cards for the time being until he felt more at ease.

A good thirty minutes had gone by before the phone started to ring. He rolled over towards his nightstand and grabbed the phone, "Yeah," he answered.

"What's up cousin, where the hell have you been?" the loud drunken voice screamed in his ear. It was Youngster's cousin Dee.

"I've been around, what's up with you? It sounds like you've been drinkin' again." Youngster said.

"And you know it!" Dee slurred out his words that was quickly followed by his amusing laugh.

Youngster held the phone from his ear. He looked at it in disgust. He knew that the majority of the time when Dee would drink too much that it would spell out trouble.

"Nah, but on the real," Dee began. "This broad that I met a few weeks ago, she got a friend that I want you to meet. I was goin' over there in a little while and I wanted to see if you wanna roll with me."

"You mean you wanted to see if I would take you over there." Youngster said.

Dee had his own transportation which was an old black Nissan truck. But when it came down to trying to impress a girl, he would prefer looking nice sitting in Youngster's Volvo wagon instead of his truck. Dee couldn't do anything but laugh at the truth.

"Alright, you got me so what's up? I think you gonna like what you see tonight."

"Well, what time you supposed to be over there?" Youngster asked.

"Whenever you ready to make that move, I'm ready." Dee replied.

Youngster glanced over to check the time, "Let me think about it for a minute and I'm gonna call you right back." There was a pause for a brief moment before he continued, "And Dee, sober up nigga. I ain't got time to be fuckin' with a drunk tonight!"

They both hung up the phone. Youngster's thoughts on going out with his cousin didn't take long to contemplate before he figured that meeting someone new just might be what the doctor ordered.

# 12

By the time Youngster and Dee hit the strip, much of the uncivilized were already out and about. The stalking of the females while cruising up and down Crenshaw Boulevard was in full effect. Youngster had to weave his way through traffic as the so-called big ballers and shot callers were slowing traffic down in their attempt to catch some fresh meat out on the boulevard. From the look of things, the females were making it real easy for the fellas by shouting their names and yelling their phone numbers over all the blasting music. They were hanging their heads outside of cars that had to be moving less than ten miles per hour indulging in flirtatious conversations. On the weekends, the majority of the population on Crenshaw were under the age of twenty-five. They didn't mind being caught by almost every red light that ran down the strip. However, there were the elderly and unfortunate small percentage sitting in their cars showing their displeasure. They were blowing their horns and shaking their heads at the clustered scene that delayed them from getting safely to their destination.

"So who is this female that you tryin' to hook me up with?" Youngster asked after looking over towards Dee.

Dee stood at five feet and nine inches. He carried a few extra pounds on him with just a small amount of facial hair above his lip area. A lot of people would kid him and call him Dr. Dre from the rap group N.W.A because of his resemblance to the rapper.

"You remember that broad Vera I was tellin' you that I had met two weeks ago?" Dee waited for Youngster's acknowledgment before continuing, "Well, she been over her friends house while we been talkin' on the phone and she asked me if I had a friend for her so the first person I thought about was you."

"Oh yeah, that's a good one but you haven't told me anything I want to hear so far."

"What are you talkin' about?" Dee asked.

"I'm talkin' about what the hell she look like and how old is she? I mean tell a nigga somethin' so I don't go over here like Stevie Wonder and shit. I don't wanna be meetin' a mud duck Dee."

"Now you know that I know you don't mess with any chicken heads and ugly ducks. These are some older broads and from what I seen last week when I met Crystal, you'll be very satisfied when you take one look at this broad."

"Dee, I've seen some of the females you have dealt with and I must say your track record ain't all that."

"Oh, you must be talkin' bout my spare of the moment broads. They don't count." After Dee finished his comment, Dee and Youngster began to laugh just thinking of some of the women that Dee has had in his bedroom.

The two women were sitting outside on the porch staring at the green Volvo wagon as it pulled up. Youngster drove slow as he approached the rather large white house sitting on Eighth Avenue. The two women had been alerted by the sounds of Bob Marley coming out of Youngster's speakers from down the block.

*Open your eyes and look within*
*Are you satisfied with the life you're living*
*We know where we're going*

Youngster turned his tape player down as he stopped in front of the house. He attentively watched the two females step off of the porch. They walked down the long concrete pavement that led to the sidewalk towards the car. One of the females was quite tall with a brown complexion, slender body, and shoulder length hair and the other one was much shorter with a high-yellow complexion, thick, and wore her hair in a short cute style.

"Yo Dee!"

"What's up?"

"Which one is which?" Youngster asked hoping that Dee would say that the short one was Crystal.

"The tall one is me, and the short one is you." Dee's answer hit him like the start of his favorite song. He hid his excitement while Dee got out the car and the women approached.

"Vera, Crystal, this is my cousin Jayshawn. Jayshawn, this is Vera and Crystal."

When Vera and Crystal leaned down to speak, Youngster couldn't take his eyes off of Crystal. Her proportions of her body were stunning. Crystal wore a tucked in colorful blouse that was half buttoned to display the cleavage of her 38dd breasts. She was wearing some tight white jeans to show off her 36 inch ass and a pair of gold hoop earrings with a gold heart pendant necklace. The chain dropped right in-between her cleavage that invited Youngster's attention more. He tried hard to keep from staring.

"Get in Crystal so we can talk," Youngster politely said with an alluring smile on his face. "This woman is too damn fine from head to toe," he thought to himself as he examined Crystal's lovely features. Her face had a glow and sparkle to it. She was wearing the right amount of foundation on her face. She had pretty brown tight eyes, nice high cheek bones, and a flawless nose that sat right above her luscious thick lips that were painted pink. To top everything off, she revealed a beautiful Minnie Mouse smile that Youngster had never seen on a woman before. He knew from the moment of observing this gift from heaven that he would soon have to have her for himself.

"So, how are you doin'?" he asked.

"I'm alright. How about you?"

"I'm good, as a matter of fact, I'm extremely good now." He gestured through his facial expression that he was very pleased to be in the company of her.

"Extremely good, huh?" She blushed.

"Indeed," Youngster shot her a smile and continued, "And I must say somethin' that I know you've heard over a thousand times already but I know that you've never heard it this honest and sincere before." Youngster paused briefly. "You are the most beautiful woman that I have ever seen on this earth."

Unknowing to him at the time, he had won Crystal's heart with that line. She began to blush and smiled from ear to ear while receiving a very warm feeling inside. It wasn't what he said because she has heard it many of times before. It was the way he said it in that deep tone of his and how he looked into her eyes. He impressed her. She was definitely feeling his vibe. Crystal's outside response was a modest one with an uncontrollable blush. Her reaction within received a tingling sensation through her body that made her sacred arena moist. It had become the closest thing to an orgasm she had ever felt without actually being touched.

Their conversation ran smoothly inside the car while Dee and Vera stood outside leaned up against the back of the wagon. They were taking in the night's fresh air in-between their intimate moments when their lips would lock. Youngster and Crystal suppressed their desire and attraction for one another. They both thought to themselves that it was too soon to feel what they both were feeling secretly within. It was unusual for them both to have such a desire after just meeting someone for the very first time. They thought it to be strange and tried to control the attraction for one another during their entire conversation.

Crystal found herself in a very awkward place. She usually would meet guys just to see what she could get out of them. The frame of mind that she had was only to use a man. Being a gold digger was not by choice but by circumstance. Crystal was raised by her grandmother because her father left her mother after she gave birth to her youngest sister. Her mother was faced with the pressure of taking care of three little girls at an early age. Instead of taking on such a great responsibility, she took to the streets and drug use. She left the burden of her young babies on her mother's shoulders while she roamed the streets and got high. So in order for Crystal to get the things that she wanted once she was old enough, she relied on her sex appeal to use men that had money. However, during the moments when direct eye contact was unavoidable between her and Youngster, it was becoming evident that her connection would be far from trying to use him.

Two hours had flown by before they would be interrupted by the vibrating of Youngster's pager. Crystal was unaware of what he did for a living due to his allusiveness when she brought the subject up prior to his pager going off. Now she would receive a pretty good idea as she pretended not to eavesdrop on his short exchange of words on his mobile phone. Crystal was well aware of the indirect language of a hustler when they would speak on phones. She picked up on Youngster's slick words that he spoke while he was talking on the phone.

It was time for Youngster to make a move but before departing from Crystal, he gave her his pager number. He also managed to plant a soft seductive kiss on her cheek. This was intentionally given from him and accepted by her as a sign of things to come. Crystal stepped out of the car and Dee hopped in. They both waved at Crystal and Vera as Youngster started the car up. He then slowly pulled off.

"So what cha' think about her?" Dee asked Youngster once they approached the end of Crystal's block.

"Damn! Damn! Damn!" Youngster dramatically shouted imitating a scene from the old television show *Good Times* while turning off Eighth Avenue. There was laughter and the slapping of hands that drowned out the sound of the music coming from the speakers. Youngster was glad that he had decided to take Dee up on the offer to get out. He felt good about hooking up with Crystal again in the near future. He definitely wanted to see what she was really about.

Youngster and Dee wore smiles on their faces as the laughter reduced. It was back to business for Youngster as they headed towards Crenshaw to make some moves.

**13**

It was approaching midnight. Youngster was laying in his bed with only one thing on his mind. He couldn't stop thinking about that Minnie Mouse smile with the 38dd's and nice ass. He lay there wondering if Crystal could see how interested he was in her. He really wanted to get to know her better. He began to think about whether or not she felt he was just running drag on her. "Was she feeling me like I was feeling her?" he questioned. His thoughts were answered as soon as his pager went off. He took his eyes off the ceiling in his dim bedroom to check his beeper. He looked at the unfamiliar number displayed across his beeper. He reached for his phone and dialed the number.

"Hello." The sweet recognizable voice answered.

"Did someone page?" he questioned just to play the role.

"Yes, this is Crystal. The girl you just met. I hope that it's not too late to be callin' you."

"Not at all Crystal, to tell you the truth, I was just layin' here hopin' that you would page me tonight."

"Oh, is that right?" The blushing could be heard in her voice.

"That's right."

"Well, I was laying here hopin' somethin' also." She dragged her sentence out kind of shy like. She aroused his curiosity.

"Oh yeah, and what's that?" he asked.

"I was hopin' that you would come and get me so we can continue our conversation from earlier. I was really enjoin' it."

Youngster couldn't drive fast enough after agreeing to pick her up. As he took the back streets towards her home, the thought of Crystal actually being the one for him kept running through his mind. He wanted a special woman in his life. He had a feeling that she just might be the one to fill that empty space.

Within an hour, he returned back to his place with Crystal by his side. They entered through the door of his town home and Crystal's eyes toured the living room. She glanced at the white Italian leather couch and matching chair.

"Very nice," she said.

"Thank you." Youngster smiled.

Crystal continued to tour and noticed a beautiful black oriental style rug in front of his couch.

"That is beautiful."

"Thank you."

She turned her attention towards the rest of the floor admiring the wall to wall oyster shell colored carpet. She looked up above the black entertainment center where there were three pictures of Jay. "Is that your son?" she asked.

"Yes it is," he answered. He started pointing towards the pictures. "That's him at three months, a year, and two years old."

"He is so cute," she said before she fixed her eyes on the tremendous amount of audio compact discs. They were neatly decorated on both sides of the entertainment center and on the side of the walls. There were so many c d's that she felt like she was at a record store. Crystal was amazed that someone would buy that many c d's.

Youngster's hobby was collecting music. He has bought over two thousand c d's that grew every Tuesday when he purchased more. He has them all organized in ten holders. Each holder held two hundred c d's in them. Youngster is proud of his collection and it showed as he wore a smile while Crystal stared at them. Youngster led Crystal towards the cozy leather couch to sit. They sat there for a little over an hour, trading funny stories and sharing personal ideas about life, love, and happiness. Their conversation ran just as smooth as the one earlier. The vibe was getting stronger between the two.

The television watched them silently in the dimmed room while Bob Marley softly wailed through the speakers of the stereo. Bob Marley soon became the topic of discussion. Crystal listened in amazement as Youngster broke down his interpretation of the messages in Bob Marley's music. He then explained what made him so hooked on listening to Bob Marley and the Wailers.

"A while back, I started a spiritual journey studyin' almost every religion that you could think of and even some that I didn't even know existed. I was really in search of the truth and I had come to terms that the only thing that I knew about religion was what my mother and grandmother had taught me. Now who's to say that it was the truth? I mean how could I actually know what they taught me was the absolute truth?" He paused for a moment only to see that Crystal was clinging to his every word. Then he continued, "If there were people on this Earth for millions of years and we as black people in America were brought over here over four hundred years ago as slaves and stripped of our language, culture, history, and names. What would possibly allow me to believe that these white people gave us a true religion written in their language and given to us in their interpretation? To cut a long story short, during my research I came across some Bob Marley songs. I began to listen to Bob and his lyrics and along with my personal studies. This led me in the direction of the teachings of the Nation of Islam. Bob Marley can be very influential if you grab hold to what he is preachin' and teachin' in his songs."

"And what about smokin' weed?" Crystal came out of her semi-trance to see how Youngster felt about Bob Marley's infamous reputation of smoking weed.

"What do you mean?" he asked the question only to stall as he sat there contemplating if he should reveal that he actually smoked weed.

"I mean how do you feel about smokin' weed? Being that Bob Marley seemed to always have been smokin' a joint. I want to know if you do."

He knew that he had to tell her the truth but he was a little hesitant. He didn't know if admitting that he smokes weed would turn her off or not. He didn't want her to lose interest in him but being honest was something he couldn't avoid.

"Sometimes," he began to answer, "I smoke some chronic but not a whole lot and not with other people."

"What do you mean, not with other people?" she inquired.

"I don't smoke weed with other people. I don't like the idea of passin' a blunt around not knowin' where the other persons' mouth has been. I smoke alone. I call myself a closet smoker." His last comment caused her to let out a burst of laughter. He looked at her glowing face and it immediately put a big grin across his.

"I'm sorry, I didn't mean to laugh." She apologized while she tried to refrain from laughing more. "But that was funny and so true that I couldn't help it. I'm going to remember that from now on. A closet smoker, I like that one."

"Oh, do you smoke too?" A sigh of relief was in his voice although he never pictured himself with someone that smoked weed.

"Yeah, I smoke but only with my sisters and Vera sometimes." She answered defensively now that she knew how he felt about sharing a blunt. She then asked, "Why did you ask if I smoke, do you have some weed here?"

"Yeah, come on." Youngster turned off the television and led her upstairs to his bedroom.

By this time, if Crystal had any ideas about using him, it had been completely erased from her mind. She strictly wanted Youngster for the wonderful vibe that she so strongly felt from him. She wanted him for his stimulating intellect. His signs of maturity really turned her on along with his personality. She felt that an intelligent man was more important than some clothes and jewelry any day. She just had never met one before. However, little did Crystal know that she would soon be receiving all the clothes and jewelry she could ever have wanted and more.

The sounds of reggae music could still be heard from downstairs as she watched him evenly spread the chronic inside of the split Philly. He carefully rolled the blunt as she looked on. She sat on the queen size bed admiring the thick black and royal blue patterned comforter, matching lamps on the nightstands, and the rest of the surroundings. "This seems fit for a king," she thought to herself. She had such a comfortable feeling within as she waited for him to finish rolling up the strong smelling marijuana.

When Youngster was finished rolling the blunt, he put it to his mouth to light it up. He then passed the blunt to Crystal while wearing a devilish look on his face. "Be careful with that," he said to her before she took a hit, "That's not your average weed."

She smiled before she put the blunt to her mouth. She took a hit and understood just what he meant right away. The coughing was uncontrollable for a good three minutes. She was not expecting it to be stronger than what she had been smoking before. She was finding out that it was the strongest weed she had ever smoked. Youngster had to start patting her on her back gently to assist her in regaining control.

"Are you alright?" he asked in a joking manner while patting her. She nodded her head. At the same time, they both started laughing together.

Things began to mellow. The mood started to shift as they continued to smoke the blunt and discuss their ideas of what a perfect relationship should be like. They shared their dos and don'ts.

They explained their likes and dislikes. Both found themselves agreeing with one another on many things while the chronic relaxed their minds and started to work on their hormones. It wasn't long before their eyes would lock on one another. The look of desire fell upon them. Youngster felt that the time was at hand for him to make his move. He turned away from her and reached for the lamp. He tapped it twice to dim the lights, giving the bedroom that candlelit effect. He then closed the gap between the two of them leaving no doubt about what was on his mind.

Youngster put his arm around Crystal. He looked into her submissive eyes and said, "I want you to be mines and I promise as long as you allow me to, I'll treat you right." He leaned towards the speechless beauty. He began to place numerous amounts of soft kisses upon her lips. He paused frequently to look into her eyes to allow his silent wants and desires to transfer into her. She didn't hold back her attraction to the persuasive spell that he was putting on her. Her sweet lips welcomed his affection.

She wrapped her arms around him as the kisses became more passionate, more deep, and inviting. He accepted her open invitation. He entered her mouth with his tongue and started swirling it around hers intensely. The tongue kissing triggered off an uncontrollable excitement that could be seen from the bulge in his pants. His hands explored her body smoothly touching every curve on her voluptuous figure, unleashing an appetite for an erotic courtship. There was no resisting temptation. He slowly unbuttoned her blouse revealing her light pink bra. The bra seemed to be having a hard time containing her large breasts. He caressed them and began to place soft wet kisses on her neck while she rubbed on his pants leg traveling towards his erection.

The foreplay lasted until neither one could stand it any longer. She whispered sensually in his ear, "I'm all yours." From the sound of her voice, he rushed to take off her blouse. He tossed it on the floor. He leaned her back on the bed to remove her shoes and jeans. He stood over her stretched out body admiring the sexy frame not yet completely exposed. Matching satin pink underwear by Victoria's Secret was the only thing left on her body. She snapped the front of her bra, freeing her breasts. She then sat up to undo his pants. She pulled down his jeans along with his navy blue boxers. She massaged his manhood for a moment. She was admiring how hard and ready it was. She then looked up into his eyes with an exotic and tantalizing look on her face. She slowly moved away only to intensify his desire for her more.

Youngster finished undressing. He walked over to his dresser to retrieve a couple of condoms while Crystal got completely naked. After she was fully nude, she retreated under the covers while he quickly joined her. He put a condom on and placed the other one to the side. He submerged completely under the covers to get a taste of her. He placed his mouth over her clit. He kissed it soft. He licked it slow. He swirled his tongue around her clit and could feel her throbbing inside. He came from under the sheets and was now directly above her. He stared into her eyes as she guided him into her sacred palace. He held himself over her while lowering the bottom half of his body. She gently pulled him into her wet and warm domain. The wish for the feeling he received when he entered her was for it to last forever. It was as if she had allowed him to enter into a world that she had prepared especially for him. He had never felt the difference inside a woman before until this night he entered inside of her. He had a feeling like never before.

The obvious difference in the feeling he was receiving began to show. After a few minutes of grinding and penetrating inside of her, his body started to lose its composure. He couldn't hold back the eruption that he felt building up rapidly. The motion of an ocean moving to a nice gentle breeze along a beautiful shore, quickly changed to that of one taken over by a vicious storm. He started to move faster and faster in the hope that he would hit her spot before he exploded. He wanted them to share that first orgasm together. He would give seven strong strokes in-between her widely spread thighs in hopes that she would *cum*.

His goal was accomplished as she felt the intensity and welcomed his passionate outburst causing her juices to flow at the same time he released his. She wrapped her legs around his back with her thighs clutching his sides obviously not wanting him to pull out. She wanted to enjoy the sensation that traveled through her body as long as she could. Although he felt drained, shame forced his body to continue to slowly penetrate. He attempted to regain full strength inside of her. He knew that pleasing her was a must. He had to execute another goal which was to sex her through an unforgettable night. He wanted to know without a doubt that she was completely satisfied. He felt he had to take her to that sexual peak so she would feel an energy that couldn't be given out from lust alone. He wanted her to feel him making love to her soul.

Round two was nothing like the first round. Youngster found himself in complete control of himself. He was concentrating on only making Crystal feel a very satisfying and fulfilling moment. A moment she would always remember. He wanted her never to forget their first intimate rendezvous. He performed like he never did before. He moved to a rhythm like that of a long impromptu jazz session. Hitting the right spots and moving at the exact tempo to stimulate her entire body. He made her reach multiple orgasms as she followed his lead. She kept up with his every move while biting down on the sheets to keep from making too much noise. He went on and on, grinding and passionately pounding his will inside of her flowing river.

After an hour, he guided her soft and wet frame to the edge of the bed. He rolled her over on her stomach. He pulled her up on all fours while he stood behind her. He stood at the edge of the bed. He pulled off the semen filled condom and replaced it with a fresh one. He inserted his hard chocolate bar back inside of her. They continued another twenty minutes in the doggy-style position while his hands were cupping her breasts, rubbing her ass, and gripping her hips. He pulled her back towards him while he relentlessly pumped forward. Each penetrating moment she let out a sound of pleasure mixed with surrender. Her feet dangled off the bed while her ass continued to back into his abs. Her body had never felt what she was feeling. She felt that her body had reached its peak of pure ecstasy and that it couldn't get any better than the feeling she was receiving. She was wrong.

Youngster shifted into a slow grinding gear just long enough to where both of their sexual senses were rekindled. He then began to move with more certainty, faster and faster, deeper and deeper, harder and stronger. He worked his libido overtime and finally, it caused both of them to lose their balance. He dropped down on her, forcing her to stretch out on the bed while he continued to stroke in and out of her. He grabbed her hands tightly as she spread across the bed. She returned the tight grip with one of her own. During this moment of intensity, she unleashed a satisfying scream that caused him to let out all that he had been holding in for well over an hour. They both exploded.

Their bodies trembled for a good few minutes. Youngster rested his drenched and drained frame on top of her backside before rolling off. He took off his condom and dropped it to the floor. He had no strength to dispose of it in the bathroom. They both soon met in the middle of the bed under the covers and cuddled until the morning. That night, they made the bond between one another official.

***

Laying on his side, Youngster was awakened by a whispering voice, "Yeah girl, I can't believe that he made me *cum* like that. His shit was the bomb." Youngster now pretended to be sleep as he continued to eavesdrop on Crystal's conversation.

"He was tryin' to get me hooked on that good lovin' he was dishin' out or something girl. I ain't gonna lie, at first I thought right before we start doin' it, that I was gonna whip it on his young ass but he ended up whippin' it on me all night long." She laughed as quiet as she could before continuing, "Yeah, he seems like everything I hoped for in a man, upstairs and down. But I'll have to wait and see. You know how niggas can change especially after you give them some." She paused and listened carefully before going on, "I know but I really couldn't help it. Now you know damn well that I don't get down like that but I'm tellin' you it's something about him and last night, it couldn't have went no other way. It was like everything was meant to be."

Crystal paused to listen to the other end of the line. She then let out a laugh that was louder than she expected. She regained her composure and said, "He didn't put anything in the damn weed, you damn fool. Girl I better let you go before you make me wake him up, I'll call you when I get home. Okay bye."

Youngster wore a big smile after hearing Crystal's conversation. It pleased him to know that he wasn't the only one that felt something special. He lay still with his eyes shut having no idea that waking up to the sound of Crystal's voice and her lovely face that morning, would be the first of many. After dropping Crystal off at home early in the day, she was right back in the car within hours. She was introduced to Youngster's world as he conducted his business throughout the day. Later on that night, he dropped her off only to grab a change of clothes. He returned for her to go home with the addition of Jay. The routine of her grabbing a change of clothes each night quickly turned into her entire wardrobe hanging in Youngster's closet. In about three weeks, she had all her things at his apartment. She had moved completely in. Youngster's clientele had started to kid them for being together so much. They would sometimes call them Bonnie & Clyde. It seemed that every time he would meet with them, she would either be the one driving or in the passengers seat. They were inseparable in the streets and at home. A family atmosphere had began to rise. She got along with Jay really well. Although Jay knew that she wasn't his real mom, he showed that he was very happy to have a female figure around him and his dad.

Youngster strived to explore new boundaries in his new found love. He treated Crystal like a queen. He worked hard at not making what he thought were mistakes in his past relationship. He showed much more affection with her than when he was with Shell. He thought that the lack of it in his past relationship, may have led to Shell cheating. He covered all grounds to make sure that it wouldn't happen in his bond with Crystal. They were sharing some of the most beautiful, fun loving, and romantic moments together. These were moments both of them had never experienced. Youngster found himself in uncharted territory. He often admitted to Crystal that he had never thought that what was being shared between them, would ever exist in his life. However, he would learn the hard way. When you are in the game, a romantic relationship is something that will always be very difficult to maintain.

# 14

The police helicopter could be heard above every roof top along with sirens and speeding police cars. The bright spotlight from the helicopter shining through the windows of households combined with the flashing blue and red lights of police cars, gave the impression that a serial killer was on the loose. But these were just typical sights and sounds of nightfall arriving in most black neighborhoods throughout Los Angeles county. Anne sat in her living room trying to enjoy her favorite game show on television hoping that the sounds of the helicopter would hurry up and pass before the next question. She loved to see how many answers she could get correct before the contestants. It would give her a feeling of joy imagining she was the one winning the cash prizes when she would beat the contestant to the right answer.

When Anne's show was finally over, she noticed that Shell hadn't been out of her room the whole day. She began to feel worried and thought that she had better check on her granddaughter. She stood up, walked to Shell's bedroom door, and knocked three times.

"Michelle," she said curiously. "Are you alright in there?"

"Yes, I'm okay." Shell answered after about a minute of silence. Her voice was filled with anguish and sadness.

"Are you sure Michelle? You don't sound very good." Anne gave the door a light tap before opening it.

"I'm alright Grandma," Shell's back was facing Anne. She was obviously sobbing.

"You have not been out this room all day Michelle. You have to realize that you can't cry over spilled milk because there ain't nothin' you can do about it. Jayshawn is hurting just as much as you are and is only with that girl to get back at you for what you did to him. He will be back, but not if you continue to cry and chase him. A man can't stand that Michelle. Get yourself together and be patient. You can only make things change for the worse by being so depressed. You want me to fix you somethin' to eat?"

"No, thank you. I'll be okay."

"Well, I'll be in my room if you need me." Anne closed Shell's door and went off to bed.

Shell would lay in her bed the whole night through crying on an empty stomach. She could feel Youngster moving further away from her despite her grandmother's speech. She didn't know what to do or just how to be patient. With him having a girlfriend, it only made things more difficult for her to cope. She had been paging him constantly trying to get his attention but when he returned her calls, he would just give her short answers. Youngster kept his distance. When he would drop Jay off, he wouldn't even go inside her bedroom anymore. It had become strictly about Jay in their conversations. Her dreams of getting back with him were fading fast. It was moving out of range to where there would be no return.

The days moved along with Shell coming to terms with the fact that there may never be a relationship with Youngster again. She needed something to ease her pain. She began to turn her attention to the compliments and the persistence of an older man that lived down the street from her grandmother's house. He would always try to get at her while she would be walking to the store. Finally, she gave in one day. She made the mistake of giving him her phone number. She had decided to use him as her rebound. She thought that having someone would help her not think about Youngster so much.

The rebound's name was Ice. His family and friends have been calling him that from the time he was a teenager. He was given the name Ice from dating girls. He was as cold to the females as the nickname given to him. Those that really knew him would say that his heart was built in the Artic. He knew all the tricks to catch women in the traps that he would lay. Ice stood a little over six feet tall. He was an average size for his height. He was light-skinned and had long wavy hair to his shoulders that he kept in a pony-tail. He had that pretty boy look and could pass for the son of Ron O' Neal's character in the movie *Super Fly*. He was a smooth talker with a hidden agenda. This was something that Shell would not discover until it would become too late.

***

All the kids were smiling from ear to ear as Youngster pulled up in front of the white house located on Hyde Park. They got so excited from the time they heard the music from Youngster's car hit the corner and saw him coming in their direction. "Mama, here comes Youngster," they all yelled over and over until their mother Diane came to the porch to calm them down.

Youngster stepped out of his car holding a small brown paper bag in his hand. He walked to the curb to get mobbed by the three siblings. There was the four year old Trevor, the six year old Terrance, and the eight year old Terry. They all rushed him to give him hugs as Diane looked on with an impatient smile on her face.

"Have you been takin' care of your little brothers?" Youngster asked Terry after she finally released his neck.

"Yes," she answered in her cute little voice.

"Good, I'll be back to take ya'll to the store after I'm done talkin' to your mother." Youngster walked towards the house stepping on the dead grass from the enormous amount of traffic that goes in and out of the house. He passed the scattered broken toys before entering through the opened door where Diane stood waiting. He followed her to the back of the house passing a few anxious customers that were sitting in her living room. Youngster entered Diane's bedroom. He took a seat on the edge of her unmade bed while she locked the door behind them.

Diane is 26 years old, five feet and seven inches, she has a medium build with very long straight hair. She has all the features of her father's side of the family who are Native Americans with the exception of her large ass which she got from her mother who is a black woman from Alabama. Although she was still young and very attractive, the street life was taking its toll on her. It added about fifteen years to her appearance.

"So, how you been Youngster?" she asked while she walked to her dresser to grab her money.

"I been okay, how you been?"

"Hangin' in there, I guess." She handed Youngster six hundred dollars. In return, he gave her the small paper bag with the ounce inside.

"What's up with those people in your house?" he asked with a chastising look on his face.

"I'm sorry but I was a little short so I had to use they money, I couldn't get rid of them before you came."

"You know I can't stand that shit."

"I know and it won't happen again. I promise Youngster."

"Have you been taking care of those kids?"

"Of course Youngster, why would you ask somethin' like that?"

"Because I know you Diane. That shit can mean more to you than them kids at times."

Diane shook her head but couldn't argue with the truth that exited Youngster's mouth. She just stood over her dresser and was breaking pieces of the cookie to serve her paid customers that were waiting for her in her living room.

Youngster stood up. He adjusted his 9 millimeter hidden inside his waist belt. He waited for Diane to unlock her bedroom door and then started to follow her out. They were greeted by the excited voices of her children yelling for Youngster to hurry before the ice cream truck drove passed their house.

"Oh, this will save me a trip to the store," Youngster said to Diane as he quickly passed her by to get outside her house. The children were flagging the ice cream truck down. Diane could only smile. She shook her head in a pleasing fashion as she watched him rush out her house just to tend to her children. She stood at her door watching Youngster give her children something that she and their deadbeat dad could never be able to give them. He was giving them the attention that they desired in their young lives. She was saddened by the thought that if their father was even close to being like Youngster, her life wouldn't be filled with a drug addiction. She felt that she wouldn't be dealing drugs to support her habit. She knew with a man like Youngster, her life would have been much better. There would be way more than just the little bit of food in her refrigerator if she had a good man by her side instead of the substituting constant use of drugs.

"Diane!" One of the males sitting on her couch yelled to get her attention. "Give me my shit so I can get the fuck out of here!"

When Youngster was done buying ice cream and candy for the kids, he jumped into his car. He rode off to return home. His conscience attempted to erase the good feeling he shared with the children. He was reminded of what was going on inside those kids home. While the children were out playing each day, he knew that their mother was getting high inside. He started to think about how each night those innocent little children slept in the midst of crack heads using the drugs that he just supplied to their mother.

The guilt traveled through his mind, as well as in his heart, before exiting. He soon accepted it all as being a part of the life he lead. A part of his daily grind in the hood.

***

Shell sat on the sofa feeling real uncomfortable about her surroundings. Ice had talked her into going with him to a gathering at his cousin's house in Watts. She sat there in the strange place questioning her decision to go along with him. Without him, she nervously sat still in the living room waiting for his return. They had been kicking it for a few days consecutively enjoying one another's company over drinks and some weed but this was a bit too much for her.

The music was blasting loud from the stereo while a group of people she had never met, drank and smoked. They all looked wild and strange to her which made her feel afraid. Ice had left her in the front of the house while he rolled joints for his cousin in the back. He would do this just to receive a couple of free ones from him. His cousin would throw these little parties every weekend and sell sticks at the party for a nice profit. Ice would always make his way over there with a new young girl on his arm. This would be Shell's first introduction to Ice's real world. A world that she would soon become all too familiar with. After an hour passed, Ice finally came out from the back to keep Shell company. The fact that he didn't look normal distracted Shell's anger causing a concern instead.

"Are you alright Ice?" she asked over the music playing.

"I'm good," he answered as he stood over her sweating profusely.

He sat down beside her on the sofa and kissed her on the cheek. He held a fat joint in one hand while he searched for a lighter in his pocket with the other. She observed the weird look on his face and took notice of his strange behavior. She could tell he was on something stronger than just weed but couldn't figure it out.

"Are you sure you alright?" she asked.

"Yeah baby, I told you that already. I just been drinkin' in the back and worked up a sweat from the heat." He lied while he pulled his lighter out, "I'm sorry I left you alone for so long, my cousin and I had some business to conduct."

Shell just continued to watch him as he wiped the sweat from his face. His eyes were wide open. It seemed that his eyes were unable to blink. He lit the joint, took a hit, and passed it to her as she remained silent. She took the joint from his hand. She noticed a smell that she was not familiar with. The smell made her feel like she had to vomit.

"What kind of weed is this?" she asked with an unpleasant look on her face.

"That's that good shit baby, hit it and you'll see." Shell still had her suspicions. She became hesitant on smoking the joint. She was feeling like she should just hand it back to him.

"If you gonna let the muthafucka go out in your hand, you can just give it back to me!" Ice yelled. His voice caught the attention of the others around them.

Shell had been put on the spot. She felt more from the pressure to hit the joint than the desire to get high. She wasn't experienced with using drugs. She had just started smoking weed recently with Ice. Youngster never allowed her to smoke or drink. She had heard that there were many types of weed, so she concluded that the weed she was holding was just a different type. A type that gave off a different kind of smell than what she had been used to. She felt for any wetness on the zig-zag to reassure herself that the joint was not laced with PCP. She then placed it on her lips. She pulled on the joint long and hard before passing it back to Ice. She immediately began to feel a rush that she would never ever forget. A rush that she would find herself chasing for the rest of her life.

Shell's heart rate increased rapidly while the stimulant traveled through her chest and brain. It reached her central nervous system which controlled her pleasure signals. She had no control of herself for the next ten minutes. She could only lay back on the sofa enjoying a high that would cause her entire life to spiral down a road of destruction and hell. She had no idea that the joint she just took a hit from was laced with rock cocaine. At that moment, as the high began to quickly vanish she was only concerned with getting another hit. She put her hand out for Ice to hand the joint back to her. She wanted another hit before he sucked it all up. Ice passed the joint back to her while wearing a wicked sly look on his face. Shell hit the joint again. The crowd that was in their presence noticed that Ice had fresh meat sitting next to him. From the look of things, it wouldn't be the last time that they would see her face. An older dark gentleman in his forties sat in the corner of the room staring. He was drooling over the thought of being the one with the opportunity to turn the young girl out. He watched her closely getting her first taste of the substance that was sure to get her hooked and doing anything for more of it. Shell had took the bait. She had entered the first stage of becoming a dope fiend. Her next couple of steps towards addiction was sure to follow.

***

Youngster and Crystal sat on the park bench hugging while Jay played at a distance on the swings. It was a break that was really needed for Youngster. And a moment that Crystal would enjoy. A time for her to soak in Youngster's undivided attention. It was an opportunity that didn't come as often as she would have liked. But when the moment came around, she would have such a wonderful feeling inside. A feeling that she wanted to hold in forever.

When Youngster decided to take time out to chill with Crystal and Jay, he would do his best to leave his work behind. Although this had become difficult, he would attempt to give the both of them the impression that it was their time and nothing else mattered at that moment.

"Baby," Crystal spoke as she looked up at Youngster who was holding her from behind.

"What's up my love?"

"Let me ask you somethin'?"

"Okay, I'm all ears."

"What is it that you see when you think about the years ahead of you?"

"Well, I see that boy over there makin' his daddy very proud of him in all the wise choices that he will be makin' in adulthood. I see him graduating college and becomin' a great defense Lawyer or a Doctor curing all kinds of shit out here. I see myself makin' my mother and sister very proud of me by actually being legit. No more of this bullshit street life. I see my mom never having to wear that worried look on her face ever again. And finally I see you." He stopped talking.

Crystal looked over her shoulders. She caught him staring directly at her. "You see me doin' what?" she asked with a curious tone in her voice.

"Well," he paused again to play with her anxious ears.

"Stop playin' and spit it out. Tell me exactly where I fit in when you look ahead at these years to come."

"Well, I see you making me very proud as my wonderful, caring, and loving wife. I see you making my life whole and us havin' a few kids together."

Youngster squeezed Crystal tight once he completed his response to her. She smiled from ear to ear before stating, "You know you got the special treatment comin' tonight so tell them toes to be prepared to curl." Together they laughed. They continued to enjoy a few more hours of peace and relaxation before the hustle would come calling in the form of a vibrating pager.

***

Shell sat in her bedroom trying to remember how she got there. The last thing she was able to remember was being in Watts with Ice. Her head was aching. Her entire body was sore. She was feeling down and very depressed. She was coming to terms with the realization that the joint she smoked had more than just weed in it. She wasn't sure what was in it but she wanted to find out. She would become very disappointed that she would desire something that she had once vowed never to try in her life. She reached for her telephone and dialed Ice's number. The phone rang four times before he answered.

"Hello."

"Ice?"

"Hey, what's up baby?"

"Please tell me what was in the weed last night?" she asked.

"It was just a little coke baby, why?"

"Just a little coke!" She screamed into the phone. "How could you do that to me?"

"Do what baby? I just gave you the best feelin' you ever had in your life so why you trippin'?"

"Ice, you know that I told you that weed and a little alcohol was the only thing that I would do. It was as far as I wanted to go when it came down to gettin' high."

"Look," Ice began, "It was just a one time deal and I'll never do that again. If you didn't like it, that's fine." Ice knew that when it came to using cocaine that for most people and all the ones he knew of, there was no such thing as a one time deal with cocaine. As for Shell, she would become just like the majority of the first time users, just as Ice hoped and planned. She would become a fiend.

Shell held the phone stunned and astounded. She couldn't believe Ice would betray her. She felt that after she had poured her heart out to him a few days prior to going with him to Watts, she could trust him. She didn't think he would hurt her or do something to trick her. She wasn't taught the valuable lesson of never showing a man like Ice a sign of weakness. A man like him would only take advantage of it instead of sympathizing with her. A man like that could never look out for her best interest. He had no compassion for a young lost girl and his lack of compassion was only just beginning to show.

"Are you there?" Ice asked.

"Yeah I'm here but not for long," she answered angrily.

"What is that supposed to mean?"

"I don't think we should see one another or talk anymore!" Shell hung up the phone before giving him a chance to say anything in his defense. Nevertheless, Ice didn't even bother to call her back. He knew that she would be the one calling him back in due time. He knew it wouldn't be long before she would be in search of the high he introduced her to. He just sat there knowing she would be soon kissing his ass and doing whatever else necessary to get that high again.

# 15

The rain fell hard on this winter night in the city of Los Angeles. The gathered clouds had made the evening darker than usual. Youngster's thoughts were on getting out of the cold. He wanted to be back in the warm presence of his sweetheart and his son. He insisted on Crystal staying in the house with Jay that morning while he made his runs. He was now missing their company while he rolled around in the heavy rain. "A couple of more calls and I'm done," he thought to himself as he turned on Crenshaw in route to another delivery. At this point in his life, he couldn't have felt any better. His business was steady and going great. His love life was looking promising, and as for the double homicide investigation, he was almost certain that the case was closed. There was one thing about the L.A.P.D. When it came down to an unsolved gang related black homicide, if it wasn't an open and shut case, it would be put on the shelf to collect dust. A case like that would stay on the shelf, and never be reopened. There was never too much emphasis put on solving a gang members death in the streets of Los Angeles. A gang member's death was looked upon as a big help more than an enigma inside the police department.

While sitting at the light on Crenshaw and Rodeo Road, Youngster was alerted by the sound of a horn. It came from a car to the right of him. He looked over to see that it was Ace in his black Mercedes Benz. Before the light could change, Ace pointed to a donut shop that was located directly across the light to the right of them. He signaled for Youngster to pull over there. Youngster pulled into the small parking lot with Ace on his tail. They greeted each other as they met at the entrance of the donut shop. They both went to the counter to purchase a cup of coffee. After they received their coffee, Ace led the way as they took seats in the far corner of the shop.

"What's going on with you my brotha?" Ace asked with a soaking wet face due to the rain.

"Not too much, I'm on my way to pay someone a visit," Youngster replied while glancing at his Guess watch. He was also showing signs of a person just stepping out of the rain.

"Well, do you remember when I said last week that I might have a proposition that might interest you?" Ace paused. Youngster nodded his head before Ace continued, "We making a move down south. We setting up shop in a few cities down there and since you got family down there all ready, I think you might be interested in making some of those Big Macs instead of these small cheese burgers you making out here."

Youngster thought about it while they both laughed from the comment Ace had made. He looked at Ace and said, "Let me think about that and I'll get back at you this weekend when I cop."

"That's why I just stopped you. We leaving before this weekend and won't be back for about two weeks. So even if you don't wanna go, you might wanna cop before Friday."

"Look," Youngster began, "I'm about to be late for my appointment so I'll be in your office on Thursday to let you know what's up."

"Cool," Ace said. They both left out the donut shop leaving two cups of coffee untouched on the table.

Youngster was never one to rush a decision when it came down to making money. He understood that one must always weigh out their options and the consequences that came along with illegal earnings. "This could be my opportunity to breakthrough," he thought to himself while carefully driving in the rain. There were two things that worked against his thought. One was that he would be working for someone else. The other thing that worked against his thought was he never was too fond of leaving out of town to hustle. He felt that if he ever did get swept up by the law, he wanted to be close enough for his son and family to visit him in prison. He didn't want to risk being far away in another state. His father made that big mistake in which the situation only put more of a strain on his family. He vowed to never do the same thing.

***

The aroma of turkey tacos smacked Youngster in the face when he returned home out of the pouring rain. Crystal had everything prepared. She was waiting on him to walk through the door so they could all eat dinner. She enjoyed sitting at the dinner table as a family. She looked forward to each time they were able to eat and share a home cooked meal.

"I am sure glad to see you," Crystal said as she walked from the living room into the kitchen wearing a red and black silk oriental style robe.

"Well, I'm sure glad to see you too, among other things." His words as well as his eyes focused directly on the way her robe hugged her shape.

"You know you have a problem, right?" she stated looking away in an attempt to conceal her blushing.

"Yeah, and her name is---" He playfully stared at her while breaking out into a big smile.

The sound of footsteps roaring down the stairs entered into the room. It was quickly followed by the appearance of Jay. He ran straight into his daddy's arms, giving him a tight hug right after Youngster picked him up.

"Well, my love, you're not the only one that's glad to see me." Youngster grinned at Crystal. He then turned his attention to his son, "What's up Jay, what you been doing all day?"

"Nothin'," Jay answered.

"Nothin'," Youngster repeated his son. "Well, are you ready to eat?" he asked while putting Jay back down to the floor. Jay responded by nodding his head. Youngster instructed Jay to wash his hands in the half bathroom downstairs before he sat down to eat.

***

The thought of leaving out of town lingered in Youngster's mind throughout the night. After putting Jay to bed, he had settled in his bedroom to contemplate. He was still full from the tacos that he had ate. Crystal was propped up against the headboard smoking a blunt while he thought and flipped channels on the television. He was trying to calculate how much more money he needed to make before Thursday when he had to re-up from Ace. If he decided not to go with Ace down south, he knew that he had to definitely see Ace before he left. The last thing he wanted to do was run out of dope with no one to cop from.

"What's wrong baby? It seems like you stressin'." Crystal stated as she handed him the blunt.

"It's just some business that I have to decide on, that's all," he replied before taking a hit of the blunt. He took a long pull before passing the blunt back to her.

"Well, don't let it worry you baby. Over there lookin' all stressed out."

"Oh, I'm not. The only thing that I'm worried about is that you don't get sleepy from all that food and this weed to where you become too tired to ride me tonight."

His comment brought a chuckle out of her mixed with a few light coughs from the weed. Youngster then moved towards her. He started to massage her shoulders. He slowly started to move his hands down her back eventually reaching around her caressing her soft breasts. He gently pinched her nipples with the tip of his fingers. He pressed up against her body from behind her. From there, she couldn't resist the uncontrollable temptation of making love to her man.

The following day, Youngster made up his mind not to go down south with Ace. He decided that it wouldn't be a good idea leaving what he had already established. He couldn't deal with the fact of building somewhere else and working under another person. It just didn't make any sense to him to take that chance.

After making up his mind, his focus shifted to meeting his daily quota in order for him to be able to cop from Ace on Thursday. He had two days to make the few thousand dollars that he was short. This would mean a little extra grinding in the streets. It meant hitting a few more corners than usual and staying out a little later than his normal closing time. Thursday had come and he had his money counted out, stacked, and stuffed in a T-shirt inside of a brown grocery paper bag. He walked inside of the office and spotted Brad behind the desk where Carla would normally be seated.

"What's up Brad, are you the new secretary?" he joked.

"Do I look like a damn secretary to you?" Before giving Youngster time to answer, Brad continued in his grimy voice, "Don't you say something that you might regret my brotha." They both smiled at one another before Brad yelled, "Hey Ace! This damn closet smoker is out here."

"Send him on back here!" Ace shouted.

The whole crew was inside the room except for Ace's mother and sister. They were the ones that operated the legitimate side of the cleaning service business. Ace and the crew were gathered around the office desk smoking weed and studying a map. Youngster spotted Ace sitting behind the desk like a General in an army. He was pointing at the map while going over their plans.

"Are ya'll goin' to war down south or what? What's up with the map spread all across the desk and shit?" he asked the crowd after stepping into the smoke filled room.

"Get your maybe next time ass in here and shut up. By the time you decide to go, we will all be rich, retired, and on an island with a whole lot of naked hoes," Ace joked. Everyone laughed while Youngster could see that Ace really wanted him to go along on the trip with the crew.

"Man, I'm out here hustlin' solo, I just can't up and leave my customers like that." Youngster attempted to explain.

Ace stood up from behind the desk and said, "I'll be right back." He then took the bag that Youngster was holding in his hand and led him outside the room. Youngster followed Ace across to the other room where Ace's mother would usually be sorting out their paper work from the cleaning service. Ace walked over to a silver file cabinet, opened the bottom drawer, and grabbed a box from it. He then handed Youngster the box that was the size of a small cereal box and tossed him a plastic bag to put it in.

"You're about to miss out my brotha," Ace stated while Youngster examined his product inside of the box. He nodded his head approving of what he saw in the box. He put the box inside of the bag, and said, "I ain't trippin'. You just make sure that you make it back in two weeks like you said. I should have enough to last me until then."

"Don't worry my brotha, I won't leave you hanging," Ace said full of confidence.

"Cool, I'm about to get up out of here." Youngster responded as he headed towards the door.

"Be safe and sound my brotha," Ace said.

"Same to you, holla at me as soon as you get back." Youngster exited the building, got in his car, and pulled off unaware that it would be the last time he would ever see Ace again.

# '16

The next two weeks flew by pretty smooth except for one minor difficulty; Shell. She attempted to disrupt Youngster's positive direction by blowing up his pager and calling his home just to hang up in Crystal's face. Her behavior had become erratic and desperate. She placed the blame on Crystal for her sudden addiction to the non-stop use of cocaine. She wanted some type of justice in her mind. Since getting Youngster back had definitely decreased, the only thing she could do was to interrupt his life. She had hoped to make his life as miserable as hers. She knew with her use of drugs, there was no chance of ever having him again. Although her addiction had remained a secret, Shell knew she was too far gone. She could only point her finger at Crystal and attempt to intrude the bond that had developed between Crystal and Youngster.

The beginning of the third week, Youngster had yet to hear from Ace. Things were not looking good because he was running low on drugs. He started to get a bit worried. He drove by the carpet cleaning office several times hoping to catch Ace's mother or sister in an attempt to get some answers. The office was always closed with no sign of neither one of them each time he drove by. He tried paging Ace over and over. He never received a call back. He thought about all possible things that could have happened to Ace. He came to the conclusion that Ace was just running behind schedule. He decided to just slow down his moves and be patient. He no longer would take the big orders that he would receive. He decided to just make sure that his loyal customers were taken care of until Ace returned.

Christmas had came and went like an ordinary day in Youngster's household. He didn't celebrate Christmas so the day was no big deal to him. He hadn't celebrated the holiday since he had left from under his mother's roof. He could never get over the idea of people going broke on a day that supposed to be Jesus' birthday. He felt that only the department stores were the beneficiaries. He had explained his reasoning to Crystal. She listened and understood. She agreed with him one hundred percent on not participating in the Christmas celebrations. It didn't even bother her at all because she felt her gifts were being received more than once a year by being with a man she had deep feelings for.

It was the day before New Year's Eve, Youngster was sitting in his living room watching television. Crystal was upstairs relaxing in the bedroom while Jay was in his bedroom watching music videos. Youngster had a few cookies left that he sold sparingly to his main customers so that kept him more at home. The clock struck four in the afternoon when Youngster turned the television station to the news. All the answers to his questions about Ace were disclosed to him in the top story. He watched in awe as he saw photos of Ace, Ali, Kareem, Eli, and Brad on the television screen. He turned up the volume on the television and listened to the report, "All five men from Los Angeles were arrested in Atlanta Georgia early this morning in connection to a drug ring with ties to the Columbian cartel. Federal agents seized a storage space that they were allegedly renting that contained ninety-one kilos of cocaine. All five men are being held with no bail and if convicted, face life in a federal prison without the possibility of parole."

Youngster sat in his living room astounded, he stared at the television screen but no longer heard the sounds coming from the speakers. The news hit him hard. He was stunned. He had turned deaf to all that surrounded him. He wasn't only feeling the loss of his only drug connection but the loss of a dear friend. Ace was like a guide to him. Because Youngster didn't have many male figures in his life to look up to, Ace had become a very important person to him.

"Jayshawn, what's wrong?" Crystal asked. She had walked up behind him without him realizing it until she spoke.

He turned his head to make eye contact with her, "You not gonna believe this shit." Youngster took a deep breath, "I just watched Ace and his whole crew on the news. They were all arrested down in Atlanta and they are all facin' life."

Crystal stood there in disbelief. She released a huge sigh. She was thankful that her man didn't go along on the trip.

"Man, what I'm gonna do now?" he asked himself aloud as he got up off the couch. He then walked past Crystal and slowly went up the stairs to his room.

Throughout the night, Ace's incarceration was on Youngster's mind. He thought about if Ace would really get all that time. He compared Ace's unfortunate event to that of his father's. It weighed heavy on his mind. Youngsters' father would take trips for a kingpin in the drug business. He transported pounds of heroin from the east coast back to the west. He eventually was caught transporting through the state of Virginia where he was sentenced to serve life in prison. Youngster wondered if Ace would receive the same stiff sentence. He thought about if Ace would do as his father did. After seven years of sitting in prison, Youngsters' father took his own life instead of giving the rest of it to the ward of the state. Youngster was ten at the time of the tragic event. It is something that he will never forget.

The following day, Youngster was completely out of drugs. He was clueless to where to cop a whole kilo. He needed someone that he could trust. He thought about who would be able to help him find another connection. He decided to give Dee a call. He wanted to see if his cousin might know someone that dealt with that kind of weight.

"Hello." Dee answered.

"Dee, what's up?" Youngster asked.

"Oh, you know I'm just bustin' bottles and broads. What's going on with you and your wife, ya'll ain't got a divorce yet?"

"Nah man," Youngster replied.

"Well, you better be careful because you know that Shell is somewhere plottin' on your ass. She ain't gonna give up on you just like that."

"Man, I'm not worried about that right now." Youngster said. "I need to know if you know someone that I can get some weight from. I've been goin' crazy after seeing the damn news yesterday."

"Oh yeah, I meant to call you about that. Looks like them niggas will not see freedom ever again." Dee paused for a minute before saying, "Well, the only person that I might know is this nigga Rob that used to stay by my mother's house. I ran into him a few weeks ago and he gave me his pager number. He told me that if I ever needed a *chicken* or two, to get at him."

"Well, hit him up after you see what he's talkin' about and call me right back." Youngster was hoping this would be a good connection.

"Alright," Dee said and hung up.

Thirty minutes later, Dee called Youngster back. He told Youngster that the ticket for the concert would be fifteen dollars and to meet him at his apartment. Youngster arrived on Queen Street in the city of Inglewood in twenty minutes. He was holding fifteen thousand dollars in a dark grocery bag standing at Dee's door. Dee opened the door to his one bedroom apartment.

Youngster stepped into the clustered living room with Dee's dirty clothes scattered on the floor. Dee had an incense burning and some music playing.

"Man, look at this bastard," Youngster said referring to Dee's messy living room.

"It's not a bastard, it's a bachelor, and this is how it's supposed to look so a broad wouldn't want to move in after I fuck her. The only thing she wants to do afterwards is get her shit and leave. But it's too late to be telling you that little secret. Crystal is takin' up more closet space than you right now."

Youngster laughed at Dee's joke. He took a seat on Dee's brown withered sofa. He then began to question Dee about his friend Rob. Dee assured him that he has been knowing Rob for a long time. He told Youngster that Rob was all right. Youngster handed Dee the bag full of money and said, "Well, you just make sure that everything is right, especially with the nigga chargin' me five hundred dollars more than what I was payin' for a *chicken* with Ace."

"Don't trip, I'm sure it's gonna be all good."

"Yeah, it better be is what I'm sayin'."

"So, have you seen that broad Vera?" Dee switched the subject.

"Nah nigga, that is your woman. I don't keep tabs on other people women."

"Well, she ain't my woman. I ain't seen the broad since she spent the night over here."

Youngster laughed and said, "That's what your messy ass gets."

Fifteen minutes had passed before there was a knock at Dee's door. Dee walked over to his door, looked through his peep hole, and opened it. A short, dark stubby guy walked in holding a large brown grocery bag. He was moving kind of fast as if he was running late for a big event. Dee introduced Youngster and Rob to one another. They both nodded their heads and exchanged, "*What's ups?*" The strange thing that Youngster noticed was that Rob avoided making eye contact with him. Rob followed Dee straight into his bedroom while Youngster remained sitting in the living room watching television. He overheard the counting of money and the rattling of bags. A few minutes later, Dee was letting Rob out the door.

"You not gonna believe this. And I know you gonna look out for me on this little deal," Dee said immediately after closing his door shut.

"What?" Youngster asked.

"Well, first he asked me was you a cool nigga and if you can move *keys* pretty fast. After I said yeah, he showed me two more *birds.* He said that he was goin' outta town for three weeks and when he gets back he just wanted fourteen thousand for each one."

Youngster stood up. He had gotten pretty excited as Dee led him to the bedroom to show him the product. Dee picked up the grocery bag that Rob walked in with. He dumped out three box shaped packages heavily wrapped in black tape on his bed. Youngster smiled. He asked Dee for some scissors to cut into one of the packages. He wanted to check the quality of the product. Dee went to his drawer. He grabbed his scissors that he uses to breakdown his weed with. He handed them over to Youngster. Youngster took the scissors from Dee and cut a v-shape into one of the packages. It was then he discovered that he had just paid fifteen thousand dollars for a box of Betty Crocker cake mix.

"Oh, I don't believe this shit!" Youngster said in a shocking and startled tone.

"What's wrong?" Dee asked looking confused.

Youngster grabbed the other two packages. He quickly cut them open receiving the same results as when he cut the first one open. His heart began to beat furiously as he stood there repeating louder and louder, "I don't believe this shit! I don't believe this shit! I don't believe this shit!" Dee just looked on speechless as he realized that he messed up from the smell of the cake mix that rushed into his nose.

"Where does that muthafucka stay?" Youngster asked angrily.

"I don't know since he had moved from over by my mother's house." Dee answered very nervously.

"You don't know!" Youngster yelled. He then picked up one of the cake mix boxes and threw it up against Dee's bedroom wall very hard. Cake mix flew everywhere as he gave Dee a mean and vicious stare. "You got some muthafuckin' lookin' to do or else I'm takin' this fuckin' loss out your ass!" Youngster stormed out Dee's apartment leaving Dee standing with his mouth wide open.

Youngster drove home steaming mad. He had just spent a little over two thousand dollars on bills. He paid his rent three days ago so his extra money was low. He just took a fifteen thousand dollar loss buying some cake mix. He was left with only four thousand dollars to his name with no dope to sell. "I can't believe this shit!" Youngster screamed. He slammed his right palm against the dashboard. "What a way to bring in the New Year," he thought to himself while driving above the speed limit. He had no idea what to do.

# '17

Youngster walked into his town home defeated, crushed, and moody. His New Year's Eve plans of spending a romantic evening with Crystal, getting high, and sipping on some sparkling apple cider had been ruined. His mind was in such disarray. The reality of getting beat for fifteen thousand dollars gave him a headache. His only desire was to be alone. He slowly dragged his feet up the stairs. He peeped into Jay's bedroom. He saw that his son was sound asleep so he turned to go into his bedroom. He slowly opened the door to his room. He stepped inside and his eyes fell upon Crystal. She was propped up against the headboard. She was wearing a purple satin chemise and a matching satin robe. She looked so sexy and attractive that it made him feel even worse than he had already felt.

"Hey baby, did everything go alright?" she asked in a soft and sensual tone.

"Not at all," he answered. He dropped his head while he walked to his side of the bed. He sat down with his back facing her and placed his head in the palms of his hands.

Crystal crawled over to him. She pressed her large and soft breasts up against his back. He felt a sensation as she started massaging his shoulders. Temptation tried hard but failed to overcome his distress.

"I'm really not in the mood my love," he said while he moved away from the affection she was attempting to give.

"What happened?" she asked.

"I just took a major loss tonight and things don't look so good my love. I can't believe that ninety-two is about to begin like this for me. I have to start from scratch."

"What are you talkin' about, what happened Jayshawn?"

"I got beat for fifteen thousand dollars tonight because my only connection got locked up. And so because Ace gets locked up, I go to Dee who doesn't know shit but weed, gettin' drunk, and playin' females for some funky ass sex. I decide to go through his ass for a hook up and I get beat out of my muthafuckin' money." He stood up and started pacing the floor, "I have to rebuild Crystal and things are gonna be tight, real tight. I'm not gonna be able to do certain things no more and so---" He stopped at the foot of the bed. He looked straight into her eyes, "I don't think we should be together durin' this shit. I'm not one to be in a relationship if I can't afford to provide and take care of it comfortably. Things are going to be hard right now, real hard."

"What?" Crystal asked. She was very surprised at what Youngster had just said.

"Look," he began to explain, "Things are really gonna be tight around here and I'm not gonna be able to buy you things anymore. Things are gonna be different for a while and I'd rather be alone durin' these times." He paused, "I'm sorry my love."

"No, that's bullshit Jayshawn!" She yelled. She then lowered her voice after realizing how loud she was. "You think I'm gonna want to leave you because of what you can't buy me? Well, you're wrong. Whether you are the richest man on this earth or the poorest baby, I'm gonna continue to love you with my all so you can forget that crap. That, "I wanna be alone," stuff is not gonna get rid of me. You are going to get through whatever it is you have to get through with me right by your side. I ain't trying to lose you over some crazy mess. And this, "afford a relationship," thing is nonsense. Love has no price Jayshawn."

Youngster stood in the bedroom with nothing left to say after listening to her words. She had truly captured him. He noticed the sincerity in her voice as well as her expression. He watched a tear roll slowly down her cheek. He walked over to sit beside her on the bed. He wrapped his arms around her tight and they kissed. Together, they kissed and cuddled in the new year.

The first day of ninety-two Youngster moped around the house. He called Dee frequently about searching for Rob. He pushed for Dee to find out his whereabouts. He also called back all the people that were blowing up his pager. He explained that he would be out of business for a minute but would soon be getting in touch with them. Youngster had only four thousand dollars left to his name. He knew that he would have to get some dope to sell real soon before he went completely broke. He decided to jump in his car and hit the streets to see what he could come up with. He allowed the fresh winter breeze of a brand new year to blow in his face while he thought deeply. His Volvo sliced through the wind while he searched the streets for a solution. He drove past the carpet cleaning service hoping to see Ace's mother or sister, but came up empty.

After cruising around another thirty minutes, Youngster drove to the spot where he cops his chronic. It was at a place near Florence Avenue & Van Ness. He figured he would get some information from his homeboy that ran the spot. His homeboy wasn't there. Youngster didn't have too many more options left. He drove around aimlessly until it was late. He finally went back home knowing that he was wasting his time roaming the streets. He had become leery about dealing with just anyone. After his loss the night before, it would be very hard for him to trust someone. He headed home very frustrated and angry. He kept thinking how stupid Ace was for going down south. Even more important, how stupid he must have been for allowing Dee to make a drug transaction for him. Knowing that Dee was naïve to the game, Youngster couldn't believe that he even called Dee for something like that.

Youngster walked through the door a little past eight that night. Crystal and Jay were just sitting at the dinner table getting ready to eat. Crystal had cooked baked chicken wings, mashed potatoes, and corn with buttered rolls.

"Hey baby, I just finished pagin' you." She said as she placed Jay's plate in front of him.

"That must be you now," he replied while removing his vibrating beeper from his hip to confirm it.

"Yeah, I was seein' how late you were gonna be so I would know whether or not to fix you a plate. And I wanted to let you know that someone called here and had a whole lot to say tonight."

"Oh, you mean she didn't just hang up after callin' you a name?" He knew she was referring to Shell's crazy phone calls.

"Nope, just wait till I tell you this one," she said with a strange grin. She then asked, "You want me to fix your plate?"

"No, I'm not really hungry right now. I'll eat later." Youngster headed up the stairs to the bedroom while Crystal and Jay ate dinner.

After Crystal cleaned the kitchen, she got Jay settled in his bed. When she finally entered her bedroom, she saw Youngster smoking a blunt on the bed.

"Are you tryin' to work up an appetite baby?" she asked as she closed the door behind her. She then hopped on the bed beside him.

"No, if I wanted to work up an appetite, you would have found me in here butt-naked waitin' on you." They both laughed. Youngster was trying to regain his sense of humor during his rough times.

"I'm glad to see you smilin' and laughin' again," she said as she gestured for him to pass the blunt. "You know your son's mother called and instead of just sayin', "you bitch," and hangin' up, she tried to actually talk crazy to me."

"Oh yeah, what did she say?" he asked while she took a hit of the blunt.

"Well," she began to answer while trying to hold in as much smoke as she could, "She said somethin' about this is all my fault and I fucked up her life. She said that I will pay for this shit whenever she sees me again. She tried to say that you and her are still fuckin' around and that she will have you back soon. Her ass then called me a bitch and hung the phone up in my face."

Youngster couldn't help but to laugh at what he felt was Shell's useless tactics. He knew she was only trying to start some mess and her words would not amount to anything. It was all a joke to him. But he failed to notice the look on Crystal's face as he laughed at Shell's crazy attempt to mess up things between him and Crystal. He had totally ignored the fact that Crystal didn't approve of the disrespecting that Shell has been doing.

"That's not funny Jayshawn," Crystal said. "How long are you gonna let her keep callin' here and callin' me a bitch?"

"I'm sorry," he said, "I've been really goin' through somethin' as you know, but I'll talk to her as soon as I can my love. She don't be pagin' me and I hear that she's not even at her grandmother's house that much."

Crystal caught herself. She decided not to press the issue any further. She realized that it wasn't the time to get into the baby mama drama mess. She quickly changed the subject. "So, how did it go today baby?"

"Not good at all. I have to find someone that has somethin' soon or else I'm gonna be in big trouble out here. I really don't know where to get some real dope from. I mean I know people that have somethin' out there but I know they blow their shit up. They only sell it hard. My people gonna complain like hell if I go that route and sell them dope mixed with that bullshit."

"Well, what you gonna do?" she asked.

"I really don't know yet, I might not have a choice pretty soon."

"Well, I might know someone if you want me to check into it."

"After what just happened to me---"

Crystal cut him off, "Well, it's my sister's husband's best friend. I know that he does somethin' and I think that it's pretty big. He's a Mexican named Pedro."

"How do you know that he does somethin' that has to do with dope?" he asked.

"He takes my sister's husband with him from time to time and she told me that each time that he comes back from a trip with Pedro, he gives her the money for the rent, car note, and other bills. Pedro must have him doin' somethin' and it's not legal."

"Oh, is that right?" he stated while giving Crystal's suggestion some thought.

"Well, it won't hurt for me to at least check it out and then you can see what's up from there," she said.

"Yeah, you're right. Well, find out if this Pedro guy is sellin' dope and if so, how much nine ounces would be."

"I'll call Tanya in the mornin' and ask her to ask Tony about what's up with Pedro. And I'll let you know as soon as I find out somethin'."

A few days had past before Crystal was able to confirm what she had felt all along. Pedro was a well connected man in the drug business. She had arranged for Youngster to meet with her sister's husband at her grandmother's house later on that day so they could hook up.

Youngster pulled in front of her grandmother's house at four in the afternoon with Crystal and Jay. Tony and Tanya were already there. They met them in front of the house. Crystal introduced Youngster to Tony and Tanya. After the formal greetings between everyone, Crystal, Tanya, and Jay walked inside the house while Youngster and Tony stood outside to talk business. Tony stood at five foot and ten inches and weighed about two hundred and thirty pounds. He had a very high-yellow complexion and wore a thin beard with wavy dark black hair that covered the top of his large head. He was a rather large man but he was well dressed for a big man. He looked as if he should be working in the field of computers.

"So what's goin' on?" Tony asked.

"I need a nice price on nine ounces of some real good dope." Youngster stated.

"Well, I'm pretty sure that my boy got what you're looking for. I just need to know when you need it and around what price range you consider is nice. And we can take it from there."

"I need it as soon as possible and at thirty-seven fifty or better. That would be cool."

"Okay, I'm going to call my boy and see if we can hook up with you tonight, if not tonight, first thing in the morning. Is that okay with you?"

"Cool, sounds good to me." Youngster replied and they walked in the house to rejoin Crystal, Tanya, and Jay.

***

A very distraught male sat in his messy apartment hurt and confused. Dee had been driving throughout the city in search of the whereabouts of Rob day in and day out. Ever since the incident happened at his spot, he has roamed the streets in search of Rob. Although he never allowed Youngster to know it when they talked, he was hurting real bad inside. He had put all the blame on himself that his cousin took a fifteen thousand dollar loss. He started drinking every single night after he would end his daily search for Rob. The relationship between him and Youngster had definitely took a hard blow. He felt the only way to repair it was to find Rob and somehow retrieve his cousin's money. The pressure of making things right was too heavy on Dee. The only way that he tried to cope was to down plenty of forty ounces of Old English with shots of hard liquor each night after returning home.

Dee had not heard from Youngster in a few days. He began to debate on whether or not he should call him. The pure shame and guilt would prevent him from calling. This would further the distance between the relationship that he once had with his cousin. Dee's guilty feeling which lead him not to dial Youngster's number, made things look suspicious from Youngster's point of view. Youngster would look at his cousin's actions of not keeping in contact with him like he could have had something to do with the whole set up. This didn't cross Dee's mind. The only thing Dee thought was Youngster was too angry with him for introducing him to Rob. The lack of communication would turn into no communication at all, leaving Dee to drown in forties and shots. He would go on feeling an emptiness while Youngster would move on suspecting his little cousin had set him up.

***

When the clock struck 9:30 in the evening, Tony and Pedro were standing at Youngster's door. Pedro was holding a small shoebox inside of a yellow plastic bag. Youngster let them inside to handle business while Crystal and Jay were upstairs. After a brief introduction, Pedro guaranteed Youngster that his product was the best. He informed Youngster that it would remain that way every time. He told him that his money would be returned to him if he wasn't pleased whenever they did business. He handed Youngster the plastic bag and said, "Go ahead and check it out." Pedro was a short heavy set Mexican that had a long thick mustache, fat ears, and short straight hair.

Youngster took the bag from Pedro. He pulled out the small shoebox from the bag. He opened the small box and pulled out

152

a clear medium size zip-lock bag that was sitting inside the box. He could immediately see and smell the white Peruvian flake. Youngster never had to taste the coke on his tongue like they would do in the movies. He was able to tell how pure the dope was just from the look and scent. It was something about the look and aroma that he would be able to tell whether or not the dope was real, fake, or weak.

"This is what I'm talkin' about, right here," he said.

"You like?" Pedro asked.

"Man, if you can keep it like this, we'll be doin' a whole lot of business together," Youngster answered while reaching into his pocket. He handed Pedro three thousand, seven hundred and fifty dollars wrapped in a rubber band. He was feeling good about the exchange.

"Just get in touch with Tony when you ready again," Pedro said after counting the money and both he and Tony walked out the door.

"Oh, for sure. Ya'll be safe," Youngster said standing at his door.

"Same to you," Pedro replied.

"Okay," Tony said.

Youngster closed his door and immediately went to work. He grabbed his triple-beam scale from the cabinet above the kitchen stove. He weighed out the nine ounces on the scale. The whole two hundred and fifty-two grams was there. He then removed the nine ounces from the scale. He began to weigh out fourteen grams from the pile of powder stacked up on the side of the scale. He put the fourteen grams into a mason jelly jar by using a playing card. He added half of a table spoon of baking soda and one-fourth cup of water. He put the jar in the microwave and set it for thirty seconds. After the thirty seconds, he took the jar out the microwave. He put the hot jar under some cool running water from the kitchen sink while using his hand to drop some of the cold water inside of the jar. This made the light-yellow gel cocaine fall to the bottom of the jar. The gel started to form into the shape of a cookie. He set the jar on the counter for it to cool down. It would take a few minutes to get hard, solid, and white. He reached for a fresh jar. He repeated the routine until he had eighteen cookies in front of him ready to be delivered.

Youngster made phone calls to all of his steady customers to let them know that he was back in pocket. He told them that he was ready when they were. Every last one of his customers were happy to hear from him. They had let him know that they would be calling him the very next day. Youngster went to bed that night with ninety dollars to his name but he wore the biggest smile on his face. He was feeling good knowing that he was back in business. Sleeping well wouldn't be a problem for him on this night. He was looking forward to getting back on the grind again.

# '18

It was like the first day of spring to Youngster as he rode off on this January day of 1992. He left Crystal and Jay at home while he engaged in his dealings through the streets. He felt brand new and very positive about his new connection. There was no doubt in his mind that he had the best quality on the Westside of Los Angeles. He knew he would soon be right back where he once was. Within a few days, he dumped the nine ounces that he had purchased from Pedro. He was looking to hook back up with him and Tony again. Right after contacting them, they delivered nine more ounces at his doorstep. As soon as they left, Youngster was back in his kitchen fixing his cookies. With quick efficiency, he wrapped up the eighteen cookies that he fixed and was off making moves again. He went about his business delivering to his awaiting customers. He was hitting corners for the better part of the day and most of the night. Crystal and Jay were now receiving less of his time and attention. The game was slowly engulfing him.

With his busy schedule in the streets, Crystal had become a very important asset to Youngster. She not only unknowingly connected him to one of the best cocaine connections in Los

Angeles, she also was there to watch Jay at a very crucial time during his rough grind back. He was hard at work in his attempt to get back to his once comfortable status. He didn't need Jay nor Crystal rolling around with him. It was a very good thing that he was able to leave Jay at home with Crystal. This made things easy for him. Gone were the days of riding around with them. The ruggedness and dangers of the grind wouldn't allow it. He was taking on all money that came in his direction. He was dealing with more than just regulars to make his money come faster. This meant accepting a type of recklessness that he had to invite with caution. Having Jay and Crystal roll with him would have made for a very dangerous situation.

Youngster was moving nine ounces in the streets so fast that you would have thought that he had a license to do so. Pedro started fronting him an extra nine ounces on consignment just so he wouldn't be seen at his doorstep so often. Pedro wanted to avoid raising any of the neighbors suspicions. Youngster was beginning to really stack his paper by copping nine ounces every time he made three thousand, seven hundred and fifty dollars. He had started to let the money he was making work for him. He would only take a little money out of what he was making for food and gas while the rest went back into his re-up.

The fifteen thousand dollar loss had been thrown in the back of his mind. It wasn't that he was trying to forget about the money nor the scandalous move pulled on him. Youngster wasn't the type to forget about anything such as a loss. The situation just had become old to him only because he knew he couldn't dwell on the unchangeable past. He had to put his effort and focus into the present. It had become all about making that new money.

Before Youngster could even realize it, in four weeks he was back to buying a whole kilo again. All his bills had been paid and he felt great. There was no need for Pedro to front him any longer. He had paid Pedro off and Pedro let him get the kilo for only fourteen thousand dollars. They had began to meet once a week just as he did when he was dealing with Ace except Pedro delivered. Youngster was very proud of his accomplishment in four weeks. Things were moving so well for him. He had started to set new goals for himself. He began to think big. He wanted more than anything to make enough money to buy a house. He wanted to buy a house and invest in a business. A business that would generate an income that would allow him to raise his son and live comfortable without having to be in the streets.

***

With the sounds of a rising new rap star, named Tupac Shakur, in the tape player, Youngster was headed towards the Jungles to make some deliveries. While making a left turn off of Crenshaw Blvd on to Martin Luther King Boulevard, he noticed K-9 making a right turn and heading in the same direction. Youngster hit his horn to get K-9's attention. K-9 drove a 1988 black Chevy Camaro IROC-Z. He had a hand controlled steering wheel column installed since he was paralyzed from the waist down. He was what Youngster considered a hustling gangster. Youngster didn't mind dealing with K-9 even though he was a well known Blood from the Jungles. He knew K-9 was more about making money than gang banging.

Once K-9 noticed Youngster, he immediately pointed to a parking lot of a shopping center for Youngster to follow him in. Youngster pulled beside K-9 in the parking lot facing the opposite direction. They both rolled their windows down simultaneously.

"Hey Youngster, what's up with you?" K-9 inquired.

"Not much, out here on this grind. What's goin' on with you?"

"Shit! I'm out here tryin' to get like you." K-9 said. "I been tryin' to get at you but you been hard to catch up with these days."

"You got my number, don't you?"

"The 5-7-9 number?" K-9 asked.

"Yeah, it's the same as before." Youngster replied.

"I stopped pagin' that number about a little over a month ago because I wasn't gettin' an answer from your ass." K-9 leaned his long head back against the headrest of his car seat. The long head, neck, and dark eyes of his resembled that of a Doberman pinscher. This is how he got his nickname K-9.

"Yeah, I was dry at that time but everything is straight now."

"Well, we need to really do some business. I'm tired of this bullshit that I've been gettin' from these niggas out here. I need some real shit."

"What you lookin' for?" Youngster asked.

"Show me some love on a nine pack."

"The best I can do is four thousand right now, if you want it soft."

"That sounds good Youngster. I'll hit you up tomorrow for sure."

"Alright then, I'll have that ready for you." Youngster said as he prepared to leave.

"Sounds good, I'll holla at you." K-9 sat up in his seat ready to pull off also.

"Be safe," Youngster stated.

"Yeah, same to you." K-9 responded just before driving off.

Youngster made his moves through the Jungles swiftly because his conversation with K-9 had him running late. Angel was his last scheduled stop. While meeting Angel and exchanging a few jokes, Gee stepped out into the alley. When Youngster noticed him, he gave Youngster a stare that Youngster didn't take kindly. It changed Youngster's whole state of mind. Angel noticed Youngster's expression on his face had switched from pleasant to unkind. She started to back away from his car and said, "I'll hit you up later Youngster, okay?"

"Alright," he said as he kept his eyes on Gee. He watched Gee get into his Regal.

Gee started up his car, pulled out of the stall, and drove down the alley. Youngster quickly followed behind him. He caught up with Gee on the corner of August Street & Nicolet Avenue. He pulled besides Gee at the corner and immediately gestured for him to roll down his window. Gee nervously complied. He heard Youngster yell, "Hey, you got a fuckin' problem with me or what?" The look on Youngster's face matched the tone in which he asked his raw and bold question.

"No, you got the problem Blood! You keep comin' around here and shit like it's all good. But that shit ain't *bool*."

"We have gone over this before Gee. And unless you gonna do somethin' about it, I suggest that you quit lookin' at me like you wanna do somethin'. Because the very next time the shit happens, I'm gonna take it as a threat and I'm not gonna take that threat very lightly. Is that understood?" Youngster paused before going on, "Believe me when I say that I'm gonna be forced in takin' some serious muthafuckin' actions." There was a brief stare down before he continued, "So, you've been warned nigga." Youngster spun out from the corner making a fast left on to Nicolet giving Gee no chance to respond after Youngster's very strong comments.

Gee sat at the corner for a moment dumbfounded. He was nervous because he knew Youngster meant every word that he had said. He realized that he had started some mess that he couldn't handle alone. His words along with his cold stares had finally pissed Youngster off. Now his back had been pushed against a wall. He had been warned and was well aware that his next encounter with Youngster would definitely not be a friendly one. He knew that he had better be prepared for war or to bow down gracefully never looking in Youngster's direction again. Gee started to think fast. He had to plan with no time to waste. He had to begin to put something into action. His first objective was to hurt Youngster's pocket, slow down his trips in the Jungles while he devised a scheme that will get rid of him for good.

Youngster continued on with his day. He headed towards Edgehill & 21st Street to meet with Black. Black has been dealing with him for a few years. He wasn't one of his daily customers but would contact Youngster once a month. He would buy two ounces that would hold him until the next month. Black's name fit him to a tee. He was as dark as the darkest African one could find on the continent of the Mother Land. Black is five feet and ten inches, very stocky, and in his early forties. He wore a clean bald head that was not by choice but due to aging.

"Hey Youngster," Black said as he approached the car with caution.

"What's up Black?"

"This bitch been hot over here Youngster. I meant to ask you to pull in the back when I talked to you earlier." Black talked fast while making the exchange with Youngster. "Them niggas across the street got this whole block hot, I'll holla at you later Youngster." Black didn't waste any time getting back into his apartment with his two ounces.

Youngster sat there before driving off to check the money. He then tucked the money in his pocket and started to drive away from the curb. He was just taking off when he heard a loud voice calling out, "Hey yo, Youngster!" He pulled into the road before noticing Willie in his rearview mirror jogging towards him. Youngster pulled back over towards the curb. He started to roll the passenger's window down while he waited for Willie to get to the car.

"What's up with you Youngster?" Willie asked once he got to the passenger side of the car. He leaned his head inside the Volvo once the window rolled down completely.

"Not much Willie, what you been up to?" he asked.

"Man, I got back out here on this grind and been lookin' for some good shit so I can sow this muthafuckin' block up."

Willie is an O.G from the Jungles. He is thirty-nine years old and stands at about six feet and two inches tall. He has a dark brown complexion with very thick lips, long ears, and a large forehead. He wears his hair in a short natural with a very noticeable receding hair line. Willie moved out of the Jungles a couple of years back. He tried to do the right thing by working a nine to five, raising his three kids, and marrying his kid's mother. But just like everyone else that has allowed the game into their hearts, Willie couldn't walk away from the game for good.

"So, what you been gettin' Willie?" Youngster asked.

"Nine ounces but this bastard I'm dealin' with only sells it to me cooked already. So you know that he puttin' somethin' on it. I need the real deal powder so I can cook it my damn self. You feel me?"

Youngster leaned back into his leather seat with a little grin on his face. He took pride in knowing that he had a reputation for having some of the best coke in Los Angeles. He looked at Willie and asked, "So when you're goin' to be ready to cop again?"

"Maybe in a day or two, dependin' on how hot these little bastards make it on this block."

"Well, get my number from Black and hit me up when you ready."

"What's the price going to be Youngster?" Willie asked.

"Four thousand." Youngster answered.

"It's all good, I'll call you as soon as I'm ready for you."

"Alright, just holla at me."

"Bet," Willie said as he stepped away from the car while Youngster carefully pulled off.

Youngster drove to the corner of 21st Street & Edgehill. He then made a left turn on Edgehill. He drove down to Jefferson and made a right turn on Jefferson to get to Crenshaw. Once he arrived at the intersection of Crenshaw & Jefferson, he moved into the turning lane to make a left on Crenshaw. He noticed a police car on the other side of the intersection in front of him coming from the opposite direction. The light turned green. He pulled out into the street with his blinkers on. The police car didn't go across the green signal. The police car sat still at the corner. Youngster paid the car no mind as he made his turn. After Youngster turned, the black and white vehicle made a right turn on Crenshaw. The police vehicle drove directly behind Youngster. Not long after that, the officers inside of the police vehicle hit their lights and siren for Youngster to pull over. Youngster checked his rearview to make sure that the flashing lights were meant for him before he followed procedures. He then pulled over right away.

The beating of his heart went into overdrive as one of the officers approached his Volvo wagon while the other one stood off to the side.

"Turn off the vehicle and put both your hands on the steering wheel," the white cop ordered as he stepped closer with his gun drawn.

Youngster did exactly what he was told while he sat there nervous and confused. He wondered why he was getting pulled over. He knew he hadn't done anything in traffic to bring about a traffic stop. The only conclusion was that he was being harassed due to the fact that he was a black male driving a nice car.

"Now, take one hand slowly off the steering wheel, open the car door, and slowly step out of the vehicle keeping your hands where I can see them!" The white officer shouted after making a complete stop near the rear car door. He was keeping a safe distance between himself and the extremely nervous young black male obeying his orders. "Walk over to the front of the vehicle with your hands up and then place both your hands on the hood."

After Youngster placed his hands on the hood of his car, the black officer approached him with speed. He began to frisk Youngster roughly. He took Youngster's black leather wallet out from his back pocket, snatched his identification out, and immediately called in on his radio to check for any warrants. The humiliation was the last thing on Youngster's mind as he faced the white officer who was inside his car. He nervously watched him search through his car. He thought about the two half ounce cookies sitting in the 28oz. Burger King cup inside the cup holder of his car. He could only pray that the officer over looked what now seemed to be a stupid prop to hide drugs.

Frustrated and agitated from finding nothing, the white officer walked over to him and said, "You dope dealing low life punk. You might not remember me but I sure in the hell remember you. You killed another one of you low life's a little over three years ago behind drugs. Now I know your black ass is still out here doing the same old shit. You may have gotten away this time, but believe me, every time I see you in traffic I am going to stop your black ass and you will not be as lucky as this time."

Youngster looked up at the white officer to get a good look at him. The officer stood about six feet and four inches tall. He had deep blue eyes, a long nose and a chiseled chin. He wore a crew cut hair style like he had just left the military and wore his police uniform very tight on his bulked up body for that intimidating effect. After examining the officer, Youngster read the name on his badge. H. Parrish was the name. He remained silent and played the humble role hoping that his encounter with officer Parrish would soon end. Officer Parrish seemed to have a major attitude towards Youngster and didn't mind showing it. However, after receiving the call on the radio that *Jayshawn King* was clean, Officer Parrish had to let him go.

Once he received a nod from Parrish, the black officer handed Youngster back his wallet. While receiving his wallet, Youngster took a good look at the very tall black man's face and read F. Trapp across his police badge. Officer Trapp was a little taller than his partner. He had a round face with large brown eyes and a flat nose. He wore his hair in a very low natural and also seemed as if he had been spending lots of his time in the gym. His chest was extremely large to go along with what seemed to be sixteen inch biceps.

Youngster would be sure to remember both officer's names. He looked on with a slight attitude as officer Trapp and Parrish retreated back to their police car. After the officers sat down in the car, they pulled off very slowly. They passed Youngster giving him a cold stare while he just stood in front of his car full of relief. Youngster walked over to get back in his car after they left. He counted his blessings as he drove off knowing just how close he came to going to jail. Although he didn't get busted, he knew from that night he was a marked man in the eyes of one officer named Parrish. He also knew that it was definitely not a good thing in his line of work to catch the eye of an officer of the law. He now had to move about the streets with an extra sense of caution.

✳✳✳

The carpet on the bedroom floor aged a few months in just one night due to the pacing of a craving young girl. Her body and mind was pulling her towards getting high again while she attempted to fight it off. Shell continued to glance at her telephone while she paced the floor. She was itching to call up Ice so she could feed her appetite. One long week had went by since she hung up on Ice. She vowed to never speak to him again but the feeling was beginning to overpower her to the point of giving in. Her desire to get high was just too strong to continue to fight.

After an hour of wearing out the carpet in her bedroom, Shell finally decided to give Ice a call. She convinced herself that Ice wasn't a bad person. She viewed him as someone who cared about her. She had come to the conclusion that he was only helping in taking her mind away from worrying about Youngster. She told herself that she needed to call him and apologize. Shell was able to reach Ice by paging him. After she received a hard time while apologizing to him, he was in the front of her house blowing his horn. He knew what he was doing from the very first time he recognized Shell's low self-esteem. Now it was time for him to put his plans in full gear. Shell stepped out into the night and headed towards Ice's car. She was leaving the days of soberness behind. She was now about to enter a world of complete darkness, pain, and clouded minds. A world that is controlled by the uncivilized and savages. This would turn out to be Shell's final destination on earth.

# 19

The four steps that he took backwards while keeping his eyes on the gang members only drew him closer to the wall behind him. He was still faced with the life threatening situation that was in front of him. The disbelief that his gun was jammed had been realized once again as he pointed his 9 millimeter towards the group dressed in red. His index finger pulled the trigger receiving the same results as before. Nothing. No sound, no bullets firing out of the barrel, and he had no way out. Death was surely on its way as the gang members stepped close enough to take his young life away. The young man could only stand there and hope he would not feel any pain in dying. He braces himself. He prepares for the end. He hears the bullets flying in his direction. Each one of them has a destination on his trembling body. The sounds of the bullets are getting closer and closer. He knows that it's all over. There will be no tomorrow. He can only shed a tear as he cries out, "Please God, not now!"

***

Crystal lay still quietly watching her man sitting on the edge of the bed. She wondered if he would ever talk to her about his reoccurring nightmares. "Will he continue to keep this to himself?" she thought to herself. This would be the ninth time she has witnessed him tossing and turning in his sleep. The leaping up, sweating, and sitting at the edge of the bed deep in thought has been seen too many times. She never would question him about what she witnessed. From the look of things, she would decide against doing so again but she was getting worried.

"Baby," she said to get his attention. "Do you want me to fix you some breakfast?"

"Nah, I'm cool, just cook Jay somethin' when you get up. I'll get somethin' a little later at Roscoe's. I have to take care of some things early so I don't have time to eat right now."

"Alright," she said as her eyes followed him while he walked into the bathroom.

Youngster stepped out the bathroom twenty minutes later from a well needed refreshing shower. He returned with only a towel wrapped around him to an empty bedroom. Crystal had left to cook breakfast. Youngster walked to the closet. He stood there trying to decide on what to wear. The nightmare had been pushed aside. It was the furthest thing from his mind. His focus was on getting dressed and the eight thousand dollars he would be picking up soon from the transactions with K-9 and Willie.

Wearing a pair of black loose fitted Guess jeans, an all white long sleeve Guess shirt, and a pair of all white Reeboks, Youngster stepped into the kitchen. He was carrying a shopping bag with a shoe box inside full of cocaine. He walked towards Crystal and kissed her on the cheek. He then walked over to Jay who was sitting at the dining table. He gave Jay a kiss on the forehead. "Ya'll be good," he said as he headed towards the door. "And I'll be back in a minute so we can go to the mall or somethin'."

"We'll be here dressed and ready baby," Crystal responded as the door was closing.

"Alright," he said from outside of the door before proceeding to his car. He was feeling pretty good about his two new customers on his team he was on his way to meet. He also felt positive about running into some more new team members to recruit.

***

The flow in and out of the grocery store located on Crenshaw was just beginning to pick up during the time K-9 parked in the parking lot. He was waiting for Youngster to pull up to meet him. The sun was just revealing itself through the partly cloudy skies while he waited for his delivery. It was a pretty fair morning as K-9 checked his surroundings to make sure he didn't notice anything strange before the discreet drug transaction took place. The parking lot was half full which made things a little easier for K-9 to scope out any unusual activities. K-9 had dealt with Youngster before. He knew that Youngster likes to meet in public areas. Youngster would stress that the person that he is to meet get there before he did. He would always say, "I should never have to sit like a duck waiting for the buyer and I will never deal with late customers unless I want to go to jail. And I don't have no desire to be in that muthafuckin' place." Youngster felt much more comfortable knowing all he had to do was to pull up on a buyer, make the transaction, and keep it moving. That was the way he wanted it.

Youngster arrived in the parking lot about ten minutes after K-9 arrived there. He parked beside K-9's car. He stepped out of his car holding a small brown paper bag in his hand. The paper bag concealed nine ounces of powder cocaine in a zip locked plastic bag. K-9 unlocked the doors to his car so that Youngster could get in. Youngster sat down in K-9's IROC. While they exchanged greetings, Youngster handed him the paper bag. K-9 then handed Youngster four thousand dollars in one large stack wrapped around two rubber bands. The rubber bands had a tight hold of the money from each end.

"It's goin' to be straight just like this every time so hit me up when you ready again." Youngster said as he started to reach for the door to let himself out.

"Yeah Youngster, I sure will." K-9 said.

Youngster closed the door. He headed back to his car in a hurry because he had Willie waiting on him at a burger stand. He agreed to meet Willie around the same time on Jefferson at a little burger spot. He didn't want to be late. Youngster pulled up on Willie just as he was ordering some food. They both acknowledged one another. Willie finished ordering his food and paid for it before walking over to Youngster's car. He hopped inside the Volvo wagon.

"What's goin' on with you Willie?" Youngster asked as he pulled away from the curb. He wanted to circle the block during the transaction.

"Not much, I been tryin' to check those young hard heads on the block, so that bitch won't be so hot when I put this bomb ass work out there."

Willie reached down in his pants. He pulled out a tightly tied plastic bag from his waist belt as Youngster carefully watched. He handed Youngster the bag. Youngster passed him a brown paper bag containing the dope. Youngster opened the plastic bag that Willie handed him. He ran his fingers through the loose bills inside estimating that the four grand was all there. Willie inspected the product he had just received at the same time. He examined the powder a few seconds and said, "Yep, this that flake here, they're going to love me." A brief sound of laughter escaped both Youngster and Willie before arriving back in front of the burger stand.

"Well, holla at me when you're ready Willie," Youngster said as Willie stepped out of the car holding the paper bag as if he had just came from the liquor store.

"I sure will," Willie replied before closing the car door. "And it won't be long," he added.

Youngster drove off to meet some regulars of his before returning home to pick up Crystal and Jay. He also needed to put away some money. He wanted to meet Pedro to replace the half of kilo that he had just sold but that would have to wait. His priority at that moment was to spend some time with his woman and son. Although the hustling itch was pulling at him to continue grinding, taking a time out for them was a must.

***

Crystal and Jay strolled through the mall excited. Youngster walked by their side feeling pretty good himself. Being able to buy the things that Crystal and Jay wanted gave him a wonderful feeling inside. To Jay, this was his Christmas. He pointed to the toys he wanted and Youngster purchased each one. He also received lots of brand new clothes. For Crystal, there would be no window shopping this day. Everything that she picked out and tried on with a smile, Youngster bought for her. She received bottles of named brand perfume, a month worth of underwear from Victoria's Secret, matching Guess outfits, and a very expensive Gucci watch. She also received a gold chain with a matching gold bracelet. It was a good day for both Crystal and Jay. This good day came to an abrupt end when Youngster's pager began to go off. After seeing the number displayed across his beeper, he was ready to leave. By Youngster being the business minded person he was, all he saw was the replacement money for the money he was spending. He hurried Crystal as she received the receipt to her last item before they left the mall. He helped Crystal and Jay unload their shopping bags into the apartment before going back into the streets. He had a number of deliveries to make. The feeling inside of him was a very satisfying one as he drove through the streets of Los Angeles knowing that their were two very happy people that he cared about with smiles on their faces.

***

A few more half ounces sat inside of the 24oz cup and things couldn't have been any better inside the mind of

Youngster. He had just made a right turn off of Vernon on to Western Avenue. He was on his way to meet with one of his customers in that area. While heading to make the drop, Youngster slowly drove past a mosque on Western. He glanced at the activities of the Muslim brothers dressed in suits and bow ties. They all wore peaceful looks on their faces as they walked with pride. They were holding Final Call newspapers with their heads held high. Youngster felt a strong desire for that peaceful look he was witnessing. He envied the Muslim brothers hoping that someday he would be able to wear that same look on his face. The look that the drug dealing business would never allow him to wear as long as he continued to take part in it.

During that slight moment of letting his guard down, Youngster failed to notice the unmarked police car that had picked up on his trail. The sky blue Caprice had been following him for a few blocks. By the time Youngster checked his rearview mirror, there was a red light flashing on the dashboard of the unmarked car signaling for him to pull over.

"Not again," Youngster thought to himself while trying to make out the two officers in the undercover car. The chances of him getting away with the dope in the drinking cup trick was looking slim. It seemed that he was about to get his car searched once again. He couldn't control the nervousness of his mind and body. The two officers stepped out of their vehicle. They approached the Volvo while Youngster did his best to stop the shaking of his arms and legs.

"You want to step outside of your car sir?" The officer on the driver's side said as he now stood right beside Youngster's car door.

Without catching a glimpse of the person speaking to him, Youngster began to slowly open his car door. While placing his right foot on the pavement of the street, he finally looked in the direction of the officer. To his surprise, the voice was that of Detective Jones.

"What is your ass doing out here still selling drugs?" Det. Jones asked Youngster who was wearing a shocked expression.

"I'm not, I'm---," Youngster was cut off from completing his lie.

"I do not have time for you to stand here and tell me a lie, Johnson and I just wanted to find out how that baby boy and Michelle is doing?"

"Are you taking care of them or what?" Det. Johnson asked while standing on the other side of Youngster's car. "Because if not," Det. Johnson went on not giving Youngster a chance to respond, "We might as well take you down to the police station where there is one officer I'm sure you know that would love to see your face."

"I'm takin' care of my son, but I broke up with his mother. So we don't see much of her," he explained.

"You mean to tell me that a girl gets shot behind your bullshit and you dumped her?" Det. Jones asked.

"Nah, it wasn't like that," Youngster responded but refused to go into explaining the whole disease story to the detectives.

"Well, we just decided to stop you and check up on you. I suggest that you find your ass a new line of work real fast though before you get stopped again. The officer doing the search might just be smart enough to open that cup lid sitting in your cup holder." Det. Jones paused before he continued, "You understand?"

Det. Jones and Det. Johnson left Youngster standing beside his car door with his mouth open. After a long minute of taking in some well needed fresh air, he let out a huge sigh of relief. He was relieved that it was those two detectives that stopped him and not some other policemen pulling him over to harass him. He also was thankful that Det. Jones made it clear to him that his stash spot in the cup holder may no longer work if he was ever pulled over again.

Youngster hopped back in his car to make his final deliveries before returning home. After running out of the dope he had on him, he decided to make a stop that would end up being a profitable one. He arrived at a light-blue house on 67th & 3rd Avenue around eight that evening. This was the residence of Stacey Williams and her ten year old daughter Sasha. This is also where his uncle named Moe could be found when he wasn't serving time in jail or running the streets. Moe and Stacey have been in an on-again off-again relationship ever since they began dating in high school. Moe was a well known hustler that was brought down by the very product that he sold. He still maintained respect in this particular part of South-Central which was the territory of the notorious Crip gang, the Rollin 60's. Moe had just been released from prison earlier that week. Youngster knew to make it his business to pay Moe a visit or he would not hear the last of it.

"Who is it?" Stacey asked responding to the knock at her door.

"It's me, Jayshawn."

Stacey unlocked the door. She and Youngster spoke to one another while Youngster stepped inside the small two bedroom house.

"So, how have you been Jayshawn?" The slim woman standing in front of him at five feet and nine inches asked.

"I've been good Stacey. How have you and Sasha been?"

"We been hanging in there. Working hard and paying bills."

"I heard that. You lookin' good though."

"Thank you Jayshawn." Stacey smiled from the compliment. Stacey was in her early thirties. She had golden brown skin, light-brown eyes and shoulder length dark brown hair.

"Where is the jail bird at?" Youngster asked.

"He back there in the kitchen. He been eating like a pig since he been out."

"Yeah, I bet."

"Boy," a loud voice shouted from the kitchen, "I was just askin' your mama where the hell you were. What's up nephew?" Moe came charging with an outstretched hand and a crooked smile. Moe shook his hand with a firm grip. He then yanked Youngster towards him to wrap his free arm around his back.

Youngster returned the love before stepping back to get a good look at his uncle. After a quick examination, Youngster said, "You always know where to go when you want to put on some weight, don't you?"

Moe is a tall light-skinned man with light brown beady eyes and a long bird-like nose. He wore his hair in a low fade and carried an athletic built every time he would touchdown after doing some time. The sad thing was that he would quickly slender down after embracing the streets and allowing himself to be consumed by rock cocaine.

"It's not like a nigga be tryin' to go to jail," Moe stated. "If I had known they were gonna test my ass that day, I wouldn't have even showed up in that damn parole office."

"That's why they call it random drug testing dummy," Youngster joked.

Stacey could not hold in her laugh. She let a burst out followed by a giant grin.

"Kiss my black ass Jayshawn," Moe quickly stated. "You got jokes and that shit cost me a whole damn year."

"Hey, you the one that got high the night before you had to go see your parole officer. So you cost yourself a whole damn year."

"Hi Jayshawn." The cutest little ten year old stepped out of her bedroom. She spoke to Youngster while heading towards the kitchen.

"Hey Sasha, where is my hug at girl?" Sasha redirected her steps. She walked towards Youngster to give him a warm embrace around his neck before continuing about her business. Sasha was conceived during one of Moe and Stacey's break ups. Moe was not her biological father but he treated her as if she was his own daughter. Sasha's real father was never around.

"So, what's the good news out here?" Moe asked.

"I just been still tryin' to handle my business and take care of Jay."

"Well, has business been good or what?"

"It's been lookin' pretty good lately."

"I've had two niggas come by this week and ask about you already."

"Oh yeah," Youngster said. "Who were they?" he asked.

"That nigga Ren and Blue, they wanted to holla at you about some work and I told them that I hadn't seen you yet but to come back this weekend and I'll try gettin' your number or somethin'."

Youngster knew that both Ren and Blue were well known Crips. More than that, he knew that if they were looking for him that it was about making some money. Youngster was all about making money. He was on a paper chase and loved to hook up with others that would be about getting their money too. He viewed it as a very important part of his building process to meet the ones that were serious about getting their money. Youngster gave Moe his pager number to give to both Ren and Blue and said, "Well, I have to get up outta here." Moe put up a minor fuss about his nephew leaving so soon. Youngster tolerated the fussing for a few minutes before he finally left to head home.

Moe was Youngster's connection to the drug dealers around that particular neighborhood. They would always go to Moe to find out who had the good dope. By Youngster being Moe's nephew, he would benefit every time. Youngster was glad to see Moe back on the streets again. "The timing couldn't have been any better," he thought to himself. He was feeling a pretty good vibe from his visit with Moe. He knew that lots of money would soon be made through the people Moe knew in the game. He had always looked up to his only uncle being that his father wasn't around. He picked up on many of his uncle's hustling ways. He admired Moe's hustle but could never figure out why and how Moe allowed cocaine to take him under. Youngster could never see how the hustling rule to *Never get high on your own supply* was so easily broken by so many like his uncle. He had much love for Moe regardless of his short comings. Youngster could only wish, just like all the other times before when Moe would get out of jail, that Moe would get his act together and lay off the coke.

# 20

The park was clear of most of the gang members that had gathered earlier except for three. They were sitting on the grassy hill next to the basketball court drinking. Nightfall crept along with a breeze of cold air blowing on the unaffected bodies of Gee, Lil' Red, and Boo. They were passing a bottle of E&J back and forth to one another keeping warm. Neither one of them noticed how quick Saturday night had come. The alcohol mixed with the conversation made them lose track of time. Lil' Red and Boo drank while listening to Gee talk. He was working hard at trying to manipulate the minds of his two younger protégés.

"Look," Gee began after taking a drink, "I know ya'll mama been dealin' with that nigga for a while but don't get soft behind no shit like that. He shouldn't mean shit to ya'll just like he don't mean shit to me. This nigga smoked one of our own homies and he needs to be dealt with. Youngster gots to go and ya'll little niggas need to earn ya'll stripes around here. We have to take this nigga out soon."

Gee was very adamant about getting Youngster in a body bag. He viewed Lil' Red and Boo as his only hope since no one else in the Jungles had seemed to care one way or the other about Youngsters' actions three years back. It never bothered them like it bothered Gee to see Youngster still making money in their neighborhood. Ever since the incident, it seemed for Gee, he had nothing better to do than to worry about Youngster. Youngster had single handedly erased his little crew that he grew up with and he wanted revenge.

"I hear you Gee," Lil' Red began to speak, "But why Youngster? He don't even bang and the shit wasn't even behind bangin'."

"It doesn't matter if he fuckin' bang or not," Gee said with anger. "This fuckin' nigga took out a homey and two other homeboys gonna rot in jail because of that nigga. Those were some down ass niggas and they gone. They were my *dawgs* and this nigga gots to pay for that shit. Do ya'll hear me? He has to pay for that shit. Whether he bang or not, he still killed a Blood."

Lil' Red and Boo looked at each other. They then turned their attention back to Gee. They realized that Gee was very serious and more anxious than ever before about killing Youngster.

"Listen Blood," Gee started back up after a brief moment of silence. "Most of these niggas around here don't fuck with Youngster and give him a pass because of his little rep, but not me," Gee lied, "I ain't afraid of his ass and I know ya'll ain't neither. We can't let that nigga get away with killin' a Blood from our hood."

Gee slowly stood up off the grass. He stood directly in front of Lil' Red and Boo, "Now if we take this nigga out with his rep that these muthafuckas around here are so afraid of, then who'll have the rep after that? We will." Gee was boosting the morale of both Lil' Red and Boo. They felt on this night they would have to make up their minds on whether or not the demise of Youngster would come at their hands. They wanted to be well known and knew that if they were to do something like kill Youngster, it would shoot them up the gangster totem pole. They would be looked up to as hardcore gangsters with hearts of steel. It would be a difficult decision and no easy task to accomplish. Their decision to actually do it would take a whole lot more persuading from the bottle of brandy and the older coward known as Gee.

***

Youngster walked through his apartment door holding a Foot Locker shopping bag that contained a shoe box filled with two kilos. It was a busy day for him. He met with both Ren and Blue along with all his regulars. Ren and Blue bought nine ounces each from him. They both were very satisfied with the product. After meeting with them, Youngster met with Pedro to cop again. From the way things looked, he would be making two thousand dollars a week off his four new nine ounce customers. In addition, he would make a seventy-five hundred dollar profit from his regulars. He could feel the bright future that awaited him. He wanted to celebrate by taking Crystal and Jay out to the movies. He had really owed them some quality time. The two kilos he had purchased from Pedro put a dent in his pocket but that's the way he liked it. He liked getting as much dope as his money could buy while having only a few hundred in cash on him. He felt that he would only grind harder if his pockets were nearly empty.

Youngster went up the stairs leading to his bedroom. He walked through his door to set the shoe box in the closet. He put his dope alongside the other boxes that actually did contain shoes in them. He greeted Crystal with a long passionate kiss before saying, "Damn baby, I wanted to take ya'll to the movies but other parts of my body is tellin' me I need to get in this bed with you right now." Crystal smiled. She ran her hands across the part of his body that he was referring to. She then looked at him and said, "I see what you mean baby. But tell him that we have all night for that after we come from the movies. Me and Jay need to get out the house for a change."

Besides the shopping spree that he had took her and Jay on, they had been stuck in the house while he hustled. Crystal really began to feel cooped up. She was hoping that Youngster wouldn't change his mind about going out to the movies.

"Alright my love, lets get ready to go." Youngster's lower desires would have to wait until later.

Crystal leaped up from the bed to get dressed. She then went into Jay's room to get him ready while Youngster took a quick shower. After stepping out the shower, Youngster changed into another one of his Guess outfits. He put on a pair of Havana Joe's black boots and a black leather jacket that hung down near his knees. Within thirty minutes they were out the door and on their way to Universal City. Taking the 110 north to the 101 freeway, it took about forty-five minutes for them to arrive at the Universal City Cineplex. Youngster drove up to the parking area to pay the parking fee. He then drove slowly searching out a good place to park. As he turned to head down another row in search of a parking space, his eyes widened as if he had seen a ghost.

"I don't believe this shit," he spoke under his breath. It grabbed Crystal's attention.

"What's wrong baby?" she asked. She noticed from the look in his eyes that something wasn't right.

Youngster continued to drive giving no response to Crystal's question. She had a feeling that she shouldn't repeat the question so she remained silent. Youngster drove slowly past the dark short stubby figure undetected. The black male was opening the passenger door to his dark blue Monte Carlo for his date. A blaze of fury shot through Youngster's entire body as he observed. A little further down in the same row, Youngster found a parking space. He made a sharp left turn to park. He glanced to see if the figure was still standing near the Monte Carlo. He then quickly turned to Crystal.

"My love!" He began with excitement in his voice, "You see that guy and girl standin' over there by the blue Monte Carlo?"

Crystal looked down the row of cars. She nodded her head before he continued. "Okay, take Jay and make sure you follow them without being too obvious. Find out which movie they gonna see and buy the same tickets that they buy. After you get the tickets, wait for me in the lobby." He gave Crystal a twenty-dollar bill while she wore a confused look on her face.

Crystal took the twenty dollars. She assisted Jay in getting out of the car and did what she was instructed to do. She was still wearing a confused look on her face as she followed behind a couple that she had never seen before in her life. She walked behind the two at a distance. She made sure that she and Jay remained close enough so she wouldn't lose sight of them.

Youngster grabbed his 9 millimeter from his stash spot and tucked it in his waist belt. He sat in his car for a few minutes so that his rage would lower to a controllable pace. He had to calm himself down before carrying out his vengeful task. He didn't want to be overexcited which would cause him to make a dreadful mistake. He knew what he was about to attempt would be a risky move. However, the code of the streets called for its necessity. Now was the time for the studying of the Mafia's ways of handling business to be put to use. He stepped out of his car calmly. Before walking towards the Cineplex, he made sure his gun was properly concealed. Since it was a Saturday night, he had to be extra careful. There were many potential witnesses out on this night.

Youngster made his way through to the lobby after purchasing one ticket to see *White Men Can't Jump*. He met with Crystal and Jay who had been waiting for him near the concession stand. Crystal informed him that the couple that she was instructed to follow was in theatre number five. Youngster then gave her the keys to the car. He instructed her to take Jay and wait for him in the car. He could tell from Crystal's expression that she had just realized that enjoying a night at the movies had been cancelled. She was disappointed but not upset. She knew that her man had definitely been distracted and watching a movie was the last thing on his mind. She felt so nervous not knowing what was going on inside of his head. Her only wish was that he would be careful. She was hoping that everything would come out all right whatever it was that her man was up to. She took Jay by the hand and lead him back to the car.

Youngster entered theatre number five. He surveyed the entire room while standing on the right side of the rear. He saw the man responsible for his change of plans. The man was sitting on the left side of the theatre with his date. The row that they were seated in only had four seats in that particular row. Youngster noticed that the other two seats had yet to be occupied. It would be a perfect situation if he could get over there before some couple took the empty seats. The lights were just getting ready to dim by the time he made it to the other side of the theatre. The seats were still empty. The couple were so into one another that they didn't even notice him as he took a seat. Youngster patiently waited before making his move as he pretended to wait for his date to join him. He frequently looked back down the aisle in-between glancing at the previews of up coming movies. The feature presentation was about to begin. The theatre darkened and not much could be seen except the giant screen. Youngster continued to wait until most of the movement had come to a halt. The theatre was now packed as everyone had taken their seats. Youngster decided to wait a little longer.

After ten minutes into the movie, he went into action like a paid hit man. He moved over one seat to get right next to the stubby male who had one arm around his girl. His face was fixed on the movie screen. He had not noticed Youngster at all. Youngster reached down into his waist belt and withdrew his 9 millimeter. He placed the barrel of his gun on the rib cage of the stunned male figure.

"Listen carefully, you are gonna tell your girl over there to continue to watch the movie. You gonna tell her not to make one sound while you follow each and everyone of my instructions or you both will be picked up by coroners tonight. Am I clear and understood?" he asked the very attentive and nervous male who recognized him immediately. He knew trouble had grabbed hold of him and there was no escaping.

"I hear you," the scared male replied. "Please don't kill me." He pleaded while his body temporarily locked on him. Every limb had stiffened from the sight of Youngster.

Rob never thought that he would get caught slipping as huge as Los Angeles was, but this night would prove him wrong. This night would make him a firm believer in the old saying, "It's a small world."

"How the fuck was you brave enough to remain out here after dumpin' some cake mix on me nigga?" he whispered in Rob's ear right after Rob told his girl to remain calm. The deadly piece of steel commanded Rob not to be stupid as he listened. "Now you can make this easy on yourself by doin' exactly what I tell you to do and nothin' more or---," Youngster paused as he leaned closer to Rob. He pressed the barrel of the 9 millimeter deeper into his side. He then put a heavier dose of venom in his voice before saying, "You can act like you have a problem with what I'm tellin' you so I can put an end to your muthafuckin' heartbeat." Rob's nervousness instantly started to reveal itself by the trembling of his face. He had no idea what Youngster had in mind, but what he did know was that he sold the wrong person cake mix. He was sure to reap what he sowed on this night without a doubt.

Youngster ordered Rob to take off every piece of clothing he had on. He told him to start with his shoes and socks first. Rob complied slowly. He undressed in the corner of the pitch black theatre as the rest of the people in attendance were either enjoying the movie or tending to their dates. The young lady that Rob had with him couldn't believe what was going on. Her date was stripping down to nothing right beside her. She watched from the corner of her eye while her face remained steadfast in the direction of the movie screen. She had only known Rob for a few weeks. She sat there thinking to herself, "If I make it home tonight, this would be the last time I will ever see this muthafucka."

In a matter of minutes, Rob's entire wardrobe was laying on the floor between him and Youngster. He sat in his seat butt-naked shivering from the cool breeze flowing through the theatre with the 9 millimeter pressed up against his rib cage. Rob had his hands in-between his legs covering up the only dignity he had left. He sat there wearing nothing but a thick gold herringbone chain around his chubby neck.

"Take that chain off and hand it to me," Youngster ordered.

Rob complied while Youngster poked the 9 millimeter into his side again. Rob immediately let out a sigh of fright. He felt that his end was near. Youngster applied even more pressure to the side of the teary eyed shivering figure. "If I see you again, you will be sure to die so save your family and friends the grief. Take your ass and what's left of my money and get the fuck outta here. I promise you that our next meetin' in this lifetime won't be in your favor." Youngster slowly withdrew the 9 millimeter from Rob. He carefully scooped Rob's clothes with his left arm and quickly made his way out of the theatre. The only thing Youngster left Rob was the keys to his car.

After Youngster left the dark theatre, he quickly walked to the nearest men's restroom in the lobby. He stepped into one of the stalls inside the restroom and went through Rob's pockets. He grabbed Rob's wallet and retrieved four hundred and eighty dollars from it. He then removed his driver's license from the wallet. Youngster put the money, driver's license, and the gold chain he took from Rob in his leather jacket before stepping out of the stall. He left the rest of Rob's items inside of the stall with his pants and shirt soaking in the toilet.

Youngster made a dash back to his car without drawing any attention. He found Crystal in the driver's seat with the car running. He couldn't help but to smile from seeing his girl on top of things. She was ready to roll as he jumped into the passenger's seat.

"Baby," Crystal began while she hurried to exit the parking lot. "You wanna tell me what that was all about?"

"Just had to take care of somethin' baby," he replied as he sat back in his seat.

Crystal hit the freeway and headed home as Jay slept in the back seat. Youngster remained silent for most of the ride. It wasn't until they were almost home when out of nowhere he started laughing out loud.

"What's so funny Jayshawn?" Crystal looked over and asked.

"I'm just trippin' off somethin' baby." He managed to say but continued to laugh.

Youngster was thinking about Rob trying to exit the theatre. He thought about the look on everyone's face when they saw a naked black man rushing to his car. He couldn't stop laughing until he saw the expression on Crystal's face. It was then that he realized that the plan was to go out and enjoy a movie. Instead, Crystal and Jay only saw the lobby of the theatre before having to sit in the car the whole time while he was busy seeking revenge.

"My love," he said to get Crystal's attention. She glanced over at him and he continued to say, "I apologize about tonight."

"Oh, it's alright baby. I ain't trippin'," she lied.

"That nigga you followed was the one that sold me that cake mix."

"Are you serious?" she asked in a shocking voice. "What did you do to him?"

"Nothin'," he replied.

"Well, what did you say to him?" she asked.

Youngster paused and smiled before answering, "I didn't say much besides that it's a small world after all." He began to laugh while Crystal continued to drive with a confused look on her face. He then reached in his pocket. He took out the money he received from Rob's wallet and placed it in Crystal's lap.

✳✳✳

The scene had shifted from Watts to the eastside of Los Angeles for Shell and Ice. Ice opened his own spot near Figueroa where he sold joints mixed with weed and cocaine. He had two girls turning tricks for him named Pam and Keisha. He was beginning to lay his trap for Shell to get her out on the streets too. He made sure he strung her along by keeping her high all night long. Shell had no idea that the sun even existed anymore. She would sleep throughout the day and awake at night to a primo stick. She had not seen her grandmother in a long time. When she would drop by to get a change of clothes and a bite to eat, Anne would be sound asleep.

All contact with Youngster and Jay had ended. Shell's world revolved around the use of drugs and Ice. She had put an end to paging Youngster. She wouldn't call his house to mess with Crystal anymore neither. She found herself too occupied to even remember that she had a son. She was very depressed. She was longing to climb out from the depths of hell that she allowed herself to fall in. Shell's hunger to get out only increased her desires to get high. She felt that getting high would get rid of the sadness. She thought it would take away the nightmare that had become her life. Things were definitely going downhill for her and seemed to be spinning out of control daily. Her life was in the hands of Ice and he was beginning to see that it was time for him to accelerate her into the direction of immoral and shameful deeds just to put money in his pockets.

***

"A pretty good day," Youngster thought as he drove down Crenshaw heading towards Black's spot. He was on his way to drop off his last order. It was all the dope he had left to sell. The sun was still high above the smog at this time of day. He had taken care of his whole clientele except for Black. This would be his last stop before returning home. An early return would be a nice surprise for Crystal and Jay. Youngster was still feeling a little guilty about not being able to enjoy a movie the other night with them. He was planning on spending some time with his woman and son before his pager would start to go off again.

Youngster had just crossed Jefferson to take the back way to Black's spot when a police car coming from the opposite direction happened to catch his eye. Just as the black and white vehicle drove past, Youngster made eye contact with Officer Parrish who was driving. He quickly checked his rearview mirror to see what Officer Parrish would do. Just as he expected, Parrish was making a U-turn. Youngster had to think fast. There was no cup this time, just a small brown paper bag that sat in his lap. The dope for Black was inside the bag. Youngster quickly thought about the liquor store a few blocks ahead. He proceeded in that direction. He increased his speed limit hoping to get to the liquor store before Parrish would be able to pull him over. He knew from the way Parrish turned back in his direction that Parrish was definitely going to stop him when he caught up to him.

Youngster reached the liquor store and made a sharp right turn into the parking lot. With his heart beating at an enormous rate, he opened the car door to step out. While getting out of his car, Youngster tossed the brown paper bag under his car. As he closed his car door, he turned to walk inside of the store. Before he could reach the entrance of the store, there was Officer Parrish pulling into the parking lot in hot pursuit. Youngster pretended not to hear the skidding sounds of the police car as it came to a screeching halt. He just continued to walk towards the store's entrance until he heard the sound of Officer Parrish's voice, "Hold it right there!" Youngster froze. He didn't take another step. Although he had not yet looked in Officer Parrish's direction, there was no doubt in his mind that there was a gun aimed at him with the command he had just heard. Youngster was dressed in a navy blue designer jean outfit. He had on a pair of black mid-cut leather boots with a thick black ski jacket to match.

"Hold your hands up high where I can see them!" Officer Parrish shouted.

Just seconds after following the instructions of Officer Parrish, Youngster found his face on the hood of his Volvo. Parrish had came up from behind him and swung Youngster back towards his Volvo. He planted Youngster's face on the hood of his car with force.

"Didn't I tell you every time I see you out here that I was going to stop your black ass?" Officer Parrish leaned over to speak directly in Youngster's ear at close range while he reached in his pants pocket to retrieve Youngster's car keys. After he pulled the keys out, he tossed them to his partner. Officer Trapp caught the keys and proceeded to unlock Youngster's car to search it.

The right side of Youngster's face begin to burn from the heat of his engine. The engine was pretty hot from all his driving around that day. The humiliating feeling that he felt was subdued by his extreme nervousness. He was hoping that Officer Trapp wouldn't think to look under his car. Youngster remained silent while Officer Parrish hand cuffed him and frisked him.

"How much money you have here?" Parrish asked as he patted down the left side of Youngster's ski jacket.

"Maybe a little over eight thousand," Youngster answered in the proper manner. The last thing he wanted to do was give Parrish a hard time. He wanted to do everything it took in order for Parrish to leave him alone, even if it meant swallowing pride.

"And how do you explain having this kind of money on you?"

"I do a lot of gambling and go to the check cashing place to get big bills after being lucky enough to win. You just stopped me after I just finished cashing in a minute ago." Youngster tried to eliminate all his slang in his speech.

"You lying ass son-of-a-bitch," Parrish squeezed the cuffs on Youngster's arms, "If my partner doesn't find anything in that car, you better not let me see you again. Because I'll do the searching next time and I guarantee you that I will find something. Do you hear me?"

"Yes Sir."

"All clear, he's clean." Officer Trapp calmly said to Officer Parrish after going through Youngster's car. Officer Trapp came up empty.

"Okay, I guess this must be another one of his lucky days." Parrish said.

"Yeah, I guess so." Officer Trapp responded while walking back to the patrol car.

Officer Parrish watched his partner get out of range before he turned his attention back to Youngster. After he saw that his partner was far enough, he took his fist and hit Youngster hard in his stomach. "You got away for the last time punk. But it's just a matter of time before I catch your ass. I'll see to it that you are behind bars where all you niggers should be. Your kind makes me sick to my stomach."

Youngster was in pain from the blow he had just received. He remained on the hood of his car while Officer Parrish took the hand cuffs off of him. After the handcuffs were off, Officer Parrish turned Youngster around to face him. He looked Youngster straight in the eye and said, "You know what boy? I hope you don't get the wrong impression and think that I hate all you niggers because I don't. You may not be able to tell but I actually have lots of niggers in my family tree." Youngster stood and stared as Officer Parrish continued, "And boy let me tell you that those niggers would still be hanging from that tree if it wasn't for the foul odor you people have." Parrish gave Youngster an evil grin. He walked away leaving Youngster standing there in disbelief. He could not believe what he had just heard from an officer of the law.

After waiting for a few seconds, Youngster walked in the liquor store. He purchased a bag of chips and a root beer. He then walked back to his car. He kneeled down and reached for his paper bag under his car. Youngster sat inside his car. He called Black to let him know that he was sorry for the delay. He told him that he would be on his way shortly. Although it bothered Youngster to have been harassed as he just did, he could only sit there counting his blessings once again. He had escaped another close call.

# 21

The rage, anger, and outburst from the minorities of Los Angeles finally dwindled to a whisper. After the Mayor of the city issued a curfew from dusk till dawn, things started to calm down. The entire police force was out patrolling the streets in an attempt to restore law and order during the wake of the numerous burnings and lootings. The uproar began a few days ago after the acquittal of four police officers for the video taped beating of a black man. The sounds of injustice rang out soon after the verdict was announced. The shocked and appalled took to the streets to display their displeasure of the justice system towards the less fortunate. Racism had slapped the so-called minorities of Los Angeles right in the face on national television and thousands of citizens decided they were not going to take it lying down.

Rioting, arson, and looting ran rampant for four whole days. Thirty-eight deaths, over a thousand injuries, and hundreds of fires blazed throughout the city. Those were just some of the results of the uproar. When the smoke cleared, army tanks rolled down Crenshaw along with troops armed with M-16 rifles. The only thing untouched or unfazed by the chaos in the streets were the movement and transaction of drugs. In fact, the drug trade increased while other businesses were decreasing or destroyed.

Youngster had turned down offers of merchandise from looted furniture, jewelry, and groceries. He only wanted cash for his product. During the days of rioting, he had made this clear to all that would call him. Although the police force were too busy to even stop a drug dealer while the city was up in smoke, Youngster had moved about the streets with caution during the days of chaos. Youngster's rise continued to move up as his steady purchase of two kilos a week jumped to six kilos twice a month. He had to start meeting Pedro at a body shop to make his transactions. A body shop that Pedro's father owned in East L.A. Youngster had to meet him there because of his heavy orders. Pedro never did mind delivering two kilos to Youngster, but six was just too much for him to deliver. K-9, Willie, Ren, and Blue were all copping a half of kilo a week from Youngster. Word continued to spread that they had the best quality of cocaine in their respective areas.

As Youngster drove through the city, it angered him to see his community destroyed by flames. But he knew it had to be done. There was no way that the so-called minorities of the city should have taken that verdict lying down. They displayed their frustration without planning and giving it much thought. They demanded that justice be served. The domino effect of the rioting had spread beyond the city limits. Many people in other states took the opportunity to yell out against police brutality in their cities. The smell of smoke, the sight of buildings and store fronts burnt to the ground really disturbed Youngster. He continued to look at the destruction as he drove across the path of Army troops. A feeling of passion and sorrow hit him as he continued to glance at the aftermath of the L.A Riots. What once was stores and places of business had become just piles of ashes. The community had spoken out in anger and rage. They were actually heard for a brief moment. However, as the smoke began to clear from each passing day, it was beginning to become obvious that the community had only hurt itself. Recovering from it all would take some years.

Youngster drove to the corner of 67th & 3rd Avenue where Ren and Moe were standing outside in the front yard. They had been waiting for Youngster for twenty minutes. As Youngster slowly parked his car, they listened to Bob Marley wail through the car speakers.

> *This morning I woke up in a curfew*
> *O God, I was a prisoner too - yeah*
> *Could not recognize the faces standing over me*
> *They were all dressed in uniforms of brutality*
> *How many rivers do we have to cross*
> *Before we can talk to the boss*
> *All that we got, it seems we have lost*
> *We must have really paid the cost*

Youngster stepped out of his car. He was not looking his usual self as he approached the steel gated fence. His mood was very dismal due to the mixture of Bob Marley's lyrics and viewing the scenery of the aftermath. His thoughts had deepened during the ride over to meet Ren and Moe. It could be noticed from the expression on his face as he entered through the gate.

"What's up fellas?" he greeted them as he walked inside the fence.

"What's up?" Moe replied while smoking on a cigarette.

"You the man," Ren said while observing Youngster's demeanor.

Youngster walked towards them and shook each of their hands. His expression remained the same as did his whole demeanor.

"You alright Youngster?" Ren asked.

"Yeah, I'm straight," he said. "It's just them damn troops and tanks rollin' down the *Shaw* along with all the burnt down stores and shit. All that just really tripped me out."

"Yeah, we tore some shit up didn't we? I know I came up the past few days. I almost came up short today with your money from all the damn clothes, groceries, and refurnishin' my apartment." Ren couldn't do anything but laugh after he made his comment. He thought about all the items that came his way in exchange for dope.

Ren is a very light-skinned guy who stood at six foot and three inches. He is built like a football player. He is a few years older than Youngster and has been a gang member of the Crips since he was eleven. His only education came from the streets but his appearance never showed it. He wore G.Q glasses to cover his slanted eyes and dressed like he was attending college. Some of his friends would even call him Mr. Student when they would see him wearing his prep clothing.

"Do ya'll realize that our community did more damage to itself by burnin' and lootin'?" Youngster asked. "Now a nigga have to drive all the way across town just to get some bread and milk."

"Yeah, but the gold and clothes has been delivered at a niggas doorstep for the past few days," Ren stated while he took out his brush and started brushing the waves on his head.

"Ren, you don't see the bigger picture do you?" Youngster asked.

"The bigger picture is that I got a whole lot of shit for damn near nothin'."

"I heard that," Moe approved.

"Yeah, but look what it took for you to get that shit," Youngster was in no mood to make light of the riots.

"What, a couple of burnt down Asian stores?" Ren asked, but not expecting an answer as he continued, "Nigga please, they got what was comin' to them. It was time for them to give back to our community. Now all we need is our forty acres and a mule from these white folks." Ren and Moe laughed but Youngster wasn't feeling it.

"It wasn't just the Asian stores that were burnt down and looted," Youngster stated. "And it wasn't them that acquitted those officers neither. Now if these bastards wanted to really tear some shit up, they should have gone to Beverly Hills and handled their business there."

"Now you know damn well niggas would have been shot up before they had a chance to light one fuckin' tree in Beverly Hills." Ren replied.

"I know that's right," Moe agreed. "Niggas would have been shot on sight out there." He added.

Youngster looked at both his uncle and Ren and asked, "So does that mean that a community has to destroy the very place where they must lay their own fuckin' heads?"

"Fuck the community!" Ren shouted. "Who gives a fuck about this community? Not us, we feed off these muthafuckas every single day and night Youngster. We are takin' these bastards for damn near all they got so our pockets can get fat and so we can eat. So fuck them!"

Ren's statement hit Youngster hard like a brick. He thought about how right Ren was and how wrong he was for distributing the poison to his people. A moment of silence past before Youngster picked the conversation back up.

"You know what?" he asked just to get their attention. "A nigga do need to stop feedin' off his own people like this."

"Who?" Ren quickly asked. "I know you ain't talkin' about me cause I'm gonna make my damn money the only way I know how around this bitch."

"I know that's right." Moe concurred.

"I'm talkin' about me." Youngster said.

"You?" Ren asked and looked over to Moe.

"Shiiit," Moe dragged out the word after removing his cigarette from his mouth. "You know damn well that nigga love makin' money too much to stop sellin' dope."

Moe and Ren started laughing. After pondering over the thought of actually putting an end to dealing drugs, Youngster joined the laughter. He knew that his uncle had made a valid point. The money was too good and it was only getting better for him each day.

"Man, you have my shit or what?" Ren asked once all the laughter came to an end.

"Yeah," Youngster answered. "It's on the passenger seat, just lay the money on the floor and get your shit up out of my car."

"Cool," Ren walked over to Youngster's car. He opened the passenger door right after Youngster hit his alarm button.

"Bob Marley got you deep in thought, huh?" Moe asked his nephew while Ren was inside Youngster's car counting out his money.

"Yeah, he be droppin' some heavy shit in his music."

"I told your ass a long time ago but you didn't listen. Crackin' your Jamaican jokes and shit." Moe turned his head away from Youngster to blow out smoke.

"Well, I'm sure listenin' to him now with some of those Farrakhan speeches here and there. I been really thinkin' about a lot of deep shit lately."

"I can see that," Moe said. "But you and I both know that you ain't gonna stop sellin' dope because of this riot, Farrakhan, or Bob Marley ass." Moe grinned.

After Ren had left the eight thousand dollars on the floor of Youngster's car, he grabbed the half of kilo concealed in a shopping bag off the passengers seat. He closed the car door and returned to where Youngster and Moe were standing back inside the gate.

"It's all there on the floor Youngster," Ren said.

"I would hope so, cause you know I'm gonna count it a few times to make sure you ain't come up short from all your shoppin' you been doin'."

Ren chuckled and said, "That's exactly why this nigga prospers, cause he's a tight muthafucka. He ain't lettin' you get away with shit."

Youngster smiled and said, "I'm out." He then headed towards his car with Moe hot on his trail.

"Alright be safe," Ren said as he walked over to the porch. He sat down holding the bag with the half of kilo in it as if it was legal to do so.

Youngster went to his car. He sat inside as Moe stood outside on the passenger side of the car. Moe was waiting for Youngster to pick up the eight grand that Ren left on the passenger's side of the floor. Once Moe saw that it was clear, he put out his cigarette. He then opened the car door and sat down in the passengers seat. Moe was expecting a little something from his nephew for the transaction that Youngster had just made with Ren. Moe sat there in the car and gave Youngster the *hook a brotha up* look. Moe felt that since he introduced his nephew to Ren, that he should get a small portion of gratitude from him.

Without much being said, Youngster grabbed a quarter ounce from up under his seat. He gave it to Moe. Youngster didn't feel like preaching to his uncle so he just watched him get out of his car. He just hoped Moe would make some money from the quarter ounce and not use it for his own personal use.

It was back to the house for Youngster with the eight grand he just made. His conscience was eating at him from knowing the giant part he played in destroying his own community. There was a battle that took place in his mind as he made his way home. But the root of all evil prevailed over the thought of the pain and suffering of the community. The money he was making by dealing the very product that helped in putting his neighborhood in such a grave condition was just too good. "One day I'll be able to walk away from this drug shit," he thought to himself as he drove by ashes that were once places of business. Stores that the community could once go to purchase their food and goods. They were gone.

# 22

Youngster's name started to fly throughout the city of Los Angeles. His reputation grew beyond comprehension. He was entering a very dangerous territory that would be uncontrollable. Although he thought he was maintaining a low profile, he was unaware of the gossip going on about him in the streets. The fact that no matter how people went about their business, when it came down to keeping the streets from talking, that would be something unpreventable. He thought that he had it covered when it came to keeping his business on the low. However, the one thing that he didn't pay attention to was the letter from the old man that read, "Jealousy and envy will always run through the heart of the streets, so never think for one minute that the streets is not plotting on you when you ever start to rise."

The streets couldn't keep Youngster's name out of its mouth. Word was that he had the best dope in L.A, the most money in the neighborhoods he was being seen in, and that his connection was the biggest drug cartel in Columbia. The rumors of his lucrative business were beginning to spread slowly towards the ears of the L.A.P.D. One very interested officer who patrolled the Jungles took a special interest in the rumors. This was none other than Officer Parrish. A man with the brains, guts, and the instincts for longevity on the illegal side of society was a challenge to law enforcers. As for Officer Parrish, he saw it as his personal challenge to capture and apprehend Youngster.

Months rolled on as Youngster continued to grow while Los Angeles tried to rebuild from the riots. He climbed the illegal corporate ladder rapidly during the year of 1992. He found himself picking up fifteen kilos within every four weeks from the body shop belonging to Pedro's family. Youngster had become a very important man to Pedro's family. Every time he would show up at the body shop, he got the royal treatment. Youngster never thought that he would be handling as much weight as he was moving. He had to rent a one bedroom apartment due to the danger of having so much weight in the same place where he and his family were laying their heads.

The apartment where he would stash his dope was located in a gated community not far from his town home. One would never have guessed that a drug dealer was occupying a space there. Youngster would only store his kilos there. He wouldn't meet any one at the apartment so no one had any idea of what was going on inside the complex. The rent was high due to all the extra amenities. The place had a security entrance, washer and dryers on each of the five floors, and underground parking with elevators. The building was full of upper-class tenants that were sure to mind their own business. The type of people to not pry in other people's business as long as a distance was kept.

Youngster's stocks had grown in the months after the riots. Over half of South-Central Los Angeles was being supplied by him. The drugs that were being purchased from him were being spread throughout the city by way of those that he directly dealt with. The quality of good dope was in high demand due to the fact that most of the drugs on the streets at that time were very weak. This was because of greed. Many dealers had started to try to push dope that was mixed with another substance to stretch the dope during the cooking process to make more of a profit. This low quality of cocaine called *Blow-up*, ran rampant on the streets of Los Angeles. Youngster never did cheat his customers by adopting this method of making more money off of a lower quality. He knew by keeping his dope at its purest, his risk of losing his loyal following would be slim. His crew of four were buying kilos from him once a week. Most of them were getting an extra nine ounces to another whole kilo for others. All others had to go through them to get the Peruvian flake that it seemed only Youngster supplied. His regulars like Betty, Angel, Black, and others were also copping extras for other people. This meant that Youngster was dumping anywhere from six to ten kilos a week.

Always on the go and making moves, the streets had taken control of Youngster. His pager had become priority. Everything else had taken a backseat to making money in the life of this hustler. His entire focus was getting it while the getting was good. He wanted to continue to keep his eyes on the prize which was to buy a house. After buying a house, he vowed he would get out of the game. He purchased Crystal a brand new silver Honda Accord. He started giving her a thousand dollars a week so that she wouldn't have to sit in the house all day while he hustled. He wanted her to be able to get around. He needed her to get Jay to pre-school and pick him up afterwards. Youngster started to spend less time with them. They were seeing less of him during his rapid come up. He was unable to take them places so getting Crystal a car was definitely a necessity.

Youngster was unaware how the game was consuming him. It removed him from his son, Crystal, and his family. He had become a workaholic in the illegal work force of pushing dope. All the money he was making made him feel like the dream of owning a home and running a legitimate business was close at hand. This drive blinded him. He was unable to see that he was changing. The game made him oblivious to just how displeased Crystal had become due to his new found success. He was so unaware of how she was feeling inside. She would have given back the new car and the weekly cash just to spend some quality time with him. Lately, Crystal would find herself sitting in the bedroom thinking of the first time she met Youngster. She would think about the times they shared at the beach, sporting events, and in the very bedroom where she now spent long nights alone. She started to fall into a depressing state. She was very unhappy inside.

One night Youngster was counting money at the edge of his bed. Crystal decided to express her feelings in which she had been holding back for the past few months. Her sudden movement had somewhat surprised Youngster because he thought she was sound asleep.

"Baby," she whispered to get his attention.

"Yeah," Youngster responded but continued to add up his earnings for that day.

Crystal had yet to figure out just how to approach him with her feelings that had been growing within her. On this night she felt she had to say something before things soared out of control. She didn't want to end up losing her man.

"What's goin' on with you?" she asked while his back faced her.

"What do you mean?" he asked.

"It's like you don't be around long enough to sit down and eat with us anymore. We barely see you and by the time you do make it home and settle down, you don't even have the time to make love to me like you once did. Is there somethin' wrong that I should know about?"

He turned to her to see if the sound of her voice was equal to the look on her face. Once he seen that her expression was just as serious as the tone in her voice, he responded, "I hope you not tryin' to say that you think I'm doin' somethin' wrong to hurt you. Like I'm out here fuckin' around on you."

Crystal sat up on the bed. She looked Youngster directly in his eyes before saying, "I'm not tryin' to say anything, I'm just askin' you what's wrong?" Without giving him a chance to answer, she continued, "Things are just not like it used to be with us. It's been lonely here without you. Jay has been askin' about you, your mother been callin' for you, your sister been worried, and I don't even have an answer for them because I haven't been seeing you enough to give an answer. I don't know what's goin' on myself baby."

"Well," Youngster began. "Nothin' is wrong my love. I'm just stayin' focused out there in these streets tryin' to reach my goal so I won't have to continue to do this shit any longer. I'm pretty close to bein' able to buy us a house and get out this game for good. I know I haven't been spendin' time with you and Jay but I promise that it won't be long before my focus will be totally on you and him. I want to spend the rest of my life with you my love. I would love for us to build a family together without worryin' about me gettin' locked up or killed out here."

The words that flowed from Youngster's mouth and entered into Crystal's ears were very gratifying to her. Fortunately for Youngster, Crystal wasn't a drama queen. She was the type that would avoid conflict when necessary. She was full of understanding. She had learned that it was much better to comprehend than to be quick to rush to judgment. She never would allow herself to talk out the side of her neck. The thought of Youngster sacrificing his time with her and his son in order for him to get out of the game, turned her on. It pleased her to know that his plan was not to hustle his whole entire life. This aroused her to hear he wanted her to have his children. It became evident that he had turned her on as she crawled over to him. She revealed that she wanted him and his full attention for the remainder of the night. She climbed on him while he sat at the edge of the bed. She rubbed her breast slowly across his face. She then gently laid him on his back so he could receive a full dose of ecstasy.

***

Early the next morning, Crystal had to shake Youngster awake just in time before a scream of fear rang out from his voice. His reoccurring nightmares were just about to get the best of him before Crystal had awakened him.

"Baby, are you ok?" she asked.

For a while there was just silence. He gave her a stare of relief as the fear slowly decreased within. The process of realizing that the multiple gunshots that he was receiving was only a bad dream was slowly taking effect. For the most part, it was still real to him at that moment. After a few more seconds, his heart rate had started to slow down. It was beginning to return to normal so that he could speak without a trembling sound in his voice. He didn't want to reveal to Crystal all the fear that had built up within him. He waited until it was almost completely gone out of his system.

"I'm cool my love, just another one of those crazy ass dreams." He glanced over at the clock to check the time. He decided to go ahead and get ready for another day of hustling. The clock had read 7:10 a.m. It wasn't the usual time for him to get up but he needed some extra time. He had to get Blue's order ready. Blue had called in an order the day before which would require him to be in the kitchen longer.

Youngster arrived at the apartment where he kept his dope just before nine in the morning. He walked straight to the kitchen through his clean one bedroom. It gave the appearance of someone living there instead of a storage place for a drug dealer. Immediately, Youngster started cooking the half of kilo Blue ordered. He weighed out other orders that he was sure to deliver during the day. He never did enjoy the long process of cooking that much dope in one day but he managed to compensate himself by putting a rewarding price tag on his services. It was a steep price for those that requested a large amount of cocaine cooked for them instead of buying it in the powder form. But they never seemed to mind.

After Youngster was all done cooking, he wrapped everything up and cleaned the kitchen. Within minutes, he was out the door and in his car. The sun greeted him by shining directly down into the windshield of his car as he pulled out from the underground parking stall of the apartment building. A nervous feeling came over him once he pulled out into traffic due to all the dope he was transporting that day. He traveled on pure hope that he wouldn't get pulled over by the police. He always carried the dope he was delivering right beside him on the passenger seat or under his own seat. There would be no chance of getting away if he was ever to see flashing lights in his rearview mirror.

It took him about thirty minutes to get to his first drop off. It was the biggest of the day. When he arrived in front of Blue's spot, a strange feeling came over him for a second time. He knew he had to go inside of Blue's place. There was too much weight and money that had to be exchanged for them to meet at any other destination. Out of everyone of Youngster's regulars that bought big packages, Blue was the one he felt most uncomfortable with. He knew he had to be extra careful around Blue. There was always a little trust that one could gain with Youngster but when it came down to trusting Blue, Youngster couldn't get himself to do it. There was just something about Blue that he felt he had to beware.

Youngster stepped out of his car with his 9 millimeter tucked in his waist belt. It was concealed under his very loose Los Angeles Dodger's jersey he was wearing. He was holding a large shopping bag in his hand as he walked down a long driveway. He had to pass a front house to get to the small one located behind it where he was greeted by Blue.

"What's up Youngster?" Blue asked as he stood in front of the door to his light blue cottage.

"Not much Blue, just tryin' to make it."

"Shit, you know you got all the money around here Youngster." Blue made his comment with a crooked smile. He opened his door for Youngster to step inside his little one bedroom flat.

Youngster walked pass Blue with caution. They both stood at the same height but Blue was much heavier than him. Blue was very dark with short black hair. He had a look of one that has been institutionalized. He wore a tattoo across his neck that could barely be seen of his name. In addition, he had two more tattoos on his right shoulder of a dead homeboy's name and the other of the neighborhood that he claimed. Rumors were spreading around that Blue had been smoking primos again since he has been out of jail. There were no signs of him using the mixture of weed and cocaine known as primos as far as Youngster was concerned. The way Blue had been buying from him on a regular basis, it was hard for Youngster to believe that Blue could be using again. However, he didn't put it past him.

"Have a seat," Blue said to him once he entered through the door.

Youngster quickly glanced around the room. He wanted to make sure that it was just him and Blue in the spot. He looked into the direction of the bathroom. He noticed the door was slightly ajar. It seemed as if someone might have been in the bathroom hiding. Youngster became leery after seeing the crack in the bathroom door. He adjusted his gun without Blue noticing. He was doing his best not allowing Blue to see that he had became nervous. He felt that if he had to be nervous when dealing with someone, that he had rather not deal with them at all. He was feeling vulnerable. This had caught him by surprise. He couldn't believe he was feeling this way. He felt like he was at a disadvantage. This was the first time he had ever experienced feelings like these during a transaction.

Youngster sat on Blue's sofa at an angle with the bathroom door in his sight. He pulled out the kilo for Blue from the shopping bag. He then brought out the thirty-six cookies individually wrapped that he had in a shoe box. He sat all the dope on Blue's glass table in front of the sofa. He looked towards Blue expecting to see the money. Blue stepped into his bedroom without saying a word. This didn't help matters as far as Youngster's uneasy feeling that he was experiencing. Blue left Youngster alone in the living room to wonder whether or not he was being set up. Youngster wanted the transaction between him and Blue to be done and over with as soon as possible. He sat on the sofa watching the bedroom Blue entered and the bathroom door that was slightly open. He had his hand inside of his jersey preparing for one false move in either direction. Blue had let off a very different vibe towards Youngster than other times when they have met. Youngster wondered about the rumors of Blue using drugs again. He thought about the possibility of the rumors being true. He attributed the rumors to Blue's strange behavior which helped bring down his nervousness a little. After a brief moment, Blue returned to the living room holding a small bag full of money. He sat the bag on the table where the dope also was sitting.

"It's all there," Blue said to Youngster as he sat across from Blue in a silver chair, "The whole twenty three thousand and five-hundred. Ain't no way in hell I would have paid an extra thousand for you to cook my shit. No fuckin' way."

Youngster took the bundle of money in his arms. He pulled it closer towards him so that he could count it. He managed to put a grin on his face before saying, "That's why you get it the way you get it and do what you please with it. But for those that want me in that damn kitchen cookin' this shit fourteen grams at a time, they have to pay." Youngster quickly went through the money. He seen that roughly it was all there. He didn't want to be in Blue's place any longer than he had to be. He decided to count the money again later at home. Youngster grabbed the shopping bag that he brought the dope in and dropped the money in it.

"Well, I'm outta here Blue," he stated while standing up.

"Yeah, you be careful out there Youngster, they been out there talkin' about you stackin' yo chips and shit. You know how that shit goes once shit like that start spreadin' around. You have to watch your back."

Youngster took a look at Blue as he approached the door and paused. He thought about responding to Blue's comment but decided against it. He knew in some cases it was better to remain silent than to speak. He chose to remain silent. While Youngster was reaching for the door to let himself out, Blue stood up to lock the door behind him.

"Alright Youngster, be safe," Blue said as he held the door and watched Youngster walk down the driveway. When Youngster was completely out of Blue's sight, Blue returned inside. He quickly grabbed his phone. He dialed a number up. When an eager listener answered on the other end of the line Blue said, "The shit will be a cinch to set up this nigga. The very next time I cop, it's on Cuzz."

***

Louise walked inside her house with a few plastic bags filled with groceries. She was very tired and weary after working her shift at the post office. She was also drained from having to deal with the grocery shopping right after she left work. She had been standing on her feet all day and the fact that she hadn't seen nor heard from her son, didn't help matters. Louise had become a nervous wreck in the past two weeks because it was unlike Youngster not to show his face for such a long time. Louise locked her front door after dropping the grocery bags on the living room floor. She stood at her door with mixed emotions. She was aware she would soon have the answers to her questions of just what's been going on with her son.

She walked into her kitchen where Youngster was sitting at her table. He was eating some take-out food from a Jamaican spot. It was another little place he would get food from when he was out making moves.

"Jayshawn, what's going on with you out in these streets?"

Youngster could not answer right away due to the jerk chicken that prevented him from speaking. When he finished chewing his food and swallowing, he responded, "Ma, what you talkin' bout?"

"You know what I'm talking about, you haven't been over here in two weeks and when I've tried to reach you at home, Crystal sounds as if she ain't seen you neither. Do you have that girl raising my grandbaby while you run these streets and hang with your crack head friends?"

206

Youngster tried to remain calm knowing that his mother was only being concerned. He didn't like the tone in her voice nor her assumptions but decided to deal with them. She was talking to him as if he was a child that needed to be reminded to look both ways before he crossed the street. However, he was used to his mother over reacting.

"Ma, everything is all right with me, Crystal, and Jay. I just been real busy and preferred that Jay stay home with Crystal."

Louise started to put up her groceries but wasn't about to let her son off that easy. "Jayshawn, why can't you just get a regular job and do right? You can't keep dodging those consequences out there in the Devil's playground. And I know you smart enough to be able to see that. Your father thought he was the smoothest man around when it came to escaping the harm out there and you see what happened to him."

"Ma, I understand what you are sayin' and trust me, I don't plan on doin' this much longer."

"Jayshawn, that's the same exact thing I heard from your father. He said one more run and that one more run landed him in prison. That is what took his life. You can't calculate an end out there when you're not on your own schedule. You are on the Devil's time out there in those streets. He controls that world you are living in Jayshawn. Don't you know that?"

Youngster continued to eat what was left in his plate while his mother lectured him. After he was done eating, he finished drinking his root beer. He looked at his watch avoiding eye contact with his mother who was standing in the middle of the kitchen. She was waiting for her son to say something that she had been praying so hard to hear from him. However, when he finally looked up in his worried mother's face, his words wouldn't come close to answering her prayers.

"Ma, we can't change what is meant to be, we can only accept the circumstance and strive to change the outcome. The circumstance is that I'm a hustler. Now I can only strive not to be like most out there and end up in jail or lose my life in the hustle. I'm not tryin' to end up like daddy." Youngster stood up and walked to the trash can to dump his plate. He then hugged his mother who was standing in silence. She was holding back her tears. She could feel her son was headed for the inevitable. She felt completely helpless in stopping it. "Don't worry Ma. I'll be alright," were the last words he said to her as he walked out of the house to return back to the Devil's playground.

***

Traffic became unbearable and disturbing to Youngster as he was trying to drive home. Frustration started to set in as there was no letting up in the traffic jam on the 110 freeway. He could see that there was a major accident ahead. What made the traffic become bumper to bumper, were all the drivers that drove pass the accident slowly just to be nosey. Youngster hated that. He decided to exit the very next off-ramp he came to. Youngster was returning from a meeting with Pedro and his family at the body shop. They held meetings there monthly to update Youngster and a few others on things such as droughts and price changes. They wanted their large quantity buyers to always be informed.

Youngster found himself on Vernon & Figueroa after getting off the freeway. His car was drug free so he thought it would be quicker getting home by shooting straight down Figueroa. This would have been a wrong thing to do if there had been dope on him. The only thing he had to be watchful for was the brake lights from the *Johns* in their cars. You could always find men on Figueroa at night rubber necking to view and attempt to holler at the prostitutes walking the streets. Most of the prostitutes walking the strip on Figueroa were not out for the money. They were out there to support their habits. Those without Pimps would give a blow-job for 10 dollars just to get a rock.

When Youngster approached the congested area on Figueroa where most of the women would hang out, he happened to notice someone out of the corner of his eye. He couldn't believe his eyes. Youngster had to give the person a double take in order to confirm that he wasn't just seeing things. He thought maybe the blunt he smoked at the body shop was taking effect on his eyesight. She was standing on the corner alone while two other women were off to the side by a parked car. She was all made up and wearing very revealing clothes. She had recognized Youngster passing by. She looked away at that very moment hoping that he wouldn't notice her. Her reaction only gave her away. This made Youngster hit the corner and go back to make sure it was who he thought it was.

Youngster pulled up the street just as the parked car that he had seen before, pulled off with the two women inside. They left the one girl that he recognized standing all alone. She was looking nervous as she looked in Youngsters' direction while he was pulling up beside her. She wore an expression like a deer caught in headlights when she made eye contact with him. Youngster drove right along side her while she attempted to walk away. He rolled his window down on the passenger side of his car and yelled, "Shell!" She stopped in her tracks. "What the fuck are you doin' out here?" he asked.

Shell had become completely embarrassed. Her high dropped which made her sober up within seconds. She slowly walked towards Youngster's car. She leaned over towards the open window dipping her head inside the car to answer his question with a question. "What do you mean, what am I doin' out here? What are you doin' out here? Your girl ain't doin' it right or what?"

"Don't play with me right now," Youngster said as he looked into Shell's eyes. "I been hearin' shit about you being missin' in action for weeks at a time and now I see you out here on the corner lookin' like a straight up hoe, what's goin' on with that?"

"Don't worry about me. I'm handlin' my business just like you handle yours." Shell looked around. She began to get impatient. Her body started to crave for more cocaine after being sobered up from the sight of the man she once thought she would spend the rest of her life with. She knew that she would have to turn a trick real soon in order to get her high back.

There was a minute of silence before Youngster would say anything. He just studied Shell's body language and thought back to when he would serve on the street level. All the signs were there that she was using cocaine. He couldn't believe it. The mother of his child was out on the streets selling her body to get high.

"Shell, get in the car so I can take your ass home."

"I'm not goin' anywhere," she said.

Shell was paying more attention to the traffic on Figueroa than Youngster. He could tell that she was on a mission. This was confirmed by her question to him, "You got some of that shit on you, Jayshawn?"

"No!" he quickly snapped. "I'm clean but even if I did, you know damn well you wouldn't be gettin' any shit from me."

"Well, let me get some money and I'll pay you back later?" Shell's craving was getting the best of her. Shame was thrown out the window as desperation showed up in full force.

"I'm not givin' you money so you can get high. Are you out your rabbit ass mind?"

"Come on Jayshawn, I promise I'll pay you back. I need it, please!"

"I'm takin' you to your grandmother's house, get in the car."

"I'm not ready to go back there, I need to get high."

Youngster couldn't believe what he was seeing nor hearing. He was so saddened by the thought that his son's mother had become a crack head.

"Shell, do you know what you doin' to yourself?"

"What I'm doin' to myself!" she yelled. "You did this to me, you muthafucka! You couldn't give me a chance to prove to you that I loved you." She began to get very emotional. "This is all your fault nigga, you and your bitch!" Shell was upset and frustrated that her high was gone. She was hurt that her son's father had seen her in that condition.

Before Youngster was able to say anything, Shell was in tears and backed away from the car. She went inside the parking lot of the motel where she was standing when Youngster had first seen her. Youngster sat there in his car in a daze. He watched the mother of his child walk away from the car still yelling and screaming, "This is all your fault, this is all your fault you muthafucka! Get the fuck from around me! I hate you!"

# 23

A loud and unpleasant odor of fried fish was floating throughout the small apartment building complex. The smell was coming from Angel's kitchen. She was almost done cooking dinner still smiling from meeting with Youngster. Things were looking real good for her now that she has been buying four and a half ounces every other day from him. She had been saving her money and looking forward to moving soon. She wanted to get her daughter away from the dangerous activities of dope dealing. She was planning on moving but she wanted to keep her spot to continue serving. Her real desire was to give up selling dope for good. But for a woman in her thirties whose only education is the streets, she felt it was almost an impossible dream. Angel called out to Trina for her to come eat as she set two plates on the dinner table. Trina yelled out, "I'm comin'," while she ran out of her bedroom. When Trina stepped into the kitchen, she sat in front of her plate filled with red snapper, mashed potatoes, and string beans. She began to eat along with her mother who was sitting directly across from her. In the middle of eating dinner, there was a knock at Angel's door.

"Who is it?" Angel yelled out before actually getting up from her table.

The response, "It's me," came from a familiar voice. Angel stepped away from the table to open the door. She was relieved that the person wasn't a customer that she had to serve. She was anxious to get back to her supper and hated to conduct business in the middle of eating dinner. She also didn't like to deal with anyone in front of her daughter. She had gotten very conscious of trying not to do business in front of Trina because she was getting older. Trina had become more aware of what her mother was doing. Angel preferred to conduct her business much later in the evening when Trina was off in her bedroom or asleep.

When Angel reached her front door, she unlocked it. She opened it slightly leaving the top chain still attached. "Hey, what's up?" she asked as she examined the male frame standing outside of her door. She was noticing something different about him. His eyes were blood shot red. His stance was that of a hardcore gangster and somewhat threatening. She watched his body sway from side to side. There was a light moisture of perspiration dripping down from his forehead. She stood there waiting for a response. She was hoping that he wasn't in any kind of trouble.

"Angel, you just gonna stare at me?" He finally spoke and continued, "Open the fuckin' door, Blood!"

"Why? What's wrong with you? Is everything alright?" she asked searching for an explanation for his strange behavior.

Angels instincts lead her to feel a very strong sense of harm and danger. She removed herself away from the crack of the door to close it shut but she didn't move fast enough. Just before the door knob reached its destination in order for it to be locked, the door came towards her like a flash of lightning smacking her in her face. The impact shocked her. She almost blanked out from the combination of the shock and pain. She fell on the floor. She found herself looking directly up at the barrel of a .45 semi-automatic. She couldn't recognize the man holding the gun because her vision had become blurry from the blow to her face. She had only remembered the last person she saw standing in front of her at the door. She thought to herself that it couldn't be him. There was no way that the man standing over her holding a gun was the same one at her door. The horrible fact that it was actually him devastated her when it was confirmed by the sound of his voice.

"Get the fuck up bitch!"

Angel struggled to stand back up on her feet. She looked over to her daughter who sat in her seat frozen and stunned. She turned her head back in the direction of the threatening .45 and the man with it in his hand. She couldn't believe it was him. "Why is Gee doing this?" she wondered.

"Get over there with Trina," Gee commanded. Angel quickly followed the order of the .45. She feared the gun more than the voice behind it. She was feeling a very sharp pain in the bridge of her nose. There was a trickle of blood dripping from it. She couldn't believe what was going on. She didn't understand why. Angel had been knowing Gee for so long and never had a problem with him. They had been speaking to one another on a regular basis for years so this was very confusing to her.

"Gee, what is wrong with you?" she asked.

"Shut the fuck up and give me all yo shit," he swiftly responded not giving her a chance to talk him out of his mission. "I want the money and the dope."

She could see that Gee wasn't only drunk, but he was also high off some type of drug. She didn't want to make him do anything that would harm her little girl but she had made up her mind that she wouldn't allow him to walk out her door with all that she had worked to get.

Gee closed Angel's front door shut. The entire apartment building had been so used to the sounds of commotion that Angel's disturbance had gone unnoticed.

"Let's make this quick," Gee said as he faced Angel with the gun pointing towards her chest. "I don't have time for no games," he added.

To make his point, Gee walked over to Trina. He placed the .45 to her head while snatching her up from the dinner table. Angel almost went into total shock seeing a gun to her daughter's head. Tears filled her eyes as she saw the look that overshadowed the expression of her precious child.

"Gee," Angel nervously began, "You don't have to scare Trina to death like that. I'll give you everything I got. Just don't point that gun at my baby please. You have her whole body shakin'."

"She will be shakin' until I get what I want so I guess you need to hurry the fuck up then, and stop talkin' bitch."

Angel turned to the cabinet where she had just stashed her dope.

"Don't try no funny shit Blood cause I swear the first to go will be Trina," Gee firmly stated.

"The dope is in this cabinet." Angel said while walking towards the cabinet. After opening the cabinet, she reached for her dope. She brought all of it out and sat in on the dinner table while Gee watched her closely.

"Now, where is the money?" he demanded.

"In my bedroom," Angel answered. She headed towards the hallway that led to her bedroom.

Gee had Trina still wrapped around one arm while holding the gun towards her. They followed closely behind Angel to the bedroom. Angel led the way to her room with no real intentions of giving up her money she had been saving. Once she entered her bedroom, she went to the side of her bed to a cigar box that she threw her everyday money into. Her .38 revolver was under her mattress right where she was standing. Quickly she tried to figure out just how she would get to her gun to defend herself without Trina being harmed. She opened her cigar box and looked in it. She knew it wasn't much in there because she just copped from

Youngster but she had decided to see if Gee would accept it. She was hoping he would take what she had in it and leave them unharmed. She had given up on the thought of doing something heroic. That thought had left her mind because she realized by trying something, the possibility of her daughter being caught in the cross fire was too high of a risk to take.

Gee held Trina close to him while standing at Angel's bedroom entrance. He was watching Angel like a hawk. He knew that he was all in and there was no turning back. There was no doubt that he would have to silence Angel after she gave him what he wanted. He knew that after robbing her, he couldn't let it get back to Youngster that he was the one. He had to get rid of Angel for sure. Just what he would do with Trina was what he had trouble making a clear decision on. His conscience ate at him when he thought about how Trina's life would have to come to an end like her mother's. He would have to weigh out his options being fully aware that Youngster's wrath was something that he wasn't willing to bear. He wanted to hurt Youngster's pockets without taking the credit for it. He knew that Youngster would come at him in full force. If Youngster found out it was him that robbed Angel, he would come at him with deadly intentions.

Angel slowly walked over to Gee. She handed him the cigar box with her money inside. Gee took his arm from around Trina to receive the box. He kept the gun steady on the side of her head while he took the box from Angel. He instructed Angel to sit on her bed and for Trina to go sit beside her. He flipped the box open. He saw that there couldn't be much more than two or three hundred dollars in fives, tens, and a few twenties inside of the cigar box.

"What the fuck is this?" he asked with a disappointing tone.

"It's all I got Gee, I just copped from Youngster earlier." She hoped that he would accept her story and just leave them alone. She figured that her five thousand dollars hidden in her closet would be enough to cop and recover from her losses. What she wanted was for Gee to just leave her and her daughter unharmed.

"Blood, I know you lyin' to me!" He yelled while pointing the gun in her direction. "This looks like less than three hundred dollars. I know this ain't all you got so break yourself or else bitch!"

"That is it Gee, plus its five ounces on the table in the kitchen for you. Just take it and go, please!"

From the look in Gee's eyes, she could tell his patience was wearing thin. She could tell he didn't believe her story. She had to do something. She thought about her .38 revolver that was only inches away from her under her mattress. She had began to feel that she might have a chance to get to it some kind of way without putting her daughter at risk. Her street pride started to creep within her mind. The thought of her allowing someone to take something from her without a fight was being pushed out. The hardcore mentality of do or die had taken its position.

The moment was close at hand to where the death toll in South-Central Los Angeles would have a few more added to its total. The unknown was smeared thick across Angel's face. She wondered if Gee would just be happy with what she had given him or would he insist on more money. She didn't want to give up her savings without a fight.

The question of just when to pull the trigger was the only thing on Gee's mind. He wasn't sure of Angel's story about not having anymore money. He had a funny feeling that she was lying. He wanted to clean her out before he took her out. Robbing Angel was not his main objective. Taking her life was the real goal. Giving Youngster one less reason to enter the Jungle while he plotted on his death was the reason he stood before Angel with a gun ready to pull the trigger. Gee's breathing became heavy. His voice changed from the knowledge that a murder was about to take place and he would be the one to commit it.

"Angel, I will blow Trina's fuckin' head off if you don't give me the rest of the money." There was no mistake that Gee was ready to carry out a killing.

Angel looked towards her closet and quickly back at Gee. The battle between the fear of her daughter being harmed and the street code of do or die had started to go to war. Grabbing her gun before Gee could react played out in her head. She slowly started to ease over towards her gun but Gee's question instantly stopped her motion for it.

"What's in the closet?" he asked. Their eyes met like a predator and its prey. "Is that where the safe is you lyin' sneaky bitch?"

She knew that she had a decision to make. She had to make it in a hurry. If she was as fast as she hoped to be, and Gee was not as alert as she prayed he wouldn't be, she would get to her .38 before he could realize what was happening. With no more time to waste, she went for her weapon. She moved to retrieve her gun but she would end up being too slow. Her sudden movement didn't go undetected as she hoped it would. Instead, she alerted Gee's attention in her direction. He was more than ready for her attempt for survival. He fired one shot from the barrel of his .45 that caught Angel in her shoulder. The impact of the bullet threw her back on her bed. Her .38 that she had grabbed went flying out her hand onto the floor. Trina sat motionless from the sudden events. She was wishing her mother would hurry and awaken her from the nightmare she hoped she was having. The reality of it all continued to play out as Angel struggled to sit up. On her attempt to sit up on her bed, she received another shot from the .45 that entered into her heart. This would become the fatal shot that would take her final breath away.

The second scream from the barrel of the .45 jolted and startled Trina. She looked over to her mother. She saw her mother stretched out on the bed, lifeless and drenched in blood. Angel's eyes were half shut. The realization had yet to sink into little Trina as she slowly turned to face her mother's killer. Her fate was very uncertain. But if the events were not all a nightmare as she had wished it to be, her fate really didn't matter to her anymore. Her mother meant everything to her, and seeing her mother no longer breathing was like the end of the world.

Gee stood at the bedroom door. He knew that he had no more time to waste. He wanted to get the whole thing over with quickly. He had to move fast. Ending Trina's life was the only thing left for him to do. She made that a difficult task by looking into his eyes. He held the gun in her direction but couldn't pull the trigger. He stood there staring at her with his finger on the trigger still contemplating. It seemed as if hours were passing by, as he thought, while Trina sat there staring at him. In fact, it was only a few seconds that ticked away before he spoke.

"Trina, if you say a word to anyone that it was me that did this, you will die just like your mother. You hear me?" Gee asked.

Trina slowly nodded her head while wearing a horrified sad expression on her face.

Gee couldn't go through with killing Trina. He decided to take his chances and let her live. He walked over to the bedroom closet. He started to search franticly for the rest of Angel's money. He felt she had more money hidden away from the way she looked towards her closet before her death. It didn't take long before he would find what he was looking for. A steel box with no lock was hidden away in the corner of the closet. The box was camouflaged by some clothing laying on the floor. He lifted the lid of the box and discovered stacks of hundred dollar bills. His eyes lit up as if he had struck gold. He was momentarily taken away from the deadly event that he was the cause of. His full attention was drawn to the money. He started to count the hundreds until a noise grabbed his attention. He turned to see what the noise was just in time. Unfortunately for Trina, she would be just as slow as her mother.

While Gee had started to count the money in the closet, Trina snapped out of her trance from the terrifying events. She had realized that her mother was beside her dead. She knew the killer was still in her presence. She wanted revenge as she looked down at her mother's gun on the floor. She leaped off the bed to pick the gun up. Gee heard the sound of Trina cocking the hammer of the gun just before she could face him to pull the trigger. As she was turning in his direction holding the gun in both her hands, Gee shot her dead. Trina's death came instantly from the one shot in her neck. She dropped immediately from the impact of the bullet and fell under her mother's lifeless legs that hung from the bed.

Gee quickly stuffed the money in his pockets. His heart was racing as he headed out the bedroom immediately after taking Trina's young life. He grabbed the five ounces off the kitchen table and exited the apartment where two bodies lay dead. Gee walked into the night after calming down. He stepped out as if he had just finished a friendly visit at Angel's place. He checked around while standing in front of the apartment door. He noticed how with all the activities that had just happened inside of Angel's apartment, things seemed to be so normal on the outside. He walked away from the apartment that was occupied by two dead bodies as if it was nothing to it. He felt as though he had just struck gold with the ounces of dope and the five thousand dollars on him. The thought of two lives being taken in order for him to receive his small fortune wouldn't even cross his mind. While he stepped further away from the crime scene, the killings became a distant memory. The only thing Gee thought about was that Youngster now would have one less reason to enter the Jungles. Gee's mission was accomplished.

# 24

July of '93 had just arrived but the afternoon showed no sign of summer. The sun had hidden its bright and shining face from the very sad occasion in progress. The clouds had gathered to mourn and shed tears over what seemed the entire city of Los Angeles. The grief could be felt in the whispering wind as it sang songs of sorrow through its dreary breeze. The windshield wipers slowly moved back and forth while Youngster sat quietly inside his car. He parked quite a ways from the other cars and small gathering that were present. He made sure he kept a distance but was close enough to view the sad ceremony taking place. Youngster fought back tears from falling from his eyes as he watched two caskets slowly being lowered into the ground. He thought about the last time he had seen Angel and how he warned her about the jealous ones that may have been among her. He told her to start being extra careful since she was making the kind of progress that wouldn't go unnoticed in the Jungles. He joked with her and told her that if someone did try to rob her, that she could always use her nice fat ass as a lethal weapon.

Youngster was able to spot Angel's mother crying her heart out while he silently said a final goodbye to Angel and Trina. At that moment, he could no longer hold back the tears from rolling down his face. He started up his car and drove off from the cemetery. There were a lot of emotions coasting through his mind and heart. He never actually knew someone that had been killed before whom he seen on a regular basis. Therefore, Angel's and Trina's death was taking its toll on him. He drove away from the gravesite feeling a pain in his heart while heading home. His eyes filled with tears every other minute as he couldn't help but reminisce on the times of his encounters with Angel. The flirting, the fussing, and the laughter that he shared with Angel flashed in his mind. The image of the happy smiles that Trina would wear on her face also added to the pain. It was a hard pill to swallow on his trip back home from the funeral. It was the first time that Youngster had witnessed bodies being put to rest in a grave. He had hoped that it would be the last time someone close to him would be killed behind the drug game. "That's too close for comfort," he thought to himself. Youngster had no idea just how close it would be the next time death came knocking.

***

Homicide detectives along with police officers were swarming the Jungles like bees to honey. They were in search of the killers of the woman and her young daughter who were found slain in their apartment. Two weeks had passed. Authorities had no real leads on who could have committed such a horrible crime. They only had the rumors that were circulating about the killings being drug related. That information didn't help in tracking down a suspect or making an arrest. During the event of the murders, no one had seen nor heard anything that would actually help. This made things tough for all those involved in the investigation of the murders. Drug spots and all the dope fiend hang outs were hotter than a forest fire during the warmest day in July. Harassments and shake downs were going on constantly. Drug trafficking became scarce in the entire area of the Jungles.

Officer Parrish thought he had it all figured out. He was looking for only one person to bring in for questioning. He had told his partner that it could have only been Youngster that committed the murders. He told him that they would be credited for the apprehension of the heartless murderer named Jayshawn King. Officer Parrish looked at this as his opportunity to make detective. He was certain that he would be the one to catch Youngster. He made it his business to do so.

"Now, how do you know it was him?" Officer Trapp asked while Officer Parrish turned on Buckingham to enter into the Jungles.

"Look, this black son-of-a-bitch has to be the one. You know how some of these drug addicts been saying that she was getting her shit from him."

"Ok, and so---" Officer Trapp attempted to get in a few words but his partner cut him off.

"And so she had to have owed his ass some money and couldn't pay up so he killed her and her child just to make an example out of them. We just have to keep snooping around and keep an eye out for him because something will come up. We will be getting promotions soon as we catch his ass."

Officer Trapp looked over to his partner. He saw a man that had it out for just one criminal in the city of Los Angeles. A man that was very determined to catch his own personal nemesis. Officer Trapp couldn't quite understand why out of all the drug dealers, gang bangers, and murderers in the streets of L.A, that Jayshawn King stood out in his partners eyes. However, it was obvious that Youngster was a definite target. The determination showed in the blue eyes of Officer Parrish while he drove throughout the Jungles in search of his murder suspect.

***

The once ambitious teenager, who just wanted a nice car to ride around in on Crenshaw to catch the car hoppin' girls, had now become a target. He was a wanted man in the eyes of a police officer and envied by many in the streets. Having no knowledge of what was beginning to build around him, Youngster sat in his apartment all alone smoking a fat blunt. Crystal and Jay were away visiting Crystal's grandmother. They were not expected to return for a while so Youngster took advantage of his alone time. He pulled on his blunt and exhaled a cloud of smoke while reflecting on how far he had come along in the game. His thoughts quickly switched to the dilemma of how to walk away from it all. With the constant nightmares of being murdered by the Bloods, the thought of his son's mother on coke, and what had just happened to Angel was too much to bear. He felt an uncertainty that he had never felt within himself. All the many nights of standing on the block selling drugs, he had never been afraid. This feeling he was now experiencing within was very strange to him. It seemed that a warning sign was flashing right before his eyes bright as the morning sun. He felt a fear within him.

Youngster blew out another cloud of smoke. He closed his eyes. He allowed the murders of Angel and Trina to eat at him more and more. He wondered if the murders were because of him, if the killers were trying to get to Angel to set him up. He was beginning to feel certain that someone was out to get him. He felt a fear within. He started trying to shake the thought off. He tried to conclude that the weed was making him paranoid. He reasoned that the red lights that were flashing was just his eyes getting red from the contact of the potent chronic. He put the blunt out. He stretched out on the couch to rest up for a while. He wanted to come down from his high. He needed to shake the fear. He didn't like being afraid.

Fifteen minutes after shutting his eyes, two roads appeared before him. One road read *Death*, and the other one read *Jail*. Elderly women were on both sides of the roads ahead. They were kneeling down. Half were grieving by wooden stakes in the ground while the other half gripped prison bars in tears. He turned to acknowledge the noise behind him. He saw that the noise was coming from his mother and sister. They were crying out for him not to go any further down the roads. The sound became clearer and clearer to him as he heard them screaming, "Don't go, don't go, Jayshawn don't go!"

Youngster jumped straight up from his short nap with his heart racing. He sat on his couch for a minute to calm down. He stared into his blank television screen. A few minutes later, he jumped up to get a pencil and some paper. He walked over to his kitchen table. He then sat down. He went into deep thought and began to write ---

Darkened by destruction and I can no longer see the light
I'm headed down a one way street where futures don't look so bright
Death or to jail is where many say that this road will lead
Trails of blood lay off to the side as mothers continue to grieve
Having knowledge of this I still can't resist
The pursuit of ghetto fortune and fame
Supplying the demand of my own people who crave to fry their brains
The selling of souls at a very low price goes on day after day
As a house full of broken dreams pass the pipe
While outside their children play
Going nowhere fast but here I come with a pocket full of dope
Hurting the kids' future and destroying their parent's hopes
Living the good life is what people think but I'm full of misery and pain
Feeling that there is no way out, I'm trapped in this hustling game
I can't turn back now, this is all I know
I've been doing this since I was a teen
I've been running my own business by way of a triple-beam
Watching over my shoulders every step that I take
For there is one thing that I know
Somethin' is out there trying to get me, is it the police or a jealous foe?
Either one I'm blinded to the facts, ignoring every warning sign
As if my fate is already sealed like a patient that knows he's dying
If I had the chance to do over again, I wonder if I would change
Live the legal life and be able to sleep at night
Unlike when you're Heavy in the Game

***

Walking zombies scattered about in dark alleys and throughout the streets. They were all in search of a drug dealer with enough heart and guts to sell during the ongoing investigation of the murders in the Jungles. The night was still young but the Jungles had the look of abandonment. There was very little movement. It seemed as if it was around five in the morning because very few were out and about. Only the dope fiends could be seen up and down the streets. Most of the working class people were inside their apartments as opposed to being out to deal with the harassment by the police and detectives who were on the murder case.

In a large one bedroom apartment, Gee stashed himself away to hide out. He was aware that the police had no leads but as hot as it was, he wasn't trying to be seen. He kept Joe, the old man that rented the place, happy by giving him a little dope each day. He wouldn't leave his hideout for anything. He had Lil' Red and Boo do all the dirty work for him while he stayed hidden away. They moved his dope while he sat back and collected the money. They became his errand boys. He sent them to the store for food, drinks, and whatever else he needed.

Gee had been getting drunk every night since he committed the murders. His conscience bothered him often when he would think of Trina's innocent face. He would feel bad knowing her life didn't deserve to be cut short. His sorrow would be erased by the thought that he had hurt Youngster's pocket. He felt that getting rid of one of his regular customers was well worth it. He would think about Youngster each night. He had became obsessed with trying to figure out how to get rid of him for good. His brain was working in overdrive trying to come up with a plan. His thoughts were broken up by a hard knock at the door. Joe walked over towards the door to see who was knocking while Gee looked on. Joe glanced back at Gee to let him know that everything was all right. He then opened the door. Soon after he opened the door, Lil' Red and Boo came walking in the apartment.

"What's up Blood?" Gee asked and threw his chin up towards the both of them.

"Nothin' Blood," Lil' Red said as he walked towards Gee to hand him the money from the drugs that he sold.

"Shit still crazy out there, Blood." Boo said as he approached Gee to pass him a bottle of E&J that he was holding in a brown paper bag. Boo then handed Gee the money he made for that day.

"Word is out on the streets that Youngster has a ten thousand dollar reward for anyone with info on the one-eighty-sevens of Angel and Trina." Lil' Red informed Gee.

"Is that right?" Gee asked. He then nervously opened the bottle of E&J. After what Lil' Red had just said, he thought about Youngster's reward. He started to wonder if anyone actually saw him coming out of Angel's apartment that night. He hadn't told Lil' Red and Boo that he was the one that did the killings but he could feel that they suspected him. From his recent come up on the dope he had them selling, he felt that they were smart enough to figure it out. Gee wouldn't allow it to show on the outside, but from within there was a strong fear that ran through his entire body. Youngster would definitely have his head delivered to him if it leaked out that he was the last one seen at Angel's apartment or if he found out about Gee's come up. Gee knew that something had to be done real soon before his situation made the headlines in the hood.

Lil' Red and Boo took a seat in the living room on a beige couch across from the matching sofa where Gee had been sitting. Gee had a blunt already rolled. They all began to smoke and drink together. While passing the blunt and pouring drink after drink in their plastic cups, Gee started thinking again. His fear along with his malice for Youngster grew worse. He had his two young gangsters in front of him getting high. He figured that it would be the right time to put a plan in motion. There was not much time left because of the reward Youngster put out. He had to eliminate Youngster fast not knowing if his two little homeys would turn on him for that reward. Gee knew he had some work to do. He took a long pull from the blunt and passed it to Boo. He held in the smoke for a while before slowly exhaling. He coughed for a good minute and then started to speak.

"Blood, ya'll mom still fuckin' with that nigga Youngster?" Gee inquired but he knew the answer to his question.

"Yeah, I seen him a few days ago." Lil' Red answered.

"I just seen him the other day in the alley." Boo added.

"It's time to get that nigga, Blood. Ya'll have to find out when your moms meet him and how often during the day his ass goes over there. We need to plan on how we can get rid of that muthafucka. We can catch him slippin' using your mom as the bait."

Gee looked into both Lil' Red and Boo's eyes. He saw they were paying close attention like young students in a classroom. He knew that through them was the best way to get rid of Youngster. He had to milk them. He had to pump their heads up to go through with the execution of Youngster. He felt that he had to take advantage of the situation before it's too late. He went on further in his pursuit to manipulate his two little homies' minds. "The time is now, Blood. Youngster must go and it's up to us to take that nigga out. Find out when your moms cop from him again and let me know. We will catch that nigga slippin' right after he meets with her. This will give us a hell of a rep and earn ya'll the respect you two lil' niggas deserve around here." Gee stopped for a minute. He took a drink. He swallowed down the liquid fire before he continued, "So, are ya'll ready to be real *G's* or what?" They both nodded in unison as the weed and alcohol boosted up their courage and bravery. It seemed that the reputation that would be gained from carrying out such a task outweighed the great possibility of someone else finding out about the murder other than their gang. This would make the murder of Youngster lead right back to them where they could face life in prison. But those consequences wouldn't even be thought about. A neighborhood reputation meant so much more to them at that moment.

The influence Gee had on them mixed with the weed and drinks they were consuming erased any thoughts of going to prison. They also didn't give any thought to collecting the reward from Youngster. They both had a pretty good idea that Gee was the killer due to his sudden actions and all the dope he had them selling for him. Lil' Red and Boo had discussed it among each other earlier that week. They both felt that Gee had to have done it but on this night, they would silently decide to remain loyal to their homey. They would choose to go after the reputation and earn their stripes. That would mean more to them than collecting a reward and betraying their big homey from the hood.

***

"What does he see in that smoked out bitch?" Pam asked Keisha as they sat on the couch smoking weed.

Ice had just walked out the door with Shell right beside him. They were on their way to find Shell some dope so that she could stay awake, or so she claimed. She had told Ice that there was no way that she would be able to turn any more tricks without a nice supply to keep her awake and alert.

"Girl, I don't know." Keisha responded. "But I tell you one thang, this bitch here is fed up with the bullshit."

"Well, I know what you mean, and I ain't gonna keep workin' my ass off just so that motherfucker can keep that bitch high." Both Pam and Keisha were on the same page. They both were headed in the same direction on their decision that night.

"What are you gonna do?" Keisha asked as she passed Pam the blunt while she put her heels back on.

"Bitch, what you mean what am I gonna do? You know that Fats been wantin' us in his stable for a long ass time. And now is the time to choose him." Pam pulled on the blunt. She exhaled a cloud of smoke before continuing, "I can't sit here and sell my shit all night just so another bitch can stay high. Fuck that!" Pam then started to put on her heels after she gave Keisha the blunt back. Their short break was over and so was returning back to Ice. They had made their minds up that Ice wouldn't benefit from their hard work just to see Shell get catered to.

Right after Pam slipped on her heels, she quickly started to pack her clothes with Keisha right behind her. After making the decision to leave Ice, they both knew they didn't have much time to waste in the apartment. They had to get out before Ice returned. The last thing they needed was an ass beating from Ice while trying to leave him. In ten minutes, all the little clothes they had were in a large bag. They were out the door. All the money that Ice had calculated earlier that night if Pam and Keisha had a good night, would now be in someone's pockets other than his. From this night and many more to come, Ice's pockets would be coming up short. He would only have Shell to put out on the streets which would not profit him at all. Shell only tricked long enough to keep her high up. She never was able to bring in enough cash for Ice. Before this night, Ice never paid it any attention because of his two thoroughbreds; Pam and Keisha. Now he would feel the full effect of having a worthless prostitute in his stable. There would be hell to pay for the loss of his main two race horses and Shell would be there to receive the full payment.

# 25

The sound of the alarm clock had awakened Crystal out of her sleep. She reached out to tap the button so that the alarm would shut off. She rolled over to check on her man to see if the alarm had awakened him too. She was barely able to cast her drowsy eyes on him. Surprisingly, she saw he was already up sitting on the side of the bed. For the last thirty minutes he had been sitting there getting over another one of his nightmares. He looked over his shoulder to make eye contact with Crystal. He had a drained look on his face as if he had grown tired of the constant nightmares. The wish that it would stop was engraved in his appearance. There was nothing that could be done to stop the reoccurring dreams is what he was feeling. But on this day, he would be wrong. Without any words being said, Youngster stood up to go shower. He left Crystal in the bed very concerned and worried about her man.

After stepping into the shower, Youngster held both of his hands against the wall while he allowed the hot running water to fall freely on top of his head. With his eyes tightly shut, he just let his mind flow. He started to think of all that he had been through in his life. All the drugs that had passed through his hands, the money that he has seen, the killings that he had committed all behind the lifestyle that he chose to live. He thought about the lives that he had a hand in destroying and had profited from. He thought about Angel and Trina. He held his eyes closed tight to prevent tears from mixing with the water that fell from his face. He started to think about Jay and the guilt overwhelmed him. He hadn't spent much time with Jay and felt bad. Youngster then started to blame himself for Jay's mother being strung out. He began to go over the poem that he wrote line by line. He thought about the vision that caused him to write it. He started to feel the presence of his mother and sister. Their voices were ringing in his head begging him to stop living the way he was living. Youngster slowly opened his eyes and turned his back to the rushing hot water. At that moment, he thought about Crystal. He thought about the conversation he had with her about his plans to buy a house. He thought about when he told her of his desires of stepping away from the game. He wanted more than anything in his life to be able to see Crystal, Jay, Louise, and Lavette happy and proud of him. "Time to get out," Youngster whispered, "Time to walk away and leave the Devil's playground for good."

By the time Youngster was dressed, breakfast was waiting for him downstairs. He arrived in the kitchen where Crystal and Jay were already in the process of eating. They had started on their food about ten minutes before he arrived. Youngster quickly ate his French toast, scrambled eggs, and turkey bacon. He stood up from the table while drinking the rest of his orange juice. After he finished drinking, he leaned over towards Crystal and kissed her on her forehead. "Don't worry about cookin' tonight my love. I'll be back early enough so that we can go out to eat." He then walked over to Jay, "Where's my hug?" Jay stood up and gave his father a hug. "You be good." Youngster grabbed what he needed and was out the door.

Youngster drove straight to his spot to get some orders ready. All he thought about on the drive there was getting out of the game. He had ten kilos left and five hundred thousand dollars in cash put away. He had no plans of buying any more kilos. He had decided that after the ten kilos were gone, he would end his drug dealing days. He would thank God for allowing him to make it through the streets without tasting death or smelling that awful stench of prison. There was no sign on this day that would warn him of the possibility of counting his blessings too soon. However, it lurked and anxiously waited to show its unexpected head.

***

The kitchen counter was lined up with cookies drying out on paper towels. Youngster had just cooked fourteen ounces of cocaine. He also weighed out a kilo and a half for Blue who had called in the order two days prior. When the twenty-eight cookies dried, Youngster wrapped each half ounce in foil. He then put them in a shoe box. He dropped the box in a shopping bag and walked into his living room. He sat on the couch after grabbing the phone to call Blue.

"Hello." Blue answered.

"What's up Blue? This is Youngster."

"What's up Youngster, I'll be ready for you a little later on today."

"Oh, okay Blue. I just wanted to touch bases with you, so hit me up when you ready."

"I'll be hittin' you up fo sho. I'm gettin' the money together as we speak. I'll page you as soon as I'm ready."

"Cool."

"Okay Youngster, I'm out." Blue hung up the telephone. He quickly picked the receiver back up to make a phone call to confirm that the set up would be definitely going down later on that day. Blue told the guys on the other end of the line to make sure that they get over to his house an hour before dark. He wanted them there early so they would be able to go over everything. He wanted to make sure things went smoothly. Meanwhile, Youngster hung up with Blue and returned to the kitchen. He went to put away the kilo and a half until Blue called for it later. After he put Blue's order up, he then picked up the shopping bag and exited the apartment. He went about his day to tend to his smaller orders.

***

Officer Parrish and Officer Trapp were still on the look out for Youngster. They cruised all around the entire Jungles. They drove on every block as well as around the outskirts of the Jungles hoping to see him. Operation *Jayshawn King* was in full effect. There would be no calling off the wolves until the goal was accomplished. Officer Parrish even had a surprise for Youngster that his partner was unaware of. If all else had failed once they were able to pull Youngster over, Officer Parrish had two ounces of rock cocaine hidden away in his patrol car. He was going to plant the coke in Youngster's car. This was his back up plan just in case he was unable to find anything to bring Youngster in on. Youngster was guaranteed to be locked away if they spotted him in the streets. Until they caught up with Youngster, they moved along questioning everyone they seen walking the streets. They pulled over all those that they knew hung out in the Jungles asking, "When was the last time you seen Youngster?"

***

Betty was counting her money in the kitchen. She was trying to see how much more she needed before calling Youngster. She had slowed down quite a bit since the murders in the Jungle. She wasn't in much of a rush to contact Youngster due to the heat in the streets. Youngster had instructed her to be careful since the deaths of Angel and Trina. He didn't want to be running back and forth in the Jungles during the investigation. He didn't want to get caught up while all the extra heat ran

238

rampant throughout the neighborhood. Betty didn't mind the slowing down of her business but it also meant she wouldn't be able to get high as often due to the unbalance of her personal intake and sales to keep her supplied.

Betty discovered that she was a few dollars short from copping again. She began to step out of her kitchen to return to her bedroom. She noticed a strange scene in her living room. Her sons were sitting on her couch in silence. They had been sitting there waiting. They were hoping to hear their mother's conversation with Youngster. A conversation that didn't happen. The plan was to catch Youngster when he pulled into the alley to meet their mother. They were to make sure that Youngster wouldn't pull out of that alley alive. Betty could see that her sons were high. She could sense they were up to something but she couldn't put her finger on it. She just ignored her strange feelings about her sons and brushed it off while she continued towards her bedroom with a suspicious mind.

***

Youngster moved about the streets feeling good about his decision to end the dealing of drugs. He hadn't heard anything on the murders of Angel and Trina. However, he felt that it was only a matter of time before the streets would come calling for the ten grand. The killer would be wearing a toe tag as soon as he received the information he was waiting for. There was a brief moment where Youngster almost allowed his thoughts of revenge to interrupt the good feeling he had inside. He reverted back to the vision of getting out of the game and started to feel good again. He thought about how happy his mother and sister would be to see that he had finally given up the drug business.

In-between drops Youngster called Crystal to discuss where they would search for a home. He talked to her about the schooling he would pursue. He made a promise to her that after he finished up with what he had left to sell, he would quit. He told her he would get out the game for good. He wanted to enroll in a community college and take up a trade. Crystal would get so excited each time she would hang up from talking to Youngster. She couldn't help but to shed tears of joy. Crystal knew she had a good man that she would now be able to spend time with. She would no longer worry each night about her man returning to her in one piece.

It was like Youngster felt liberated as he drove delivering his cookies throughout the streets of L.A. It was as if he had seen the light at the end of the tunnel with a sign that read *Freedom.* No more looking over his shoulders. No more staring through his rearview mirror with that silent fear of death or jail that would always run through his veins. The thought of walking away from the game brought a bright smile to his face. It made him very happy within. Youngster had yet to go into the Jungles as he drove through the city making his drops. And eventually, there would be many that wished he had never entered the Jungles on this day.

***

Ice sat across from Shell with a cold look on his face. It had been three whole days that had passed without a sign from both Pam and Keisha. It was beginning to look like they were not returning. Shell's jealousy and her addiction to drugs had caused too much friction within Ice's stable. She wanted too much of his attention as well as dope. Pam and Keisha had decided that they would be better off with another pimp that wouldn't have a jealous crack head hanging all over him and getting high all the time. Ever since they packed their belongings and left, Ice's anger had been building. It had been growing to a boiling point. The explosion was very near.

Shell was very confused. She felt very frightened as she sat still with a blank look on her face. She was too afraid to say a word to Ice so she remained silent. She was hoping that the situation would blow over soon enough before she started to crave for a fix.

"You know you done fucked up my money right?" Ice asked in a very serious and stern tone. "You no good bitch! You hear me talkin' to you?" he raised his voice and Shell jumped. He startled her from the sound of his voice. She was afraid to make eye contact with him.

"Are you playin' deaf on me bitch?" he asked.

"No Daddy, I'm---," Shell didn't respond fast enough. She was rewarded with a firm introduction to his fist. The impact of his closed hand connecting to her left cheek caused her to fall from the couch on to the floor. After his initial leap towards Shell, Ice's rage only grew as he stomped on her. She squirmed around in the fetal position on the floor while he kicked her again and again.

"I'm sorry! I'm sorry!" Shell screamed repeatedly as she attempted to cover up. She was trying to avoid being hit in the face by the bottom of his shoes.

"I know you sorry bitch," Ice shouted. "You're one sorry bitch! Now I have to teach you a fuckin' lesson." He reached for her. He pulled her up by the neck with a firm grip. He then pushed her up against the wall. He began to slap her with an open hand. Blood started to seep from her bottom lip instantly. She cried out, "Please Daddy, don't hurt me no more!"

"Fuck you! You fucked up my money so take what's comin' to you, you funky bitch." Ice swung from all angles. He prevented Shell from falling to the ground. She was unable to cover up. She was pinned against the wall. She received blows to the side of her body and to each sides of her face. Blood flowed freely from her mouth and nose. She could only shed tears and cry out for the next twenty minutes until he tired out. After Ice felt he made his point, he stormed out the front door leaving Shell against the wall in tears. After a few minutes, she managed to find some comfort on the floor where she would cry her heart out until she eventually fell asleep.

***

Gee called over to Betty's apartment every thirty minutes to check on Lil' Red and Boo. He kept going over the plans with the both of them. He made it clear that they had no room for error. Gee constantly reminded them how big they would become after they carried out their mission. He gave a boost to their confidence every chance he could get. He told them how they would be the ones to run the drug trade in the neighborhood. He repeated over and over that they would be the ones feared in the Jungles. He filled their heads up each time he called leaving no room for the thought of backing out of the plan. He didn't want to take a chance on them choosing Youngster's reward over their desired neighborhood glory.

Lil' Red and Boo were beginning to get anxious from all the phone calls from Gee. They had shared a blunt and had been drinking just enough alcohol to keep their courage up. Reneging wouldn't be an option. In fact, the only thing holding them back was time and Youngster's arrival.

***

Youngster sat at the light on Crenshaw & Florence waiting for it to turn green. The day was coming to a close. Nightfall had began to move in over the city. He was down to a few ounces. He was on his way to his mother's house to chill until he received a page. It had been a while since he had seen his mother and sister. He felt the desire to get there to see them. He was hoping they both would be home. He wanted to give them the good news of his retirement plans. He was sure that it would put a smile on their faces. He felt certain it would lift the burdens on their hearts.

The light turned green and Youngster proceeded down Crenshaw. A few minutes later while passing Slauson, he received a page from Blue. He picked up his mobile phone that was laying on his lap to return Blue's call.

"Hello." Blue answered.

"What's up Blue?"

"Hey Youngster, what time can you get here?" Blue asked.

"Give me about an hour cause I have to go get it for you."

"Cool, I'll be here."

"Alright, I'll see you then," Youngster assured Blue before hanging up. Before the page, Youngster had figured Blue wasn't getting his order that day because it had gotten so late. But he was glad to get the call from Blue. He wanted to dump all the dope he could as soon as possible.

Blue hung up the phone after speaking to Youngster and nodded his head towards the two guys standing across from him. They were holding guns in their hands with mean expressions on their faces. Blue stood up and said, "Get ready ya'll, he'll be here in about an hour. Let's not fuck this up Cuzz. Remember, as soon as ya'll see him steppin' towards the house, get his ass."

***

Before arriving to his mother's house, Youngster received another page. He looked down at his pager. He saw Betty's number across the screen. He dialed her up while passing his mother's house without noticing his mother and sister standing on the porch. They were trying to flag him down. They screamed his name a few times but Youngster didn't notice them. They would stop in their attempt in getting his attention thinking that he would be right back.

Youngster figured that it wouldn't make any sense to stop at his mother's house knowing Betty wanted something from him. He decided to meet her first before stopping. He didn't want to stop at his mother's, call Betty, and then have to leave right back out. He wanted to meet Betty first so that he would have more time to spend with his mother and sister.

"Hey Betty," he spoke as soon as she answered the phone.

"What's up Youngster, I'm ready."

"Okay, I'll be there in five minutes," Youngster hung up his phone and headed towards his possible doom.

Lil' Red and Boo listened to their mother's short conversation with Youngster. They immediately put their plan into action. They ran out to the alley where Youngster would usually pull up. They were sure he would be there because it had been so hot. Driving anywhere near the front of the building to meet their mom would have been an open invitation to get stopped and searched by the police. Lil' Red rushed to the parking stall across from their building to post up while Boo hid by the entrance. Lil' Red would be the one to keep an eye out for Youngster while Boo kept watch for his mother and witnesses. It wouldn't be long before they would be participating in one of the biggest hood stories of the year. A story that would put them in position for their claim to street fame.

# 26

Youngster's pager began to vibrate once again as he sat at a light on the outskirts of the Jungles. He glanced down at his pager while holding the button to display the number. He saw the digits of his cousin's home number. He wondered what Dee wanted. They had only spoke once or twice since Youngster had recovered from the loss he had took. Youngster had felt unsure about whether or not Dee really had something to do with the loss. His lack of communication with Dee didn't sit well with him which only made his suspicions grow. He had been meaning to call Dee to find out what was going on. This would be a good opportunity to discuss it with him.

When Youngster arrived at another red light, he decided to return Dee's page. He dialed his number while he waited at the light.

"Hello." Dee answered.

"What's up Dee?"

"Nothin' at all." Dee responded in a strange way.

"You alright over there my nigg?" Youngster asked.

"Yeah Jayshawn, I just need you to stop by so we can talk."

"Alright cool, give me a few and I'll come through." Youngster hung up the phone as the light turned green. He felt a little worried about the way Dee sounded. He was definitely not feeling a good vibe from the tone in Dee's voice. He felt he should go see about his cousin and attempt to clear the tension between them. Youngster had a feeling that would slightly erase his suspicions. He replaced his suspicions with the thought that maybe Dee was just too ashamed to call him after the way things went down. Youngster wanted to go straighten things out with Dee. He felt it was a good time to do exactly that.

***

Dee dropped the phone down to the receiver. A tear from his eye fell at the same time he hung up the phone. He couldn't believe that he had just went through with the phone call he had made to his cousin.

"So, how long will it be before that muthafucka shows up?"

"He said he will be here in a few minutes." Dee nervously answered with a .357 magnum to the back of his head.

"Good, you did very good nigga. Thanks for your services."

"Please don't kill---," Dee was only able to speak those three words before taking his last and final breath.

Rob didn't give Dee a chance to beg for his life as he pumped a single bullet from the magnum through the back of Dee's head. Blood shot straight to the ceiling as soon as the bullet made contact. The blood continued to pour out of Dee's splattered brains rapidly as he fell out of his seat on to the floor. The only thing Rob needed from Dee was to make the phone call to Youngster. From that point, Dee was useless to him. Dee's lifeless body was now stretched out in his own puddle of blood in the middle of his living room floor.

Rob had returned to L.A with a deep vengeance in his heart. The encounter with Youngster inside the theatre over a year ago was the most embarrassing thing that had ever happened to him in his life. Having all those people stare at his naked body while he jogged to his car was unforgettable. He had swore the very next day while on a plane that he would return back for Youngster. He would definitely make Youngster pay. Rob sat inside of Dee's apartment with Bear, a friend of his that was a hardcore gang member from Watts, waiting for Youngster to arrive. Youngster had made one of the biggest mistakes against the street code. He pulled a gun on someone and allowed that someone to live. "It won't be long," Rob thought to himself. He would make Youngster pay for such a crucial mistake. It was just a matter of time before Rob would get to hand out his revenge. Little did Rob know, there were a few people ahead of him. They were also plotting on Youngster's life and his wealth. The chances of Rob getting to Youngster first was not at all in his favor.

***

Youngster entered the Jungle by making a left turn off of Martin Luther King on to Coliseum Street. He had just missed Officer Parrish and Officer Trapp by seconds as they had just turned up Nicolet Avenue before he approached the same street. When Youngster made his turn on Nicolet, Officer Parrish was able to recognize the Volvo wagon in his rearview mirror while heading up the block. Parrish slowed down to make sure it was Youngster's green Volvo wagon he had seen. Parrish then quickly steered the wheel to turn around. By the time Parrish finally turned the patrol car completely around, Youngster was gone. Officer Parrish franticly began hitting corners. He was speeding up blocks while Officer Trapp took on the job of an extra pair of eyes for his excited partner. Officer Parrish made the mistake of passing up the alley on Nicolet. That was where Youngster had turned into. Parrish headed to August Street instead. He made a right turn on August Street speeding towards a drug spot located on Coco Avenue. He thought Youngster might have been on his way there to make a delivery. This would end up being a crucial mistake. A very costly one that possibly made the difference on the outcome of the upcoming events.

***

Shell sat in the one bedroom apartment off of Broadway in pain and distress. It was late in the day and she was just waking up to an empty apartment. Ice had been gone since the night before. She wasn't sure if he was ever coming back to her. She found herself laying there hurting more over the thought of him leaving her than over the pain he had caused her from the beating he gave her. Ice had blamed her for losing both Pam and Keisha. He called her a home wrecker and beat her for a good forty minutes the night before. His fist made contact all over her helpless body until she was nearly unconscious. Shell's jealousy and her need to feel wanted revealed itself one too many times. It had caused too much friction between her and the other two girls.

Shell didn't know what to do after she finally stood up to check out the damages that Ice put on her. She walked to the bathroom very slowly. She stared into the mirror unable to recognize herself. Her eyes were badgered and her lips were swollen bad. Her face was a mess. She couldn't even cry from the excruciating pain that it caused when she attempted to shed tears. The last place she wanted to be was on earth. She couldn't remember the last time she had seen her son. Depression was beginning to set in. She felt she had lost another man in her life. Her body started to cry out for dope but as she stared into the mirror, she realized drugs wasn't the answer to her problems. The use of drugs had only been the reason for the nightmare that had become her life. The depression started to become overwhelming. She didn't want to cope with it any longer. She felt a sudden urge to end it all as she opened the medicine cabinet. She reached for a bottle of sleeping pills. She opened the bottle of pills. After closing the cabinet back, Shell stared at a young girl in the mirror that she didn't want to see any more.

***

Youngster made a right turn into the alley and a sharp left. He was just a little ways from Betty's apartment building so he slowed down before approaching her back gate. He wanted to call Betty and have her come out before he reached her building. He didn't want to be sitting out there in the alley for a long time. He reached for his mobile phone as he continued to slowly cruise up the alley. He was listening to Tupac Shakur rap about how the streets was like being on death row. He listened as the rapper dropped a verse about how the game was difficult to let go since it was all that he knew. Youngster related to every word coming from his speakers. He thought about actually preparing to get out the game. He smiled from knowing he would soon be letting it all go. The drug dealing would soon become just a distant memory to him.

There was no one in the alley from what Youngster was able to see. Darkness had fallen over the city to prevent him from spotting the two predators that were awaiting their prey. He became focused on dialing Betty's number after turning his music down. He took his eyes off his surroundings. While Youngster was dialing Betty's number, this gave Lil' Red and Boo just enough time to launch their attack.

Lil' Red looked at his brother to make sure there was no one coming in the alley from their building. Boo gestured to Lil' Red with a slight nod signaling that it was all clear from his end. Lil' Red then looked up and down the alley making sure there wasn't anyone present before making his move. He crept out slow. Once he saw the Volvo cruising ahead with Youngster busy dialing, Lil' Red sped up his pace towards the vehicle with his weapon drawn. He reached the hood of the moving vehicle on the passenger side and let off a shot that shattered the front windshield of the car. This made a loud noise upon impact. The sound of the loud bang combined with his shattered windshield alerted Youngster that danger was near. He ducked instantly and reached under his steering column for his gun. His attempt to mash on the gas and flee the scene was met by a barrage of bullets as Boo left his post. Boo started letting off rounds into Youngster's car from one side while his brother covered the other side. The Volvo was full of holes by the time it crashed into an empty parking stall just passed Betty's building. Youngster had lost control of his vehicle after trying hard to keep his steering wheel straight while ducking. He had been hit several times during his attempt to get away. Youngster had just missed an elusive Lil' Red by inches before his head-on collision into the parking stall. The car came to a halt with the hood badly damaged from the collision. There was hot steam shooting out from under the hood and glass everywhere.

Lil' Red and Boo both ran towards the wrecked car to make sure that they did their job properly. They wanted to confirm that Youngster was no longer breathing. Boo arrived to the car first. He leaned into the wrecked vehicle by way of the broken glass on the driver side. He was greeted by a bullet immediately in the middle of his forehead. Lil' Red watched his little brother fall back. He saw that his brother was dead before he even met the concrete. After witnessing his brother's death, Lil' Red didn't hesitate to abandon all plans of finishing Youngster off. He ran out the alley as fast as he could. He headed towards Gee's hide-out shaken from the events.

Youngster struggled to sit upright in his car but the energy he used to pull the trigger on his 9 millimeter, took a lot out of him. He could hear the sirens coming from afar but his vision was becoming more and more blurry. Reality began to sink in that the end of the road was near. He realized that his life had reached its final destination. He managed to laugh for the last time as he thought about his illegal journey. It had came full circle. His life would end where he started off in the game. It would end in the back of an alley while he was trying to get his serve on.

***

Officer Parrish and Officer Trapp were the first on the scene. They pulled into the alley with on-lookers already forming into a rather large crowd. They ordered everyone back but had trouble pulling Betty away from her slain son. She was gripping Boo tight in her arms while sitting on the ground. Her back was against the wall of the parking stall. She could only scream, "Why? Why? Why?" She held her son while rocking back and forth. Officer Trapp finally was able to pull Betty away as the sounds of the sirens from the ambulance, police cars, and the roaring helicopter drowned out her screams of sorrow. Officer Parrish, with his gun drawn, approached Mr. King's Volvo cautiously. He would be the first to view the lifeless body of the young black male who was known as Youngster. With only a few weeks from walking away from the streets, time wasn't kind to Youngster. Time didn't allow him to escape the elements of the streets that had just claimed his young life.

Officer Parrish looked in disgust as Youngster wore a peaceful smile on his face from the last few thoughts he had before he took his final breath. Moments before Parrish had arrived, Youngster was able to think about no more nightmares, no more drug transactions, and no more watching over his shoulders. He thought of his mother and sister not having to worry about him any longer. These thoughts gave him a good feeling within. He felt at peace knowing that his son was in good hands. Youngster thought about how Jay would now have three strong women watching over him. Youngster thought about Crystal making good use of the half of million dollars that he left behind. He felt she would make sure to carry out his plan of Jay getting the best

251

education in a private school. He was confident that she would make sure Jay stayed away from the street life. At the last thought he was allowed to have, a smile came across his face. This smile was from the thought of what the old man wrote to him. It was one of the last letters his father sent to him from prison. Youngster was only ten years old at the time he first read the letter. He never understood the meaning of what was written until he was seconds away from losing his life. It was only then that he was able to fully understand. This caused him to smile by actually realizing what the letter meant that read, "When you're heavy in the game, the devil becomes the only one you'll ever have to answer to. And it is only when you are ready to walk away from it all, you will find that the Devil don't play fair."

**It's not over,**
**_"The game don't wait"_**
**is coming soon.**

**www.jlovebooks.com**

# ABOUT THE AUTHOR

J. Love was born and raised in Los Angeles, California. He was voted most likely to succeed while in the 9th grade when he attended Audubon Jr. High school. By the time he reached the 12th grade at Dorsey High, his life took a turn in the direction of obtaining a degree in street knowledge instead of keeping his once 3.6 grade point average up and attending college. He dropped out of school to pursue the american teenager's dream of having a car. He started with a $50 dollar double-up pack and from there built his little empire. Fatherhood soon followed the start of his illegal career and so he took on the single parent role while grinding it out in the streets. It was only when all had been lost and after serving three years in prison that J. Love realized that his 11th grade English teacher was right suggesting to him back then that he should be a writer. After 13 years of hustling, he has now taken his life experiences and put them in the novel "Heavy in the game" and is presently working on the sequel, "The game don't wait."